The Final Wish of Mr. Murray McBride

Joe Siple

Black Rose Writing | Texas

This is a work of fiction. Names, characters, businesses, places, events and incidents are either the products of the author's imagination or used in a fictitious manner. Any resemblance to actual persons, living or dead, or actual events is purely coincidental.

ISBN: 978-1-68433-613-5
PUBLISHED BY BLACK ROSE WRITING
www.blackrosewriting.com

Printed in the United States of America
Suggested Retail Price (SRP) $18.95

The Final Wish of Mr. Murray McBride is printed in Cambria

Praise for
The Five Wishes of
Mr. Murray McBride

"In less than 250 pages, Joe Siple had me laughing out loud in public places, and crying where I could not see the page. I'm not sure how he created such emotional depth."

—Lisa, San Francisco, CA

"It isn't often that an author can completely draw you in and have you deeply invested in a story. This story tugs at your heartstrings and will bring tears to your eyes."

—Ruth, New York, NY

"This book makes you realize that every moment with a loved one counts and that we have to make the best of it. Keep the tissues nearby when reading this book as you will need it. I finished this book early on a Saturday morning crying my eyes out. If I could give more stars I would, as it is I would recommend this great novel to everyone, you can't not read it.

—Natasha, Ermelo, South Africa

"No words can describe how this book made me feel. Love? Kindness? Hope? They are the best words in the world and together they are what this book means. Can not recommend this highly enough."

—Lauren, Tasmania, Australia

"This story resonated powerfully with me. It is funny and poignant without being sappy. I promise you, you will be glad you read this book."

—Catherine, Canada

"What's not to love about a book that left me with a heart about to burst and adoring the characters so much I wish I could meet them in person? Amazing to finish a book feeling as though I'm a better person myself for having known these people through its pages, even though they were fictional!"

—Elizabeth, Woodstock, VA

"This was one of the best books I have ever read, full of wisdom about how to conduct one's life, touching in so many ways. Read it!"

—Nancy, Labelle, FL

"If Hollywood doesn't make this a movie they are crazy. Most emotional book I have read in many years. I loved it, and so will you."

—Susie, Bristow, VA

"*The Five Wishes of Mr Murray McBride* by Joe Siple is an extraordinary tale, one I'm so glad to have read. I spent much of my reading laughing, and I will admit to tears; I couldn't see the last few pages for them."

—Brenda, New Castle, Australia

"This story is full of lessons of life, love, and second chances. I recommend this book to everyone."

—Fajriy, Indonesia

"The characters are wonderful and they will stick with you for a long time. You will laugh and you will cry. Keep the tissue handy. A great story. Recommend it no matter what your age is. When you give you receive. A very strong story."

—Linda, Deming, NM

"This book delves into some of the hard issues in life: What it means to truly love and live, and how we can affect others. The love in these pages is something we all so desperately need to recover these days."

—Holly, Tecumseh, OK

"As good as it gets. This story reminds us of the whole point in showing up to this existence: to live life to the fullest without fear, to love and to remember to show our love, and to believe in the synchronicities that makes our particular lives special and unique. Most of all, to remember that the whole point is to live joyfully and with the idea of possibility in all things."

—Theresa Young, U.S.

For Anne.
With too little acknowledgment, you've been my greatest support.
For so long, my own wishes have been about you.
Thanks for making them come true.

Acknowledgements

Many thanks to my publisher, Reagan Rothe at Black Rose Writing. You took a chance on Murray McBride when no one else would, then did everything you could to get him into the hands of readers who were looking for this type of story.

David King is the unheralded genius behind the cover artwork for Black Rose Writing books. His work speaks for itself. I'm convinced that a good portion of my book sales start with people being intrigued by his art.

And Christopher Miller, promotions guy extraordinaire, thank you for your efforts, especially in the world of social media. Your work has allowed me to keep a safe distance from something of which I have an irrational fear and aversion.

Without the diligent eyes of my editor, Kim Catanzarite, this story wouldn't be complete. Your insights helped make this the book I was trying to write. Thank you.

As always, I'm deeply indebted to my writers' group. We call ourselves the "World Where the Books are Written," and the WWTBAW has, once again, come through with invaluable feedback and ideas. Thank you David Sharply, Laura Mahal, Sheala Henke, Sarah Roberts, Ronda Simmons, and Amy Rivers.

A special thanks to my neighbor, Laurie Matson, for your expertise as well as sharing your personal experience with type 1 diabetes. The information you shared over a glass of whiskey helped the authenticity of this story immeasurably.

And a final "thank you" to all the readers of *The Five Wishes of Mr. Murray McBride*, especially those who have written such touching reviews on Amazon, Goodreads, and other sites. When my writing was at its lowest and I couldn't see the way through to this latest story, reading your words inspired me to continue.

Thank you. And I hope you enjoy the sequel.

The Final Wish of
Mr. Murray McBride

I'm starting this silly thing because Father James said I should. Ridiculous, if you ask me. Not that anyone would ask my opinion these days. But I respect the good Father, and Jenny had one of these journals, so I guess it can't be all bad. Don't plan to write much, though.

The only thing I'm going to say today is that young folk don't understand how much emptiness hurts. They think if you have pain, there must be a cause. Something real and substantial and. . . what's the word I'm looking for? Tangible, that's it. But they don't understand that what hurts more than anything else in the world is nothing at all. Pure emptiness. Sometimes I think I'd pay good money for a little pain. Give me something, anything, except for this confounded emptiness.

—From the Journal of Murray McBride

Chapter One

JFK Center for the Performing Arts

The stage curtain closes in front of me. A puff of dust billows off the thick fabric and the three thousand people seated in the theater disappear from view.

Under my perfectly pleated tuxedo, my slicked-back hair, and a bit of stage makeup is an amazing amount of pain. My heart hurts. Figuratively, sure, but that's not what I mean. I'm talking about the squeezing in my chest. The physical ache that has grown into much more than discomfort.

It reminds me—as if I needed a reminder—that my heart is not my own.

I ignore the pain and heave a sigh. After twenty years of studying, practicing, and traveling from one show to the next—each seemingly bigger than the last—I've finally given my best friend, Tiegan Rose Marie Atherton, her fifth and final wish.

I know she's watching, wherever she is. Right along with Mr. Murray McBride, most likely. Chewing on some Milk Duds or hitting heavenly home runs with that beautiful swing of hers, just like when we were kids.

The excitement of the moment makes my heart thump, and I squeeze my eyes shut, focusing on the ache, embracing the pain. Tiegan's heart sends the blood of life through my veins. It's a concept I doubt I'll ever fully wrap my mind around. It's a debt I'll certainly never fully repay.

My mom is here, walking backstage from the wings with tears in her eyes, holding Collins' hand and beaming. Her embrace feels warm and familiar, despite the time that has passed. But I can't focus on it because of what I see over her shoulder. Della—Tiegan's mom—staring at the floor, unable to meet my eyes.

I recognize the confused furrow of her brow and the vacant stare, pointed at nothing. It's a mirror image of what's inside me. Something I didn't anticipate but now realize I should have.

Emptiness.

Since that day twenty years ago when I awoke in a hospital bed in Chicago with Tiegan's heart pumping in my chest, I've been laser focused on one thing. If I could become a well-known magician, I could earn enough money to make Tiegan's final wish of raising a million dollars for the homeless a reality. If that singular focus and determination also helped me deal with the loss of my two best friends—one an old man and the other a young girl—so much the better.

And it worked. Until now. Until the distraction is gone, and all I'm left with is a gaping hole and an uncertain future.

Funny that I would think of my goal as a distraction. The truth is, it's been my entire life's meaning. But I'm finding Cervantes was right: the journey is better than the inn. And now I'm faced with a question, so soon after reaching my goal: what comes next?

I have no answer, and it paralyzes me.

Forget the questions about the future of my career, or my relationships, or any other big picture things. I can't even figure out where to move my feet. Standing here behind the curtain, I hear the loneliest sounds I've ever heard.

The fading of the crowd's applause.

The clicking of seats folding into position.

The shuffling of feet as they exit.

The silence that covers the theater like a plague.

"Jason?"

It's my mother's voice. The fear and sadness in her eyes make me feel even worse, so I try to smile. "How'd I do?"

"Amazing," she says. "It was truly amazing." But after watching me stand motionless for several long moments, she touches the shoulder of my tuxedo gently. "What's wrong?"

Staring straight at the backside of the curtain, I shake my head. "I'm lost, Mom."

There's a squeeze of my shoulder. I can tell she wants to hug me again and I wonder if she's holding back because of the distance I've created in the name of focusing on my goal. "If you're lost, you can always come home," she says.

I want to ask her: what home? I haven't had a home since I woke up in that hospital bed twenty years ago. The last time I had a home, I snuck out of it and into Murray's car in the middle of the night. Together, we journeyed. We adventured. We lived.

And we lost so very much.

But I've caused my mother enough pain as it is. First, she had to live with the uncertainty of my health, then she surely believed she'd lose me to a failing heart. After that, I surprised her by surviving—only to disappear on a quest as soon as I was old enough, the motivation for which I could never adequately explain.

So I nod, give her a hug, and kiss her cheek. "Okay, Mom," I say. "I'll come home."

■　　　■　　　■　　　■　　　■

The heart is such a mystical thing. It's so much more than an organ. So much more than a muscle that pumps blood through the body, delivering oxygen and nutrients. Over the years, it has come to symbolize love itself. Thanks to the combined ideas of a philosopher and a physicist.

Aristotle once described the heart, not quite accurately, as having three chambers with a small dent in the middle. Then, in the Middle Ages, Italian physicist Guido da Vigevano drew the shape he imagined from Aristotle's description: the modern "heart" shape we see on Valentine's Day cards.

Needless to say, I've spent a lot of time thinking about the heart.

It's been years since my heart and I (which I think of as two separate things) have set foot in my hometown of Lemon Grove, Illinois. I returned for a while after the transplant. Long enough to finish elementary school, middle school, and high school. But it's amazing how little of those years I remember. With all the hours I spent reading about magic, practicing magic, even performing magic the last few years I was there, I barely remember anything after Murray picked me up in the middle of the night and drove me to Chicago, where so many of my wishes came true.

Along with my worst nightmares.

It's the nightmares that haunt me. I wish I could remember the feeling of kissing Mindy Applegate, or watching the baseball sail over the fence at Wrigley Field, or punching that bully to defend Tiegan's honor. But all I can think about is what happened to Murray and Tiegan in the end. All I can remember is waking up with them gone. All I can feel is guilt.

I suppose this is how Murray must have felt before he met me. Worn out, washed up, and having outlived what should have been his life. If he hated himself for living when others died, if he had a void that felt too big to fit inside him…well, then I guess I'm getting to know Murray better now than I ever did during our adventures together.

I can't get out of D.C. fast enough, so I take a redeye to O'Hare, then rent a car and drive up to Lemon Grove. But I don't go home. My mom wouldn't be there anyway. Everyone who was in D.C. for the show is still in D.C., except for me. So despite being the middle of the night, I drive straight to the old house where Murray McBride used to live.

I never actually visited his home when Murray was alive, but I used to take the city bus to this neighborhood and walk by when I was in middle school, after he was gone. I'd look in the windows and try to imagine him eating his bran flakes. I'd crack up at the thought of him getting ready to go to his art class, where he was a nude model, although in his case, *nude* only meant removing his top shirt. It was one of the few things that could make me laugh in those days.

It doesn't make me laugh now.

At some point, I must have fallen asleep in the rental car because when I startle awake, the sun is up. The driver's side seat is fully reclined, which I don't remember doing. I must have been exhausted from the adrenaline of the performance followed by the flight here and car rental. I probably didn't even get here until 4 a.m.

I glance at my phone: 8:48 a.m.

For all the times I visited Murray's house in the years after his death, I never knocked on the door. I don't know why. Fear that the people who live there now might feel intruded upon? Fear that the memories of Murray would be too much? Whatever the reason, it doesn't affect me now. So I step out of the car, straighten my wrinkled tuxedo as best I can, and walk straight up to the door.

And I knock.

Chapter Two

Been thinking about my boys a lot recently. Since meeting Jason, I guess. Been realizing all the things I did wrong. Wishing I could do it all over again. But time doesn't allow for that, I know that much. So I guess we just have to try to do it right the first time around.

But there's one other thing I'm learning from my time with the kid. Even if we mess things up real good the first time around, time keeps on ticking. So maybe there'll be another chance, of sorts. And if we're lucky, maybe we'll do better the next time around.

—From the Journal of Murray McBride

The woman who answers looks like she could be Murray's age. She's stooped over so far that her thin, white hair dangles in front of her wrinkled face. Her voice, when she speaks through the screen door, is raspy and hollow.

"Yes?" she says, confused by the appearance of a relatively young man at her door. The skepticism in her voice suggests the only thirty-year-old men who have knocked on her door in the past have been pushy vacuum cleaner salesmen.

"Ma'am," I say, suddenly unsure why I'm even here. Is it because I expected Murray to answer the door? Or his grandson, Chance, maybe? Neither of those would make any sense. Maybe I just want to see the place where he lived. Maybe I'm hoping it'll bring back a piece of my old friend, if only in my mind. I could use a friend right now.

"What can I do for you?" the woman asks.

"That's a harder question than I thought it would be," I say. Of course, the woman looks confused by my answer. I'm even confused. "I was friends with a man who used to live here. A long time ago."

She looks at me in the way a botanist might study a new species of flower. "Come in," she finally says. "Let's see if you can find what you're looking for."

I follow her in and shut the door behind me. The living room we enter is small. Cramped, actually. I could probably walk from one side of the room to the other in five strides. Through a small arch, I see a dining nook where Murray must have eaten his Chef Boyardee. The place where he'd taken his life-saving pill each morning.

"My name's Jason," I say.

She nods, like it's an acceptable name. "Betty."

Of course her name is Betty. How could it be anything else? "How long have you lived here, Betty?"

"Oh, let's see. It'll be nine years in October, I guess. Feels like less. The years go so fast nowadays."

My heart sinks. If she'd been living in the house for the entire twenty years since Murray died, maybe something would have remained the same. Maybe something of Murray's would still be around. Of course, even that was a silly thought: that someone would live in a house for two decades and not make it her own. And now I know it's not possible; Betty wasn't the one to buy the house after Murray's death.

"Do you plan to live here for a while, or do you think you'll sell?"

It's another strange question that I can't rationalize. It's not like I'm going to buy the house, even if it goes up for sale. I've got a bit of a nest egg, but I've donated most of the money I made to make Tiegan's final wish come true. More than anything, I'm just making conversation. Trying to make it seem natural that I'm here, despite the fact that Betty is no doubt starting to realize just how unnatural it is.

"I couldn't sell it if I wanted to," she says. "I'm just a renter."

"You rent?" I say, and an unexpected spark of hope flares in my chest. "Do you know who owns it?"

"My landlord," she says, as if I must be a special kind of stupid to have to ask.

A landlord. An investment property owner. The kind of person who purchases a house, clears it out, and churns through renters. And maybe, the kind of person who doesn't pay much attention to the nooks and crannies of a place.

As if called to it by Murray himself, my eyes flick to a square on the ceiling, near the corner of the room. A small handle suggests an entrance.

"Have you ever been up there?" I ask. "In the attic?"

Betty follows my gaze and startles as if noticing it for the first time. "I never thought to," she says. "Do you think there's anything up there?"

"I'd like to check, if you don't mind."

Her face crinkles tightly. "I don't know about that. What if there's something important up there, and my landlord comes to get it someday?"

"I promise I won't take anything without permission," I say.

After a long moment of consideration, Betty nods, then shuffles toward the kitchen. "I'll go put on a pot of coffee."

I wait until she rounds the corner and is out of sight, then quickly slide a heavy recliner a few feet to the right, until it's directly below the attic entrance. The amount of effort it takes surprises me. My heart squeezes tightly and I have to stop to catch my breath. I must be overly excited about the idea of the attic, the possibility of what I might find.

I take a deep breath and my chest starts to feel better. I step up onto one of the armrests of the chair, careful not to tip it over, and reach to the ceiling. My fingers slip into the handle and I pull.

It doesn't budge, but there doesn't appear to be a lock of any kind. I slide my finger along the edge and realize the problem. It's been twenty years since Murray lived here. This ceiling has been painted over. Multiple times, by the looks of it.

I grab the rental car key out of my pocket and use it to chip away at the paint along the edges. Once I get some space, I slide the key along like I'm opening a package, and suddenly the panel drops open, revealing a dark space above.

A wooden ladder is retracted into the space. I grab the lowest rung and pull but, like the entrance itself, it's stuck. This time it's just age and wear and with a second pull, something releases and the entire ladder swings down, knocking me off the recliner and onto the floor, where I grunt from the impact. The squeezing in my chest flares again, and I rub at it hard until it subsides.

Betty scurries around the corner and pulls up short when she sees me sprawled on the carpet next to a ladder leading into a dark attic she didn't even know existed. Her eyes bulge, and she studies the situation for a long moment. Then she turns around and goes back into the kitchen without a word.

I'm not sure if it was silent permission to continue or if she's dialing 911 right now. I hope it's the former and pick myself up from the floor. I give the ladder a good tug to make sure it's not going to collapse on me from above. When I'm relatively sure it'll hold me, I stretch my hand toward the highest rung I can reach and begin to climb.

. . . . .

The space that opens above me is a cross between an antique shop and something out of a scary movie. As soon as my head clears ceiling level—which is also the floor of the attic—I enter another world. Below, Betty's living room still exists with its shag carpet and peeling wallpaper. But above, I'm transported to another era. One of wooden rafters, cobwebs, and relics from the past.

My heart pounds, and I take a moment to listen to it. I try to hear Tiegan's voice. I focus on feeling what comes from her heart. It's hard to describe this connection I have to her, but it's real. That much I know. It's my guiding light. Like a conscience, but more personal. Like a voice in my head, but deeper. For my entire adult life, I've listened to it in times of turmoil. She's never let me down. And right now, my heart is telling me to continue.

So I climb the rest of the way into the attic and step fully into the space. As my eyes adjust to the darkness, I see a single, bare lightbulb dangling from one of the wooden rafters. I pull the string connected to it and, with a click, the space is bathed in the soft, yellow light of a bulb that's barely able to conduct enough electricity to function.

The dusty room reminds me of a museum's storage space. Nothing is displayed, but boxes are everywhere. The first box I open contains pictures of Murray with a woman who must be his wife, Jenny. There aren't many photos, maybe eight or ten in all. But they span the different eras of Murray's life: One of him in a Cubs uniform. One that looks to be in this very house, with Jenny, who's trying to wrangle two little boys who are showing no interest in sitting for a picture. And one of Murray as I remember him. Or close to it, anyway. Old and weathered, but beaming like I never saw him before, with his arm around Jenny. I don't think I ever saw him so happy. So carefree. With me, he was satisfied, maybe, or content. Proud, surely. But not blissful like he is in this picture. He was a different man with Jenny.

I put the pictures down and open the next box. It's an old turntable with a few records next to it. I don't bother to look through the records because another box catches my eye and my vision gives in to vertigo for a moment. When my eyes clear, I look at the old cardboard box again to make sure I'm seeing correctly. Sure enough, the box has small, handwritten letters in faded Sharpie.

Jason

I grab the box like it's a treasure and clutch it to my chest. I carry it directly under the lightbulb, set it back on the floor, and peel open the top flap.

Inside is one treasure after another. The baseball glove I brought to Wrigley Field—which until this very moment I never realized I didn't get back. The gaming console I brought with me, along with that ridiculous game I used to love—All-Powerful Gods and Blood-Sucking Aliens. I gaze at the dusty cartridge and remember all the times I wanted to play just so I could ask Murray for answers no human has. Answers about life and death and fairness and pain.

I set the cartridge back into the box and sit back hard, feeling like I've just taken a body blow in a boxing match. Twenty years is a long time. But apparently some memories are stored in their original, raw form and can be brought back with unexpected power.

I start to fold the cardboard flap closed when a notebook catches my attention. Normally, a notebook wouldn't stand out, but among these things, its presence doesn't make sense. What use would Murray have with a notebook? And why would he have kept it in the box of my things?

The pages shake as I open to a dog-eared page partway through and read:

8/16: Met a kid today. Found his list. Want to give it back.

8/17: Met Jason Cashman today. Well, met him before but properly introduced now. Father James helped. Calls me dude. Have to help him learn. Disrespectful, but sick with heart problems. Good kid, I think.

On each page, Murray's sloppy handwriting charts the progress of our time together in short, choppy notes. I want to sit and read them all, and I vow to do just that when I'm in a place with a bit more privacy. For now, I just flip through the pages, trying to see the words without reading them. Just to be with them.

But when the pages thin and I'm near the end, something about the entries changes. They get longer. The clipped phrases and three-sentence entries become full, flowing paragraphs. The handwriting continues to decline in legibility and everything about the script exudes urgency. I can't help myself. I stop near the very end of the notebook and read an entry.

What has this all been for, I can't help but wonder. An old, washed-up man, missing his Jenny more than breath, ready to see Saint Peter, and then along comes the kid and everything changes. Life is worth sticking around for again, that's what. But the Good Lord dealt him a bad hand, and I can't understand why. I did what I could. But I wish I could have done more.

How do you like that? I want a wish. Just like Jason and his five. A hundred years old, and I want one for myself. Maybe it's selfish, maybe it's useless, but there you go. I have a wish.

And here it is: I wish the kid would survive somehow. Get that heart he's been waiting on. And I wish he'd grow up, grow old like me. Most important, I wish he could meet someone like I did when I met him. Wish he'd get to know the joy and satisfaction and, okay I'll just say it, the love I feel for that little boy.

Yep. If I could have one final wish, I'd wish Jason could have his very own Jason Cashman. Then he'd know why living this life means so much. He'd have purpose and meaning, just like he's given me. It's just the wish of a dying old man, but still, it's my wish.

■   ■   ■   ■   ■

Betty gives me a strange look when I descend the ladder. Part fear, part confusion. But it morphs into something like sympathy after she sees the expression on my face. She holds a steaming cup of coffee toward me, but I shake my head.

"I'm sorry. I can't stay." I hold up the box that contains my things. "Can I take this with me?"

Betty pauses to study the name on the fraying cardboard box. "That's yours?" When I nod, she stares at the box again, a deep crinkle in her brow. "I don't think my landlord even knows about it, so if it's useful to you, it's yours."

I think of that phrase—"useful to me." I wonder if it will be.

"Thank you for allowing me in, Betty."

I want to say more. To tell her about what I've found. To tell her the whole story of what happened to me, and Tiegan, and Murray. But my throat constricts and I can't say anymore, so I try to show my appreciation with my eyes. Then I leave Murray's old home behind.

Chapter Three

Doc Keaton told me I should go to a painting class today, so that's what I did. Don't think the good doctor knew what he was setting me up for. But he wanted me to be social, so that's where I went. So much of life is about where we decide to go, and who we meet when we're there. Those two things: where and who. They end up making all the difference.

—From the Journal of Murray McBride

When I get to the car, I put the box in the back seat and take a long, deep breath. Again, I have to think about where to go. It's strange, not having a home. I know my mom would say her house is my home, and I guess it is the closest thing I have. But it belongs to her and Collins now, as it has for the past twenty years. I'm welcome there, I know. But I'd be a visitor. It's not mine anymore. My "home" has been a years-long string of hotels. Now that I've left that life behind, I have no home at all.

So I go to the Catholic church on the corner right near Murray's old house. I have no idea if the person I'm hoping to see is still there, but something tells me the stone building itself couldn't exist if he wasn't inside its walls.

Sure enough, as soon as I walk through the front doors, colored light from a stained glass window paints Father James Gonzalez in a kaleidoscope of colors as he sweeps the stone floors of the entry way.

We stare at each other for a moment. I recognize him right away. The dark beard is now gray and his hairline has receded quite a bit, but his eyes are the same piercing black that I remember.

Recognition takes him a moment longer, which makes sense. He was an adult when I knew him. He's aged a bit, softened and grayed. But he still looks remarkably like the man I knew. I, on the other hand, was a ten-year-old boy when he knew me. I only saw him a handful of times in the "after" years, when my mom would still make me go to church, and thought it would be a good idea to go where Murray had gone.

So recognition dawns slowly for Father James. But when it comes, he smiles wide and extends his arms even wider. I step into his embrace and squeeze him tightly.

"Well, if it isn't Prospero, Master of the Impossible," he says.

I chuckle. "Actually, it's not. Not right now anyway." He gives me a searching look, so I clarify. "I'm sure I'll go back to performing someday. It's my livelihood. But right now I'm trying to figure some things out."

Father James leans his head back in understanding. "So that's why you're here."

I shrug sheepishly.

"Come back to my office," Father James says. He turns to lead the way, but then stops as if hit by an idea. "First, pray for five minutes. Something tells me you could use it."

I try to object. To tell him I don't believe in God the same way he does. That prayers coming from me would surely not be answered. But he has already turned his back and is out of sight before I can get a word out. I don't want to disobey him so I take a seat on a pew and take in the surroundings that used to feel so comfortable.

Comfort is definitely something this place used to provide—at 10 a.m. most Sunday mornings. But comfort was also the extent of it. With all I was going through before my transplant, I never thought to turn to religion. I figured if I didn't have much life left to live, I needed to live it, not spend my time praying for a miracle that would never come.

And then it came. But at a price. And that price has defined every moment of my life since. So when I stepped into the church just now, it wasn't to find God—only God's messenger. The man who helped me find Murray in the first place. Or rather, who helped Murray find me.

After a few moments of pretending to pray, I follow the steps Father James took and end up in a back office where he's just ending a conversation on the phone.

"Thanks, Juan. I appreciate it." He hangs up the phone and smiles at me. "I'm happy you're here. I've often wondered what happened to you . . . after . . . " He seems to search for a reaction. Some sort of indication of how lightly he might need to tread. But I've spent nearly as many hours perfecting my stoic face as I have my magic tricks. Finally, he continues. "I've heard about your career, of course. But, I mean personally. How have you been personally?"

"There hasn't been much *personally* for me," I say. "I guess that's why I'm here."

Father James's piercing stare seems to break right through my poker face. And then he says the most amazing, most perceptive thing possible. "Feeling empty, or feeling guilty?"

If my jaw physically hit the floor, it wouldn't surprise me any more than what he said. How could he possibly know about the void that consumed me the moment the curtain closed on my last show? And the feeling, every single day of my life, that Tiegan is the one who should be alive. Not me. I had a bad heart. I was supposed to die. But Tiegan. . .well, Tiegan was perfect. And she should have spent the last twenty years sharing that perfection with the world. Instead, I stole that chance from her.

Father James has been watching me, and I can't help but feel he's somehow heard every word that's gone through my mind. He nods sadly. "There's nothing I can say, I'm afraid, to make it better. I've seen enough heartache to know that words simply don't have that kind of power. Not in the short-term, anyway. But there is something that helps. Something your old friend found, just before it was too late."

"Murray?" I say.

"Murray."

"What did he find?"

Father James leans forward, his eyes burning my own. "Purpose."

I shake my head. It's exactly what Murray said in his journal. But how does someone go about finding purpose? I spent so much time and effort and thought focusing on one, all-consuming goal, I don't even know who I am without it. How's that for purpose?

"What about raising more money for the homeless? That's what you've been doing all this time, right? And it provided you purpose? Why not continue, if it was meaningful?"

I try to keep the anger out of my voice, but it's not something I can control. "It was meaningful because it was Tiegan's fifth wish," I say. "I know I should have been doing it for the people getting the money, the people in need, but I wasn't. I was doing it for Tiegan. Only for Tiegan. Now that I've hit the number she set, it just wouldn't be the same."

Father James is more comfortable with silence than I am, and he lets it fill all the empty space in the room. "Things just change so much," I finally say.

"Of course they do," Father James says. "That's what life is all about."

"But I don't want it to change. I don't want to move on or find some other purpose."

"What *do* you want, Jason?"

"I want to go back to when I was ten. When Murray was driving me all around, sneaking off to Chicago. When I could watch Tiegan hit a baseball in that old lady's garden and give her a hard time about something, and she could call me out on it and we'd laugh. I don't want those things to change."

"But they already have."

I'm not sure where the words come from when I say, "Then I don't want to be here!" It's as if they've been inside me all along, and I'm no longer able to keep them in the dark recesses of my mind. "I was allowed to live when I shouldn't have been," I say. "But what if I don't want to live? What if I want Tiegan to be the one who lives? Why can't I have that?"

"That past is not something we can change, Jason."

"Maybe not. But if I can't have my past back, maybe I don't want a future."

Father James's eyebrows curl deeply inward. I can't tell if he's angry or sad. I expect him to lecture me about how ungrateful I am. How I should thank God every day that I've been allowed to live. That I have no right to feel the way I do. But that's not what he says.

"Strange, isn't it? The feelings life can force upon us? Sometimes they make no sense and yet that doesn't make them any less real. And certainly no less powerful." He leans back in his chair and looks to the ceiling. After a long moment, he turns his stare back to me. "You didn't kill Tiegan. You need to understand that."

"But if she hadn't gone out in that storm . . . she only did it for me."

"And she'd done a hundred things like that a hundred other times. It was an accident. An accident that you didn't cause. And the fact that you lived as a result of that accident does not make the fact that it happened your fault. Your survival was a blessing. A silver lining."

I stand, feeling something solidify inside me. A knowledge. A certainty. "That's where you're wrong," I say. "The fact that I got to live because she died—*only* because she died?" I shake my head and feel the familiar burn somewhere deep in my chest. "No matter how anyone tries to rationalize it, that fact is simply unforgivable. And I don't know if I can live with it anymore."

■   ■   ■   ■   ■

I leave Father James in his office, once again with no idea where to go next. I've come to my hometown seeking something, but I don't even know what. Purpose, like Father James said? Like Murray wished?

Maybe so. But I'm not finding it anywhere. And no one left me an instruction manual.

On the way out of the church, I notice an assortment of candles set up in a corner, which stops me in my tracks. I don't believe God decided I should live and Tiegan should die. I don't think there's some grand plan, and all I have to do is go to church every Sunday and say the rosary and everything will turn out like it's supposed to.

But still, I find myself drawn to those candles.

When I get there, it's a pretty depressing sight. Only about a quarter of the candles are lit. The others look drab and neglected, and add to the darkness that covers the entire alcove. I stare at one of the unlit candles for a long moment, wondering what my prayer should be. Is it selfish to pray for purpose? For a reason to live? Especially when I haven't prayed at all for several years? Although I don't have an answer, I find a lighter on a small shelf, flick it to life, and touch it to a dark wick. Soft candlelight warms my face.

"What was your wish?"

I'm so startled by the voice behind me that I drop the lighter to the floor, where it clanks and echoes against the stone walls of the empty church. I squint into the darkness, where I can barely decipher the form of a girl hidden in the third and final row of chairs set up in front of the candles. I'd completely missed her until now.

"I'm sorry," I said. "You scared me."

The girl doesn't say anything and the silence soon becomes awkward. Finally, she says, "I asked what your wish was," as if she's been waiting for an answer.

"Oh." I try to come up with something. "It's a pretty long story."

The form of the girl shrugs. She stands from her chair and walks up to the candles. She reaches her index finger just inches from a flame. "This one's mine," she says. "It's so I can stay in America and not be sent away."

"Sent away?"

The girl looks at me with round, brown eyes, and I try to figure out how old she is. Ten, maybe? Somewhere around the age I was when I met Murray, which immediately makes me fond of the kid. She has flowing dark hair, and in the candlelight I can tell her skin is darker than mine. Her face has distinct Latina features. She has a fanny pack buckled around her waist and when the candles flick light on her shirt, I see red, white, and blue stripes along with several stars. It's like she's wearing an American flag for a shirt.

"I like stories," she says, and I notice she doesn't have an accent. She must have been raised in the states.

I try to figure out what she's talking about with the stories comment. I don't have a book in my hand or anything, so why would she randomly tell me she likes stories?

"You said your wish is a long story," she says. "I like stories."

I shift from one foot to the other, then back again. "I guess I'm not exactly sure how it works, but I think they're actually prayers, aren't they? Not wishes?" Prayers, admittedly, are something I don't know much about. Wishes, on the other hand...

The girl shrugs. "Same difference."

I consider arguing the point, but it seems inconsequential. Besides, she might be right.

"So what about your story?" she says.

I wonder for a moment about her insistence on learning my wish, or prayer, or story, or whatever it is. Maybe I shouldn't have asked her about her wish—about being sent away—because now I feel like I owe her an explanation about mine.

"How much do you want to know?" I ask.

She settles into the first pew like she's ready for a long retelling. Her eyes shimmer in the candlelight. "Just the good parts, I guess."

I chuckle and consider what the "good parts" of my story would be. "Well, I met an old man once and we became friends. Despite an enormous age difference."

"Was he, like, as old as you are now?" she asks.

"Much older, believe it or not." I try not to be offended by her skeptical look. After a long silence, I say, "Things turned out differently than we anticipated, and I guess I was wishing ..." I try to think about exactly what it was I was wishing for when I lit that candle. "I guess I was wishing that I could turn back time."

"But that's impossible," she says. "Why would you wish for something impossible when you know it can't come true. It's a waste of a wish, don't you think?"

"Yeah," I say. I stop myself from saying that my entire life has been a waste. At least in comparison to what Tiegan's would surely have been. Tiegan probably would have raised the money for the homeless and gone on to find the cure for cancer or something.

Okay, that might be a stretch. But that's the thing: I'll never know what she would have been capable of. I'll never know what she might have achieved in her life, because I stole that opportunity from her. But this girl doesn't need to hear all that.

"How was it different?" she says.

"What?"

"The ending. You said things turned out different than you thought they would. How?"

I have no idea who this girl is or why such a young kid would be alone in a church by the candles. Or why she's asking so many questions. But I'm surprised to realize I haven't spoken this comfortably with anyone in years. Maybe not since Tiegan. So, ridiculous or not, I tell her.

"Well, my heart?" I say. "It's not actually mine."

The girl's face turns to complete befuddlement. "Then whose is it?"

"A girl named Tiegan. Tiegan Rose Marie Atherton. She was my best friend, back when I was your age."

"That doesn't make any sense at all," the girl says, sneaking fleeting glances at my chest. "How did you get her heart? How does she live without a heart? Did you trade with her?"

"I'm sorry, that was a really bad explanation," I say. "She died, very unexpectedly. A long time ago. And I was sick and needed a new heart, so when she died, I got hers."

The girl stares at my chest unabashedly now. I can see the wheels turning in her mind. "You can do that? You can take someone else's heart?"

"Crazy, I know," I say.

"Well that was lucky." She shakes her head as if she's said something wrong. "For you, that is. Not for her."

"Yeah." I can't help but chuckle while I figure my way through my amusement at the girl's innocence and the pain brought on by her bluntness. "Unfortunately, when that happens, the heart doesn't last as long."

"Wow," she says. "So someday you could get another person's heart? How many people's hearts do you think you'll have before you die?"

"Just one," I say, chuckling again. I wonder if Murray ever felt this way with me. Entertained. Connected. A bit befuddled. Parental, even. "Well, two I guess," I say. "If you count the one I was born with. But I would never get rid of Tiegan's heart. I couldn't do that to her."

"Do what to her?"

"Cut her out of my life like that."

She cocks her head to the side. "But she's not alive anymore, is she? She wouldn't feel it, would she?"

"Well, no. But there's also . . . oh, nothing," I say, catching myself. But the girl is insistent, as I somehow knew she would be.

"No, tell me," she says. "It's okay, I'm old enough."

"It's not because you're young," I say. "It's just, well, it sounds a little crazy."

"That's fine. So far, everything you've said has been crazy."

"You might have a point." I try to figure out how to put into words what I've only ever felt before. "Ever since I woke up with Tiegan's heart, I've felt like she's been guiding me. Like she's somehow still alive in me, or through me, or something."

"Like an alien?" the girl says, looking again at my chest. Although this time she looks like she just ate something that might have been moldy.

"No, not like that. More like . . . a companion. Like she's my conscience. Or a sixth sense, maybe."

"Wow," the little girl says. A little crinkle forms in her brow, as if she's thinking deeply about something. Then she rotates the fanny pack so the storage area is in front, unzips it, and removes a few small devices I don't recognize. She puts one up to her finger and I hear a clicking sound.

"What's that?" I ask.

"I have to test my sugars. I'm feeling a little lightheaded."

"Your sugars?"

She ignores me, scoops a tiny droplet of blood onto a test strip, and slides it into the other device she removed. She sees my questioning stare. "It only takes about fifteen seconds."

"Are you a diabetic?" I ask.

Her eyes, which have been so friendly up to this point, flare at me. "No, I'm not 'a diabetic.' It's not my identity. I'm a human being who happens to have type-1 diabetes."

"I'm sorry," I say. "I didn't mean to be insulting."

She fiddles with the device, squinting at it in the near darkness. "Once, when I was little, my sugars got so low I passed out and my dad had to give me a glucagon shot. I don't remember it, but it completely freaked out my dad. So now I'm super-duper responsible about it. I test my sugars exactly twelve times every single day. Rain or shine, as my dad likes to say."

"Twelve? That seems like a lot."

She ticks them off, one by one. "Before and after every meal. That's six. Right when I wake up and just before bed. That's eight. And four times throughout the day, between my meals. Twelve."

She squints at the meter in her hand. Apparently satisfied with whatever number it came back with, she returns everything to her fanny pack, zips it up, and spins it back behind her. Then she turns her gaze back to the candles, and I notice she's staring at hers. We've spent the entire time talking about my wish, and I still know nothing about hers.

"I bet you wish you didn't have diabetes, huh?"

She shakes her head. "I already told you my wish."

She seemed reluctant to open up about it earlier, so I skirt the issue and point to a piece of paper she's pulling from her pocket.

"What do you have there?"

"It's why I'm here. My dad sent me to bring it to Father James. So, bye."

She's halfway to the altar before I figure out she's leaving. Talk about an abrupt departure. "Hey wait," I say. "What's your name?"

She comes all the way back to me and extends her hand. "Alexandra Lopez," she says. "It's nice to meet you, Mr. . . . . "

She lets her voice trail off, waiting for my reply. I consider how to answer. I could say "Mr. Cashman." Murray would sure get a kick out of that, considering I always insisted on calling him "Dude" when I was this kid's age. In the end, when Murray told me he was okay with me calling him "Dude," I don't think he ever knew how much that meant to me. It was the first time I truly realized we were friends.

"My name's Jason Cashman," I say, shaking her hand. "But if you wanted to call me 'Dude,' I'd be okay with it."

Alexandra looks at me sideways, squinting a little as if trying to figure out why I would say something so obviously stupid. "It's nice to meet you, Mr. Cashman," she says.

And with that, she's gone, leaving me shaking my head and feeling like a complete idiot.

■　　　■　　　■　　　■　　　■

A complete idiot, yes, but there's also something else. I'm filled, somehow, at least partially. Or maybe it's more accurate to say that during my few moments with Alexandra Lopez, I didn't feel quite as empty. She reminds me of someone, and it doesn't take long to put a finger on who.

Tiegan.

Tiegan was strong and independent, like this girl. She was brave and unafraid—or at least able to overcome any fears she did have. Maybe that explains why I wait until I see Alexandra leave the church—having delivered her paper—then head back into Father James's office. Doing so sounds better than going back out into that big, empty world, that's for sure.

Father James is sitting at his desk, writing something with pen and paper. Something about the old-fashioned method of communication takes me back to Murray. But not Murray writing letters. Murray on his email machine, and the hilarious messages he used to send me.

Not that he found them funny. The poor old man had no clue just how clueless he sounded in those emails. But for the first time, I'm hit with another thought: he probably thought my emails were every bit as strange as I found his. It's a crazy idea, and probably just as crazy that I'm only having it for the first time now.

"You're still here?" Father James says. He sets his pen down and gives me his full attention.

"Yeah, I . . ." I stumble over a few words, unsure how to say *I met a girl out there* in a way that doesn't sound very different from what actually happened. "Did you just talk to a little kid back here?" I ask.

"Ah! Alexandra. You had a chance to say hello?"

Something about Father James's expression is off. He's too chirpy—almost excited—considering the state I was in when I left his office just minutes ago. Then, slowly, I start to put two-and-two together.

"Did you . . . orchestrate our meeting?"

"Whose meeting?"

"Me and Alexandra."

"Why would you think that?"

"Because right when I'm at my lowest, I happen to meet a girl who seems like she could use some sort of help. And you have a history of pairing people who need each other at just the right time."

Father James shrugs. "Her father needed to deliver something to me, and I may have made a phone call while you were praying before you came back to my office to make sure she got here when you were here. So, in a way, the prayers I had you say were answered."

"I didn't actually pray," I say.

The twinkle in Father James's eye doesn't falter. "Alexandra is a wonderful little girl."

I don't know why I'm disappointed that Father James doesn't take my bait on the whole "I didn't pray" thing. Maybe I was hoping he'd challenge me and we'd end up in a long, philosophical discussion that would lead to my understanding of all things divine. But Father James doesn't seem to be in an answering mood. Will wonders never cease?

"So let me get this straight," I say. "You set me up to meet Alexandra, knowing I'd talk to her, get to know her problems, and want to help her?"

"Not knowing. I can't see the future, after all. But hoping."

"Just like before, with me and Murray."

Father James gives his little shrug again. The one that coincides with a flicking of his head that suggests it's no big deal. "It worked out last time. Why not try again?"

"I wouldn't say it worked out last time. People died."

"Murray was ready, Jason. He'd lived a long—"

"Tiegan wasn't. You think she would have chosen to give her heart to me? To die in my place?"

Father James lets my words bounce around the room until they fade and all that's left is the humming and clicking of the old, metal radiator along the wall. His dark eyes stare right at mine, as if challenging me.

But about what? About whether Tiegan would have chosen to die in my place? She was such a thoughtful, loving person. If she had known I was about to die, and that she had the power to save me but the cost would be her own life, would she have chosen to die in my place?

It's ridiculous to even contemplate. We were ten years old. Ten year-olds shouldn't have to think about things like that. They should spend their time running around and hitting baseballs and playing video games. Being kids.

I take a deep breath and focus on my heart. I feel Tiegan inside my chest, and along with her, a calmness. It's as if she's saying, *Don't worry about it. It's okay. Focus on the girl.* And that allows me to remember the reason I came back to Father James's office in the first place.

"So, Alexandra," I say to Father James, in control of myself once again. "I didn't get the whole story, but she told me she's diabetic—I mean, that she has diabetes. And she said something about being sent away somewhere?"

"Indeed."

"What's that mean?"

"Nothing more or less than what she said." Father James sees my confusion, I'm sure. He adjusts himself in his seat as if readying for an explanation. "Alexandra was brought here from Guatemala, as a toddler, immediately after her diagnosis. This is the only home she's ever known. But, to the government, she's a . . . what's the phrase? Illegal alien?"

"Really? But she doesn't even have an accent."

"Which, unfortunately, doesn't mean she gets to stay." Father James's eyes home in on mine again, like a magnet. "When Murray met you, your life was on unstable ground. Your survival was uncertain. The same is true for Alexandra right now. Here, in the United States, she is healthy, happy, and has a bright future in front of her. She can effectively manage her diabetes. But in Guatemala, the health-care system outside its large cities isn't nearly as robust, and Alexandra's father is a farm worker, so they would have no choice but to live in a rural area. In those places, insulin is hard to find, and her father's wages wouldn't be able to pay for it even if they can find it." He shakes his head as if unwilling to let his thoughts spiral downward. "Her chances of survival wouldn't be much better than yours were. And, unfortunately, she has no Tiegan Rose Marie Atherton available to provide her with a miracle."

What he's asking is too much. Does he want me to somehow prevent her from getting deported? Does he think I'm an immigration lawyer or something? I have no idea what I could possibly do for this kid.

"What about her mother? You mentioned a father, but no mother?"

"Her mother didn't survive the journey to the United States, I'm afraid."

"She died?"

"It's a very dangerous trip to make. Those who attempt it know this, but sometimes they're left with no choice. Type 1 diabetes is a serious condition, Jason. In fact, if Alexandra were to lose access to insulin—if, for example, she was in rural Guatemala and the power were to go out and the heat ruined the insulin—she would only survive for about twenty-four hours before succumbing to something called ketoacidosis."

I know what he's thinking. It's just like Murray, who could only survive for about a day without the pill he had to take for his condition. I don't know whether to feel closer to Alexandra because of the connection, or manipulated by Father James.

He rips a page out of the notebook he was writing in when I entered his office and hands it to me. "There's a deportation hearing next week. It's very important. The time and location are on this paper."

I take the paper and put it in my back pocket, feeling like I'm on autopilot. But really, what could I possibly offer this kid?

"Look, Father," I say. "I see what you're doing. Murray was lost, and then he met me and his last days were fulfilled. And you want the same for me. Apparently Murray does, too," I say, thinking about his journal entry. "But you guys don't seem to understand. I'm not Murray. I just don't think I'm the right person to do it."

Father James looks at me for a long moment, his eyes flicking from my chest back up to my face. "Actually," he says. "I think you might be the only person who can do it."

Chapter Four

Hospitals are the most depressing place in the world, so I'm not sure why I went to one when I met Jason. I knew going in I wouldn't enter a room with a bed. I'll never do that again. Not while I'm conscious, anyway. Not after Jenny died. Hospitals are terrible, terrible places, and that's the truth. Terrible things happen there.

Except, strange as it is, they do have one redeeming quality: whenever we're there, we tend to be in the presence of the ones we love. And that's no small thing, I've found.

—From the Journal of Murray McBride

As soon as I step out of the church, there's an ache in my chest. I get these aches a lot and have for quite a while. It's different than when I feel Tiegan, but it's hard to explain. When I feel like Tiegan's guiding me, it's more like an instinct. Like I just know what I should do in a situation, and that knowledge, that instinct, comes with a certain pressure. A squeezing in my chest. But it's not uncomfortable. Actually, I've come to need that feeling.

This current feeling, on the other hand, is painful and purely physical. I rub my chest hard. That usually does the trick, but not this time. It hurts enough that I try to figure out how long it's been since my last checkup. The answer is long enough that I can't even remember. Which isn't good when you've had a heart transplant.

So I drive to one of the many medical clinics in Lemon Grove, my vision blurring a bit, then recovering. Since I'm on Murray's side of town, I wonder if the clinic I pull into could be the same clinic he used to go to, and the thought gives me some comfort.

I park and make my way to the front door, still rubbing my chest hard, to no avail. There's a list of doctors who work in the office, but the doctor Murray used to see, Dr. Keaton, isn't one of them. I'm reminded again of how much time has passed.

Inside, I go through the normal back-and-forth with the receptionist. No, I don't have an appointment. No, this isn't an emergency, but I have had a heart transplant and am due for a checkup (this always gets their attention). Yes, I'm willing to see a new doctor. Yes, I can wait a half hour. Thank you, I'll be reading *People* magazine until you call my name.

When a young woman in blue scrubs calls my name, I follow her to an examining room, where she takes my vitals with a scowl and I wait for the doctor to arrive, which he does a few minutes later.

But when he asks me the first question—I'm not sure what it is—something very unusual happens. I start to get lightheaded, my vision begins to swim in strange swirls, and I can't seem to catch my breath. It feels a lot like when I was a kid and needed a hit from the oxygen machine, which is a feeling I could definitely do without.

"Mr. Cashman?" the doctor says.

I try to look at him. I open my eyes wide and blink several times, but a darkness creeps in from the sides of my vision and before I know it, I'm sliding off the examination table.

■   ■   ■   ■   ■

I wake up in a hospital. I know because of the smell of the bed. Every hospital bed smells the same, and a hospital bed is the only place in the world I've found that smell.

The fact that I'm here is ridiculous. My heart has been fine for all these years, and now, when I've finally found a little girl I might be able to help—and who might be able to help me find that meaning I'm searching for—my heart decides to give out?

Before I fully regain my bearings, a beautiful face appears over me like she's been waiting for me to wake up.

"How are you feeling?" she asks.

All I can think about is how round her eyes are, how deep and brown and perfectly framed by long lashes. But after a few moments, I clear my head enough to remember she asked me a question.

"I'm fine," I say. While one truth is that I don't want such a gorgeous woman to see me so vulnerable, it's also true that I don't feel any ill effects from passing out. Which apparently I did.

"Good," the woman says. "Do you feel up to answering some questions? If not, I can have someone come back later."

"No," I say, because I don't want her to leave. "I'm fine." I sit up a little to illustrate the point.

"Take it easy," she says. "You can lie down for this." She thumbs through some papers—undoubtedly my medical records—and shoots occasional glances at me. I get it a lot. It's not often you see a man my age with a heart transplant. "My name is Rachel Sparks," she says. "I'm the transplant coordinator here at the hospital."

"Transplant?" I say. "I can't get another transplant."

She seems stumped, like she has no idea what to say to that. Finally, she ignores my answer and moves on. "How long have you been experiencing issues with your heart?"

I actually laugh. "Since I was born."

"Yeah," she says, consulting her chart again. "I see that. I'm sorry."

With all the bad news about my heart I've received over the years, I've never had someone say those words so simply, and with such sincerity. I feel my throat tighten and try to reign in a wave of emotion. "Thank you," I finally manage.

Rachel pulls a chair up to the bed, sits, and leans forward on her elbows. Through sheer force of will, I keep my eyes away from the loosening of her shirt as she leans forward. Thankfully, her eyes make the task easier.

"But recently, I mean. You've been experiencing problems?"

I shrug. "I don't know. Why?"

"Well, one part of the calculus of where someone gets placed on the wait list is how immediate their need is. If it's bad enough for you to lose consciousness, it's likely been getting worse for a while. These things don't usually happen out of the blue. But the progression has probably been relatively slow. Sometimes that can make it sneak up on you."

"I guess I have noticed a little more discomfort than normal lately."

"What do you mean by *lately*?"

I usually hate these questions. Normally, I'd downplay the pain and tell little white lies so I could leave sooner. But I find it impossible to lie to Rachel. "I first noticed a difference about a year ago. Since then, it seems to get worse for a while—more painful squeezing and stuff—but then it goes away and I convince myself it's fine."

She leans back in her chair and crosses her legs. "Do you know how long the average heart lasts after a transplant?"

"About fifteen years?"

"Even less if the donor is the opposite sex."

"I know, but this was Tiegan's heart."

She pauses for a moment, as if considering whether to ask what I mean, but then she moves on. "Then you know your heart is nearing the end of its life."

The words feel like a stab straight into this heart we're talking about. I'm immediately short of breath. I feel a drop of sweat rise from my hairline and find it hard to swallow.

"I'm sorry," Rachel says. "I didn't mean to scare you. There are options for you. That's what I'm here for. I didn't mean to imply this was a death sentence, because it's not. We'll get you on the list for another transplant. We can get that started today."

I shake my head hard. There are two very good reasons for me not to get another heart transplant. The first is impossible for people to understand. How could anyone who doesn't have Tiegan's heart in their chest possibly comprehend the depth of the connection I have to her? They can't. I could talk until I'm blue in the face about the guidance I feel when faced with a big decision and the certainty that somehow, in some way—despite knowing it's physically impossible—the source of what I'm feeling is a little girl named Tiegan.

It's too much to ask someone to comprehend because it doesn't make any sense. I know that. To most people, the heart is an organ that pumps blood, nothing more. It's not a device for transmitting emotion, despite the symbolism it has held throughout history. And it's not the source of love, despite what Hollywood tells us. It's simply an organ made of cells and has a singular function in the body.

Well, that's true for most hearts, anyway.

And that's why it's impossible for my mom, or my doctors, or this beautiful transplant coordinator, or anyone else to understand why I can't simply remove the organ currently in my chest and swap it out for a newer, healthier model. For me, despite what I know, it's not just an organ. It's so much more.

"You don't understand," I say, still struggling to catch my breath after the idea of a new heart knocked it out of me. "My heart . . . it's Tiegan's heart . . . she's . . . important to me. I can't . . . "

"Okay," Rachel says, putting her hand on mine and squeezing. To my surprise, my breath immediately comes back. I stop sweating and I'm able to swallow again. "I'm sorry. I didn't know," she says.

We sit there for a long moment in silence. Finally—and I like to think reluctantly—she pulls her hand away from mine. "Look, Mr. Cashman—"

"Jason," I say. "Please, call me Jason."

She looks pleased by that, but I can't tell if she actually is or if I'm just projecting my own feelings. "Jason," she says, "you don't have to do anything you don't want to, obviously. If you decide you don't want a new heart, and you just want to live until your current heart gives out, that's your decision to make. Not mine, not even your doctors'. But I wonder if you'd do me a favor."

"What's that?" I almost say, *Anything at all for you,* but I manage to control myself.

"We give out cell phones to patients on the heart transplant list so we can get in touch quickly. When a heart becomes available, we only have about four hours to get it into the recipient."

I know all this, of course. This isn't my first time facing someone who wants me to cut Tiegan out of my life. But I don't say that because I'm hatching a plan that has everything to do with the second reason I could never get another heart. And that reason is very simple and easy to understand: there are others who need a new heart.

If there were unlimited hearts in the world and everyone who needed one could simply go to the transplant center and get the latest model installed, then maybe it would be a hard decision for me. But that's not the case. For every heart available for transplant, there are many people needing that heart.

Hence, the waitlist.

And the names on that waitlist aren't just made up. They're actual people with actual families and actual lives. As someone who has more or less disconnected himself from his friends and family, it seems like I should be the last person to get another heart.

"You want me to take a hospital cell phone?" I say, responding to her previous comment. I feel bad, toying with her like this. But there's something I need, and this might be my only chance. "But I just told you I can't get another heart."

I'm banking on the fact that she doesn't want to see an otherwise-healthy thirty-year-old pass up a chance at better health. I can't help but feel guilty when she plays right into my hand.

"That's fine," she says. "Like I said, it's your choice. I'm not suggesting anything that will change that. I'm just asking that you take the first steps, because if you don't, and then you change your mind, there's no way you'll get a heart. This way, if a heart becomes available, we'll call you. If you still feel the way you do now, all you have to do is decline and we'll give it to the next person in line who matches well. But at least you'll have the option." She spreads her hands out like she's showing me the entirety of her argument. "That's all I'm asking. No strings attached. As a favor to me."

"Okay," I say. "But it doesn't mean I'm considering another transplant."

"Trust me," Rachel says. "You've made that clear."

"Good."

She stands and walks to a computer near the corner. "Let's go ahead and get you started."

It takes a little longer than I anticipate, but before too long I hear the words I'm expecting.

"This can't be right," Rachel says.

"What's that?" I ask, all innocence.

"Your name. It's already on the list. Not only that, it's been on here for quite a while."

She stares at the screen—at the list she's brought up—and shakes her head as if to clear it. "I just need to make a call," she says. "I'll be right back."

Just as I was hoping, she leaves the exam room. The computer is facing away from me—probably intentionally—so as soon as the door closes behind her, I scamper over to the front of the computer, and there it is.

The wait list.

Like Rachel said, my name is on it. Not only that, it's below only one other. Somewhere along the line, a doctor must not have liked what he saw. The only way I could be this high on the list is if they decided my need is very "immediate," as Rachel said.

I continue scanning the list. Beneath my name is the problem: many, many more names. Not just names though. People. Most of whom—maybe even all of whom—desperately want a heart. And here I am, terrified of the thought of having my name called.

The list is pretty basic, actually. It's just a list of names, ages, addresses, blood types, and what must be the disease they have that makes a transplant necessary.

I have no idea how long Rachel will be gone, and the thought of her walking in on me makes my hands shake. I grab my phone from a bedside table and swipe until I find the camera. I snap a quick picture of the computer screen, then rush back over to the hospital bed. Almost as soon as I get my feet off the ground, Rachel returns, looking flustered.

"You must have known you were already on the list," she says. "That's not something that happens without patient consent."

"Oh yeah," I say, and I try to chuckle, but it seems obviously fake to me. "I guess I just blocked it out. You know, since I don't want a heart."

"Okay," she says in a voice that suggests she's struggling to decide whether to believe me. "But it looks like our hospital put you on the list. Meaning we must have already given you a phone, like we talked about."

"I guess I must have lost it," I say. "It was a while ago, now that I remember."

The truth is I threw the phone in the garbage the day they gave it to me. I had tried to tell the doctor I didn't want a new heart, but I'm pretty sure he was worried about being sued, so he insisted until I relented. Not that I had any intention of answering the phone call. Or even keeping the phone.

"Well, I think the doctor wanted you to get an oxygen machine. So I guess we can just get you that and a new phone, and you can be on your way," she says, still sounding skeptical of the situation. "Sound fair?"

I hate the idea of an oxygen machine. I haven't had to deal with one of those miserable contraptions since I was a kid. But I've already put up enough of a stink for Rachel to deal with. "Sounds fair," I say.

She nods, turns, and heads toward the door. "All right. Another nurse will take care of that for you. It was nice to meet you, Jason. Good luck."

As she's about to leave, I'm hit with the memory of my first wish, all those years ago. Kissing Mindy Applegate. I remember the fear I felt when I almost changed my mind about going through with it, but then I had remembered Murray's story about his wife, and what he said next.

Life's not worth a pile of beans if you don't live it.

I don't know that I actually decided to do it, but somehow Rachel's name comes from my lips, and she turns back to face me. When I realize what I've done, I start to lose my breath again. But then I remember the overwhelming elation I felt while running back to Murray's car after that first kiss. So happy I couldn't help but skip. Joy absolutely erupting from me.

"I know you must get this ten times a day," I say, "but I won't be able to live with myself if you leave and I never see you again, and I'll always have to wonder what you would have said."

"Said about what?" The sparkle in her eye tells me she knows exactly what.

"Do you think I could take you to dinner sometime?"

There. I said it. Now I can live with myself even if she shoots me down. And why wouldn't she shoot me down? I must look pretty pathetic lying here in a hospital gown, in such bad health I need a new heart—and not even wanting one.

She bites her lower lip, which is about the most beautiful thing I've ever seen. "Do you live in Lemon Grove?"

I look at her with genuine surprise. She knows where I live? She shakes her head like I'm ridiculous and stifles a grin. "It's in your chart."

Oh. That should have been obvious. And would have been, if her beauty wasn't so distracting.

The longer, more truthful answer is that I'm not living anywhere. I haven't lived anywhere in particular in a long time. But that would require a lot of explaining, and she must already think I'm strange. Besides, I'm sure she has other work to do, so I just say, "Yes."

"My college roommate lives up there and I'm going to dinner with her tomorrow night at Tasty Harmony. It's a vegetarian restaurant. Do you know it?"

"It's a pretty small town," I say, although I don't know the place she's talking about.

"Well, I'll tell you what. Maybe I'll stay for a drink after dinner. If you happen to show up, we could probably talk. Just as people, not as transplant coordinator and patient. Think you can make it?"

I crack a wide smile that I don't even try to contain. "Definitely."

And for the moment, despite the guilt resulting from my ruse about the list, my heart feels just fine.

Chapter Five

I never wasted much thought on wishes back when I was a younger man. Seems to me, a man makes his own luck through hard work. Wishing never did anyone any good.

Then I met the kid. And now I'm not so sure I was right. Maybe there is something special about making a wish, if it's not just a selfish thing. So here's what I believe now: wishing is all well and good, so long as you have someone to wish with.

—From the Journal of Murray McBride

Being back in the Chicago area has brought on a whirlwind of emotions. The most recent one I'm fine with. It's been a while since I've felt that kind of rush in the presence of a woman. And tomorrow night can't come soon enough. In fact, the very first thing I do when I leave the hospital is google the restaurant she mentioned. I couldn't forget the name even if I tried— I've been repeating it in my mind ever since she said it. But still, I don't want to take any chances.

Of course, things are never simple for me. The giddiness I feel about meeting Rachel is tempered by the old wounds that inevitably come to the surface when I'm back here. And the wounds are numerous. The loss of my good friend, Murray. Turning my back on my family in the name of Tiegan's final wish. And most of all, of course, is Tiegan herself. Being forced to think about my heart makes me think about her. Not that I needed any prompting.

For years, I used my profession as a magician to mask the terrible pain I felt. The pain of loss and the pain of survival in the form of guilt. I became very good at it. Any time the guilt became too much, I'd throw myself into the minute details of the trick I was working on. And it worked on both fronts. I was able to become one of the best magicians around, and more importantly, I was able to sweep painful emotions under the rug.

But now that I'm back, it's all right in my face. And since I'm ripping off the Band-Aid and facing things I've been hiding from for so long, I know what I have to do. Once I'm discharged from the Chicago hospital—with my brand-new portable oxygen concentrator in a bag with a shoulder strap—I drive back to Lemon Grove, toward my house, and park in the street across the way. But instead of going inside, I veer to the right, having left the oxygen in the car, and climb the three concrete steps to the place next door.

Tiegan's house.

I can almost see her running around the corner to meet me. Pigtails bouncing around her favorite All-American Girls Professional Baseball team hat. Smiling. Always smiling.

When she wasn't rolling her eyes at me.

I turn back to the door, take a deep breath, and knock. After a few moments of silence, I hear footsteps, and then the door opens and Della is looking at me with an expression I can't read.

"I knew you'd come," she says.

I can't tell if she's happy to see me. She showed up at my show in D.C., when I finally hit the goal of one million dollars for the homeless. But I remember her vacant stare after the show. I remember how little she said. And I wonder if she was happy to have come, or if she regretted the decision. Back here, in the place where she's certainly reminded every moment of the daughter she lost, her reaction to me is guarded.

"Come in," she says, which is at least better than the alternative.

I follow a step behind her. I don't know whether I should look at the pictures, breathe in the scents, and try to hear Tiegan's laughter, or close my senses down for the sake of self-preservation and pretend it's like any other house, any other room, and not the house where Tiegan lived. Not the place we used to run for snacks on a hot summer day, when we needed a break from the sprinkler. Soaked from head to toe with grass stuck to our legs and water dripping down our shins, and shoulders, and cheeks.

Della hands me a tissue and I realize the drips down my cheeks weren't just memories. "Thank you," I say, and I follow her into the living room, where she sits on the very edge of a recliner and leans forward. I settle into the couch opposite and wipe my cheeks dry.

"What is it you want, Jason?" she asks.

"I want..." I pause, because until this moment, I don't really know what it is I came here for. "I guess I just want to know."

"To know?"

"What happened. The night Tiegan died."

She stares at me, her eyes widening with either fear or anger, I can't tell which. Maybe both. "You came over here to make me relive the most excruciating moments of my entire life?"

"I'm sorry. I didn't mean it like that. I just . . . It's just that I woke up all those years ago and I was alive and everyone said there was an accident. I was ten years old. I'm not sure I ever processed it. And now I'm trying to figure things out and I just met this little girl that reminds me so much of Tiegan, and I want to help her because she might get deported and I just . . . I was hoping maybe you would . . . "

"Is what I already did for you not enough?"

I'm stung by the words. They hit me like a sucker punch. They're the last thing I expected coming from the person who created the SBK greeting for her daughter. Strong, brave, and kind. It was such a beautiful reminder of her love for Tiegan. But right now, all I see in Della's eyes is pain and anger.

I can see that my request was a mistake. I should have known it would be. The loss of a child is something I'll never understand, but I can tell by the look in Della's eyes that the pain never goes away.

"I actually have something I want to offer you," I say. "Maybe it will help somehow. I don't know."

"There's nothing that can help, other than getting my daughter back."

Obviously, I can't bring Tiegan back. But there is something that might be close. At least, as close as I can get. "Come over here," I say, and I reach out my hand. Despite a deep furrow in her brow, Della comes, moving slowly, full of uncertainty.

"What?" she says, taking my hand when I extend it to her.

I gently pull her onto the couch beside me. I lean back slightly; just enough so I can guide her head to my chest. Before her ear makes contact, she pulls up quickly, as if insulted by what I'm doing. But then I see it in her eyes: understanding. It dawns on her and changes her expression from sadness and anger to strong, overwhelming need.

She bumps her ear onto my chest so hard it gives a hollow thump, and she squeezes. I feel the lub-dub of my beating heart pulsing through my chest and into Della. She's listening to her daughter's heart for the first time in twenty years. She wraps her arms around me and squeezes, pressing her ear tighter and tighter against me. I'm nothing but a vessel. A receptacle that contains Tiegan's heart. And that's okay. I'm more than willing to offer Della whatever I can.

After a few minutes, Della's head begins to shake. Moments later, I feel moisture on my shirt. She cries silently yet uncontrollably for several long minutes before she lifts her head from my chest. Her eyes are red, and I can't read her expression. She shakes her head and says, "I can't . . . it's not . . . I never want to do that again. And I'd like you to leave now."

A deep sadness creeps into my bones. It's not unusual. Thinking about Tiegan brings about many things, pure joy among them. Also chuckles at the memories, sometimes even full-on laughter. And dismay, an inability to believe how mature she was, how caring, how funny.

But always, always sadness.

"I'm sorry to have bothered you," I say, getting up. Della remains on the couch, her head turned toward the window, although her eyes are closed. I know I should respect her wishes and leave, but find it impossible not to say more. "I miss her too, you know. I realize that, as her mother, you loved her in a way I'll never understand. But I loved her too. She was my friend. She was my very best friend and ever since then—"

A shake of her head cuts me off. Her meaning is clear. My words are only causing more pain. It's time to go.

So without another word, I retrace my steps until I'm out the front door. Crossing the street—still not ready to go to the house where I grew up. Stepping down into the driver's seat of the rental car. Resting my head on the steering wheel.

Crying.

As the moments stretch on and slowly turn to minutes, and eventually to hours, my forehead doesn't move from the steering wheel. I realize what I was looking for from Della: absolution. Understanding. And maybe, subconsciously, even permission to cut Tiegan out of my life. Maybe I was hoping if I let her listen to Tiegan's heart, she'd be able to say goodbye.

A tapping against the window jars me out of my thoughts. My neck is sore from being in the same, uncomfortable position for so long, but when I see Della outside the car, I forget about the pain and quickly roll down the window.

Her eyes are swollen and still wet from the last few hours spent doing the exact same thing I've been doing. As different as our situations are, we'll always be connected by grief.

"Jason," she says, her voice croaking. She tries to speak, but when no words come out she just shakes her head. "I didn't mean to . . . "

I open the door slowly and stand from the car. I open my arms and she immediately lunges into them and sobs into my chest. "I know," I say. "The pain sometimes speaks for us, and it's not always kind. It's okay."

After several long moments, she gets herself together enough to wipe her eyes and sniffle. "She'd be so disappointed in me. After all I taught her about how to treat people. And then I go and say those terrible things to you."

"No," I say. "She'd be amazed at you. At your strength."

She nods and steps back. For a moment, we both look at our shoes awkwardly. "Maybe, sometime, you could come back and let me . . . " She gestures to my chest, unable to finish.

"Of course," I say. "Anytime you'd like."

She looks uncertain, as if she isn't sure she should have asked, or isn't satisfied with my answer. "Tiegan always loved the wishes thing you guys did," she says. "Your list, her list. Trying to make them come true."

I nod and smile, remembering how full of joy Tiegan was each time we checked a wish off a list. But I'm not sure why Della's telling me this now. Her reasoning becomes clear when she touches my elbow and tries to meet my eyes. She fails, but her words are soft.

"You said you met a new little friend who's in trouble. Maybe she would like it, too. To have some wishes."

I see the effort it takes for her to talk of these things, because as soon as she finishes the sentence, the tears come back. So she quickly turns away and runs back into her house.

■　　■　　■　　■　　■

My time with Della leaves me exhausted. For years, I knew she must be the only person in the world who felt more pain than I did after the loss of Tiegan. But it was always from a distance. I never had to come face-to-face with it like I did when I stepped into her house. It has left me emotionally spent.

But I can't let that fatigue stop me from doing what I need to do now. I realize perfectly well that what I'm about to do could be seen as ridiculous. Certainly it's illegal. But I can't help it. I need to know who I'm competing with for this theoretical heart. Maybe it's more accurate to say I want to know who I'd be stealing from. An eighty-five-year-old man who spent half his life in prison for murder and still cheats on his taxes? Okay, that might not give me the greatest excuse for passing up the heart. But that's unlikely. The people on this stolen list are probably people like me, or even people like I was when I had to wait for a heart as a ten-year-old kid, unsure if it would arrive in time.

Okay, they're probably not kids. As Murray learned in his final days, an adult can't get a kid's heart, nor vice versa. But as I pull my phone out and scroll through the names, I'm sure there are plenty of young adults here. Good people with good reasons to live. Better than I have, certainly. The most important is that they actually want the new heart.

The first name on the list is a woman, and although it's not unheard of for a woman to receive a man's heart (I'm a living example of cross-sex donation) the fact that rejection is less likely with same-sex donors makes it seem likely they'd try to match males to males and females to females. So I scan down to the second name on the list, mine, and then the third— Andy Tart.

According to the list, Andy is twenty-one years old, shares my blood type, and has Dilated Cardiomyopathy. No other details of his disease are listed, but fortunately there's an address. Before I can talk myself out of it, or realize all the reasons this is a terrible idea, I grab the keys to the rental, plug Andy's address into my phone, and start driving.

Heart transplants are different than other kinds of transplants because hearts need to be transplanted more quickly than other organs. Because of that, geography plays a bigger part in who gets a heart than it might with other organs. Fortunately, that means I only have to drive a half hour before I pull in front of a neat, two-story house complete with white picket fence and everything. It's a perfect example of Americana.

As soon as I get out of the car, I'm out of breath. It's possible that whoever the doctor was that moved me up the list knew what he was doing after all. So I grab the backpack with the oxygen concentrator and toss the strap over my shoulder. The last thing I need is to be passing out left and right.

The woman who answers the door is silver haired but still youngish. Andy's mother, no doubt. She eyes me skeptically when I explain who I am and why I'm here.

"And you want what, now?" she says, her head tilting slightly.

"I was hoping to meet Andy. To get a chance to hear his story."

"Because you might want to give him the next heart?"

"That's right. My name is on the list before his, but I think he might be a better candidate than me."

I don't try to explain why. But maybe I should have. It might have prevented the next question, which I should have seen coming.

"How do you know the order of the list?"

I murmur something about someone at the hospital who shared the information with me, which is certainly stretching the truth. And how I didn't get the list through illegal means, which is an all-out lie. The woman's skepticism grows, but the possibility of her son receiving a heart sooner convinces her to invite me in.

"Andy's upstairs in his room," she says. "I'll go get him. You can sit there." She motions to the dining room table. "Want me to brew some coffee or something?" she asks, but she's already on her way upstairs and I'm not even sure if she hears my "No, thank you."

When she's gone, I pull out one of the wooden chairs, scraping it against the hardwood floor, and sit. Just the effort of making it inside has tired me out, so I unzip the backpack, unwrap the tubing from the oxygen concentrator, and put the nasal cannulas up to my nose. When I turn it on, fresh, cool air fills my lungs and I feel a jolt of energy. It makes me wonder how long I've been slowly, imperceptibly declining.

It feels like an invasion of this family's privacy to sit here, breathing through my concentrator while I examine their home. But I can't resist looking at the framed pictures set up around the room.

A wedding picture of the woman who opened the door, much younger, with a smiling husband.

That same woman several years later, holding a newborn infant, still in a hospital gown.

A young boy in a football uniform, hidden behind his helmet and face mask.

A senior picture of a teenage boy, his hair swept casually to one side, wearing a Brown University sweatshirt.

Slow footsteps descend the stairs and then the same boy appears, only this version is hunched over and his features, which were so young and vibrant in the photo, are gaunt and hollow. He struggles to walk, which makes the picture of him as a boy in a football uniform seem cruel.

His mother helps him sit in a chair opposite me. He takes a deep breath, as if the effort has exhausted him, and finally turns his eyes to me.

"I'm sorry to bother you," I say. "I won't take much of your time. I was just hoping you'd tell me about your illness."

"My illness?" he says, and I realize the stilted feel of my words. But he shrugs. "Apparently I've had it my whole life, but I never had any symptoms until my freshman year at college."

"A lot of times his disease is associated with alcoholism or diabetes," his mother says. "But Andy didn't have either. No family history..." Her voice trails off, as if she's overcome by confusion.

"You were at Brown?" I ask.

Andy nods in a casual way, but his mother chimes in proudly. "It was always his goal to go to an Ivy League school. It was a dream come true. He was studying engineering. He and his professor were working on inventing a carbon capture device when he fainted and—"

"Mom," Andy says. "Just stop. It's not important."

After an awkward silence, I smile as gently as I can. "It's fascinating to me, actually. It sounds like you were on your way to doing some great things."

Andy nods again, but it's an empty gesture. As if we're talking about someone else. "Halfway through my sophomore year, it got worse. I went to the doctor and . . . "

He shrugs, as if what happened next was inconsequential.

"And now you're waiting for a new heart," I say.

"It's our only hope," his mother says, and I notice the use of "our" instead of "his." I'm reminded for a moment of Della, but I push her from my thoughts. "He's gotten a lot worse, just in the last couple weeks. We're hoping they'll move him up the list."

That clinches it for me.

"I've taken enough of your time," I say, even though I've only been here for a few minutes. I've seen what I needed to see and heard what I needed to hear. If I accept the next heart that becomes available, I will be moving this innocent, Ivy League young man one step closer to death. "I want you to know that if I get a call for a heart, I'll turn it down. Andy can have it. I already checked and we have the same blood type."

The look they both give me validates my decision, not that I needed validation. Their eyes overflow with gratitude. Andy's mother stands and takes my hands in hers.

"If you would do that for Andy, we would be eternally grateful."

She gives me her phone number, which I enter into my cell. Then I squeeze her hand, and we both look at Andy. He already looks better than when I first saw him. It's amazing what hope can do for a person.

I drive away feeling lighter than I have in years. I start doing the math. If a new heart becomes available every four months on average, and I manage to hold on for another year? Who knows, maybe even two or three years? I could save a dozen lives.

Now that's something that seems worthwhile to me.

Chapter Six

When Jenny passed on, I thought I'd never get out of bed again. Wouldn't have, either, if I didn't have to take the damned pill to keep breathing. And soon enough, I decided not to take that anymore either, and be done with it once and for all. But then came the boy's list. The five wishes. And somehow, even for an old, washed-up man like me, that changed everything.

We all need a reason, and that there gave me mine.

—From the Journal of Murray McBride

So much of my life has been about me. *I* was the sick kid who got everyone's attention. Murray helped make *my* wishes come true. Even when I was trying to make Tiegan's final wish come true, I was the performer. I was the one people were watching.

So it's been nice to give back, at least a little. First letting Della listen to Tiegan's heart, then telling Andy and his mother that he has moved up on the list. But I'm most excited for the next thing on my list: to make wishes with Alexandra.

Father James's opinion about the wishes is one thing—and I value it. But without realizing it, I was seeking Della's approval. No, actually, I was needing her approval. After all, I'd be re-creating something I did with Tiegan, which could be interpreted as a betrayal.

But now that I have Della's approval, the idea is blossoming in my chest like a sunrise. Tiegan is guiding me. She's telling me this could give me a sense of purpose and reward before her heart gives out for good. Like Murray, it's some good I can do in the limited time I have left.

It would probably surprise some people to know that the whole "limited time" thing doesn't scare me, as strange as that may seem. Okay, maybe it scares me a little. I mean, who wouldn't be a little scared about death and all the uncertainty that comes with it? But this isn't my first time around the block with this stuff. For years, I faced the possibility that I might not wake up the next day. Even after I received the new heart, there were daily risks. Life has never been guaranteed to me like it is to most people. So knowing it will end soon doesn't scare me.

What scares me is the thought of cutting Tiegan out of it.

I wake up in a hotel, which is nothing out of the ordinary for me. But I'm hoping what I do this morning will start something extraordinary—granting five wishes, just like Murray did for me.

So I get in the rental car and look at the paper Father James gave me.

Cook County Courthouse, September 14, 9 a.m.

And then below it:

Alexandra Lopez (Juan) 2912 Cottonwood Dr.

I put the address into the map on my phone. Ten minutes later, I pull in front of a small house stuck very close to the two on either side.

The house itself is tiny, especially compared to the other houses in the neighborhood, which aren't exactly big. But Alexandra's house can't be more than a thousand square feet. It's not much bigger than a shack.

I leave the oxygen in the car this time. I'm hoping to meet Alexandra's dad, and I don't want him to see me looking sick. Maybe it's silly, maybe it's egotistical, but there you go.

I knock on the door and hear footsteps sprinting, increasing in volume as they approach the other side of the door. There's a pause, as if the person on the other side is looking through the peephole, then the main door swings open and Alexandra is there on the other side. She's wearing a red shirt, blue shorts, and tall white socks, and the same fanny pack she had on in the church.

She's carrying a book, still open, as if she'd been reading it while sprinting to the door. I cock my head to the side to read the title: *Our Founding Fathers*. Pretty dense stuff for a kid.

"Mr. Cashman," she says. "What are you doing here?"

"It's Jason," I say. "You can call me Jason."

She doesn't seem to hear me. Or maybe she's just ignoring me. "Is it okay if I come in? Is your dad here?"

"No and no. Sorry, Mr. Cashman."

"What?" I don't know why, but being turned down wasn't in my plans at all.

"No, it's not okay if you come in. Because, no, my dad isn't here. I'm not allowed to let anyone inside the house when he's gone, and he's working now."

"Oh. That makes sense." I shift my weight, feeling awkward. I remember what Father James said about how serious her diabetes could be, which makes me uncomfortable with the idea of her being home alone all day. "I figured you'd be at school. It's not Labor Day, is it?"

Alexandra shrugs and the pages of the book flop around. "No, but my dad's worried. He heard some story about families being rounded up at school, and people with diabetes don't get the treatment they need in those holding places, so he decided I should stay home until after the trial. I have all A's anyway, and I still study at home."

"Oh," I say. I wonder how long she's been staying home. How much school she's been missing. And whether the precaution is necessary. Does the government actually "round people up" from their schools, and then fail to provide medical care? Seems unlikely to me. "Well, can you come outside?" I ask.

She thinks for a long moment. "I don't think my dad would be comfortable with that since he's never met you."

"Oh. I see." For a long moment I feel even more awkward. I have no idea what it's like to be a kid these days. What's safe, what's reckless, what's acceptable. "Well, can we just talk through the screen door then?"

"I don't see why not. That's what we're doing right now."

"Great," I say, but I've never had a real conversation with someone through a storm door, and I'm not sure how to start. Finally, I just jump right in. "Father James told me about your . . . " I pause, wishing I had come up with what to say before I was standing in front of her. ". . . immigration status."

She takes a small step back from the door. "Okay."

"No, you're not in trouble. I mean, I couldn't get you in trouble even if I wanted to. I'm not with the authorities. But I definitely don't want to. Actually, I want to help."

Her left eye squints, like she's aiming at a target. "You want to help me . . . with my immigration status?"

"Not exactly. I mean, yes, I'd love to help you with that. But I'm not qualified. Besides, there are lawyers for that. I just thought . . . " I rub my eyes and wish I'd brought my oxygen concentrator. "Look," I say. "I know you must be worried about getting deported."

One thing about kids is they don't even try to hide it when they feel fear. "I hear Guatemala is beautiful," she says tentatively. "And the village where I was born is very peaceful. But they don't even have a medical clinic. Where am I supposed to get insulin?"

"I don't know. And I can't imagine how terrifying that must be for you."

We avoid eye contact for a long moment. "Look," I say. "I'm not sure what I can do to help with your immigration problem. But maybe there is something I can do to help with, like, everyday stuff."

"What do you mean, everyday stuff?"

"Do you remember the friend I used to have? The one I told you about at the church?"

"The one even older than you, right?"

"Right," I say, chuckling. "I was facing something terrible, like you, and he helped me. Not with the terrible thing, because there was nothing he could do. But he helped make my wishes come true, and that meant everything to me."

"Your wishes?" Alexandra closes her book to give me her full attention.

"Yeah. I came up with a list of things I wanted to do." I almost say *Before I died,* but since I'm here, alive in front of her, I stop myself. "I was thinking we could come up with a list for you. Of things you want to do."

"There's only one thing I want," Alexandra says firmly, "and that's to not get deported. To stay in America, and become an American. That's all."

"No, I mean . . . " I feel like she needs to know about me. My story. But the door between us acts like a barrier I can't reach through.

As if she reads my mind, she looks behind her, purses her lips, and says, "You're not some secret kidnapper or anything, are you?"

"I promise you I'm not."

We smile at each other, which is a little awkward. I can't figure out how to smile at a kid in a way that's friendly, nonthreatening, and most of all, not creepy. I try to remember how Murray acted around me. He never seemed nervous or unnatural. He was just there to help me. Maybe I can channel him, somehow.

I can't see my own expression, but I must not mess it up too bad because she opens the screen door and sits on the top step. I sit next to her, leaving plenty of space between us. She swings her fanny pack around and unzips it. With complete nonchalance, she begins the steps to test her blood-sugar levels.

"You better not be a kidnapper because my dad will be home any minute," she says as she pricks her finger. "And the neighbors are watching, too. And the police come around sometimes, just to check on the neighborhood and make sure the kidnappers aren't around."

"I give you my word," I say. "Would Father James let a kidnapper into his church?"

Alexandra thinks for a moment as she slips the test strip into the meter. "Not intentionally, I'm sure." She looks at me out of the side of her eyes for a while, then nods. "Okay. I trust you." She looks at her open fanny pack, then at her hands, which are full at the moment. "Can you grab me a fruit snack out of this pocket."

"Ah," I say, feeling very uncomfortable with the idea. "How about I take one of those for you?" I motion to the things in her hands.

"Sure. Take the lancet for a second."

She hands over the thing she used to prick her finger, then rifles through the fanny pack until she finds what she's looking for. She unwraps a little snack and pops it into her mouth.

"Do you need some insulin or something?" I ask.

She recoils and stares at me with wide, round eyes. "Insulin? Are you trying to kill me?"

"No! Of course not. You mean, insulin wouldn't help?"

She shakes her head in disbelief. "Insulin brings blood-sugar down by letting the sugar into your cells. My sugar is already low right now. If I took insulin, I'd probably be dead in, like, thirty minutes."

"Oh. Sorry. I guess I should learn a little about diabetes."

"Nah," she says, chewing her snack. "I know what to do. So, about these wishes."

"Yes?"

"How many do I get?"

"I don't know. There aren't really any rules about it."

"How many did you have?"

"I had five."

"Why five?"

"I guess it seemed like a reasonable number. More than just one or two, but not so many they couldn't all come true. I actually didn't think much about it when I made my list. I was pretty young. How many do you want?"

"That depends. Did all five of your wishes come true?"

The question brings back so many memories. Mindy Applegate's perfume. The feeling of standing up to a bully. The ivy of Wrigley Field. The man who became my stepfather. And just the other day, the real magic of making Tiegan's wish come true. "They did," I say.

"Then I should do five, too."

"It's a deal," I say. "Any thoughts on what you want them to be?"

"I already know four."

"Really?"

"Yep. Baseball, hot dogs, apple pie, and Chevrolet."

I try to figure out what she's talking about. How could hot dogs be a wish? Then I realize I've heard those words strung together before, although I can't place where. I try to step back and see Alexandra anew. It only takes a moment for it to hit me. Always wearing red, white, and blue. Reading about the Founding Fathers. Her desire to become an American. When I look at her that way, the lyrics of an old commercial suddenly come back to me.

As American as baseball, hot dogs, apple pie, and Chevrolet.

"I like it," I say. "But I'm not sure how to make those things into wishes. So how about this? How about we come up with five things typical American kids do, and try to do them before your deportation hearing?"

She's quiet for a moment. "Yeah," she says. "While I still have the chance."

Part of me wants to contradict her, to say she'll be fine and that she'll end up being able to stay. There's no reason to rush her five things because the hearing will go her way, she'll continue to get the medical care she needs, and everything will be okay.

But I've lived this before. I've had my own "while I still have the chance." I know unexpected things can happen—some good, some bad. So I know better than to make a promise I might not be able to keep. She needs to know that I understand. That I won't sugarcoat.

So I say, "Yeah. While you still have the chance."

She runs back into her house and returns a minute later with a pen and a notepad. She sits next to me and after a few moments leans back onto her elbows and looks up toward the sun. "Water parks," she says.

"Excuse me?"

"Water parks. Absolutely full of American kids," she says. "On a hot summer day."

"It's September, though. Water parks are closed until next summer."

She gives me that sideways glance again. "You're not very good at this, are you? How did your wishes ever come true?"

I chuckle. It's a reasonable question. "Well, I had help."

"So, can I keep *water park*, or not?"

She holds her pen over the pad of paper. I have no idea how to get her to a water park when none of them are open, but still, I say, "Sure" and she writes it down. Her penmanship is a hundred times better than mine was at her age, I notice.

"Okay. Number two. I want to sing the National Anthem at a baseball game. I prefer football, but for some reason they call baseball the Great American Pastime, even though it's boring."

Remembering Murray and his love of baseball—and how good to me the Cubs were—I almost argue about the entertainment value of baseball. But in the end, I decide it's probably a losing battle. Chalk it up to kids these days and their short attention spans. "You're telling me lots of American kids sing the National Anthem at baseball games?" I ask.

"No, only the *most* American ones get to. Sometimes it's a cute kid with an amazing voice or a pop star. Sometimes it's a whole class from an elementary school. I guess I'll shoot for the first one, since my school doesn't even have a choir. And I'm not going to be a pop star because I'm going to be a scientist and stop climate change."

I chuckle. Not because her goal isn't possible; based on the little I know about Alexandra, I'm betting she'll be able to accomplish just about anything she puts her mind to. The certainty of childhood makes me chuckle, and I realize I miss it. "So you have an amazing voice?" I ask, back to the wishes.

She shrugs as she writes it down. "I don't know. Sounds pretty good to me when I sing One Direction songs in the shower. What else should I do?"

I don't know how to answer. Was I this ridiculous when Murray helped me with my wishes? It doesn't take more than a quick rehashing of some of the things on my list—Hit a home run in a Major League

Baseball stadium? Be a Superhero?—to realize Alexandra's list is looking like a piece of cake compared to mine.

Of course, I'm no Murray McBride.

"Oh! I know," she says. "This is the best one so far. It might be the very most American thing I can possibly think of."

"Wow. Okay, what is it?"

"I want to vote."

"Vote?"

"You know, it's kind of weird how you repeat everything I say as a question. I happen to know for a fact that I don't have an accent, so I know you can understand me."

It's true. She speaks perfect English. But it's the words, not the accent, that keep throwing me. "You know you have to be eighteen to vote, right? How old are you?"

"Eleven and a quarter. And you never said the wishes had to be easy."

"Okay, fine," I say. "So what do we have so far?"

"Ah, let's see." She consults her notepad and taps the bottom of her pen against her lips. "One: Go to a water park. Two: Sing the national anthem at a baseball game. Three: Vote."

"Okay," I say, bracing myself. "Two more. Do you have more ideas, or should we think about it for a while?" I'm hoping that if she takes some time, maybe she'll come up with more thought-out answers.

"Well, I feel like I should say 'shoot a gun,' but I really don't want to do that at all. Guns terrify me."

"That's understandable," I say.

"Maybe I could eat hamburgers every day for a month. From McDonalds."

"Gross," I say. "Really?"

"Well, I don't want to. I prefer chicken nuggets. But hamburgers are more American."

"I'm not sure you should go the food route," I say. "There has to be something healthier to wish for, doesn't there?"

"Well, I think American kids should all visit Washington D.C. at some point," she says, kind of offhandedly. "That's America's capital, if you didn't know."

I chuckle at the memory of explaining baseball to Murray—a man who had spent a large chunk of his life playing the game professionally. "I know all about Washington D.C., believe it or not."

"Great. Then that's number four. I've never been out of Lemon Grove, so that's going to be super-exciting."

I find it hard to believe she's never left this small town, but what do I know? It's not like I've spent a lot of time with undocumented immigrants in the past. Maybe staying near home is a way of staying safe. I'm sure her diabetes is a factor, too.

"Now for the last one," she says. "Since it's last, it has to be the biggest, most ginormous one."

"Agreed."

I mean what I say, but I'm also a bit apprehensive about what "the biggest, most ginormous" wish will be, considering the difficulty of several of her first four. Not to mention, fifth and final wishes have a history of being nearly impossible. The combination of mine and Tiegan's took me twenty years to accomplish. "Do you already know what it is?"

"Kind of," she says. She squints at the sky, deep in thought. "My dad tells me all the time, over and over and over, that America is the greatest place in the entire world because we help people who need it. Because we're the richest country in the whole world and instead of keeping it all and being selfish, we give more money than any other country to help poor people around the world. I want to do that. I want to be a real American and help poor people in the village in Guatemala where I was born."

A tsunami of thoughts bombard my mind. I know another girl whose biggest wish was to help others. I've spent the last two decades trying to make that wish come true for her.

But I've recognized that Alexandra is very different from Tiegan. Beneath the lighthearted, happy-go-lucky veneer, she has a layer of seriousness that Tiegan didn't, because she was never forced into it. Tiegan might have developed that more serious side of her personality if she'd been given the chance, but she never got that chance.

I force my thoughts back to Alexandra. I'm tempted to challenge her assessment of American generosity. The way I see it, our country could do a lot more for people in need. But rather than quibble about total dollar amounts versus percentage of GDP, I decide to adopt her view.

"I like that one," I say. "Any idea how?"

"Nope. None. That's what you're here for, isn't it?"

"I thought I was here mostly for moral support. But I guess I can try to help with some of the details."

"Great!" she says. "Here. Memorize this."

She hands me the paper. A corner bends in the breeze, so I flick it straight and read what she has written.

My Five Wishes
1. Go to a waterpark (So American!)
2. Sing the National Anthem (Star-Spangled Banner) before a baseball game.
3. Vote
4. Visit Washington D.C. and see the monuments.
5. Help poor people in El Remate.

"I like it," I say. "It's a good list. And I have some experience with lists of wishes."

This makes her smile as she takes the list back. "Let me know when we can do the water park," she says. "We only have a week until the hearing."

No pressure or anything. Of course, all I have to do is remember how I was with Murray to realize this is just karma coming back to me. So I sit on the steps in front of Alexandra's house and rack my brain for ways to make her wishes come true.

I startle at the feeling of Alexandra's head on my shoulder. I'm about to scoot well out of reach when I see the little contented smile on her face. "Thanks, Mr. Cashman," she says. "You're the best person in the whole entire wide world."

I pat her shoulder three times, awkwardly, thinking of Murray the whole time. But as uncomfortable as I feel, her smile convinces me to stay right where I am, enjoying the feeling coming from Tiegan's heart.

Chapter Seven

Sometimes, even now, I think back on Jenny in her wedding dress. It takes my breath away. Eighty quick years and it was over. Oh, how I wish I could do it all again.

—From the Journal of Murray McBride

I go back to the hotel to get cleaned up for my big date. At least, I've been thinking of this get-together as a date. And Rachel did suggest I meet her, and she hinted that we'd be talking and getting to know each other. So that's a date, isn't it?

Either way, I've met the young man who will receive the heart I'm slated to get, I've created five wishes with Alexandra, and now I'm meeting a beautiful woman. Those three things have gone a long way to helping with my emotional state after my time with Della.

As soon as I pull up to Tasty Harmony, I see Rachel through a large window, sitting across from another woman, apparently deep in conversation. She tosses her head back in laughter at something her friend said, which mesmerizes me to the point that I would have smashed into a stopped car in the parking lot if he hadn't honked at me. The driver throws his hands in the air as if to ask what my problem is. I avoid eye contact and park far away.

But even from this spot, I have a visual of Rachel through the window. She seems to be enjoying herself, which somehow gives me a feeling of happiness, too. It's like her laugh is contagious, even if I can't hear it.

I feel like I need some time to prepare witty things to say, or maybe the appropriate compliments. It's been quite a while since I've been on a date. But before I'm ready, Rachel and her friend stand and hug each other, then her friend walks out of the restaurant, and Rachel sits back down.

I turn to the back seat and stare at the oxygen concentrator. Do I bring it and risk looking fragile and pathetic? Or do I leave it and risk passing out in front of the woman I'm trying to impress? Reluctantly, I toss it over my shoulder.

In my excitement to get inside, I hit my head on the car door. It's hard enough to leave a welt, I'm sure, but I barely feel it. I rush through the entrance and approach Rachel, sitting perfectly comfortably by herself at the table, looking into space with a slight smile on her face.

"Hello," I say. "I found you."

"So you did." Her smile grows and pretty much turns me to putty. She motions to the bag on my shoulder. "I'm happy to see you're following doctor's orders."

I'm not sure if she'd say that if the nasal cannula was in, but at the moment I'm glad I brought it with me. She motions to the opposite side of the booth and I sit. As soon as I do, her brow furrows as if something's wrong. I rack my brain, trying to figure out what I could have messed up so soon. Is my hair all over the place? Food on my chin? But then she reaches over the table and touches my head, right at my hairline. I flinch at her touch.

"What happened?" she asks. "Are you okay?"

"Oh," I say, feeling the welt on my head for the first time. "I just hit my head getting out of my car. Real smooth, I know."

What am I doing? If I can't say anything charming, I should just keep my mouth shut, but I find myself unable to edit my thoughts around her. "I guess I was in a hurry to get inside," I say.

Her knowing smile tells me she understands. She seems either embarrassed or flattered, but I can't tell which. After a moment, she gathers herself again.

"So I did the requisite Google search," she says.

"There's a requisite Google search?"

"You didn't know? I guess it's probably different for men. As a woman, the rule is, don't go out with a guy you don't know without checking him out online first."

"Really?" I say. I wonder how I didn't know this, and like always when I feel a little clueless, I'm reminded of when I was young. Back then, I thought I knew everything and the old man with me had no idea about the most basic ways of the world. Oh, how the tides have turned.

"I suppose even a creep could put up a pretty good online presence," Rachel says. "But you can usually rule out the serial killers that way."

"Good to know I passed that test, at least."

She smiles and I can't help but watch the perfect shape of her mouth.

"At the hospital the other day, I didn't realize I was in the presence of a celebrity."

She still has that smile on her face, but I can tell the comment is more of a question. People—women especially—seem either drawn to my small amount of fame or repelled by it. They either assume I'm amazingly talented and rich or that I'm egotistical and narcissistic. Since Rachel's smile hasn't changed since her comment, I'm guessing she's the latter. Most reasonable people are, I've found.

"*Celebrity* is a pretty strong word for it," I say. "I'd be somewhere around an E-list, if there was one."

Some tension releases from her shoulders and I know I was right—she's not the kind of woman drawn to famous people. "Still," she says, "it must be a pretty interesting life to live. Traveling around, doing shows. You probably have groupies, don't you?"

I laugh so loud I startle myself. The idea of me with groupies? "I'm not that type of celebrity, I'm afraid. It was really just a means to an end for me."

She asks what I mean and, surprisingly, I tell her. Not just the basics—that I was trying to raise a million dollars for the homeless because it was the wish of a dear friend. No, I tell her things I've never told anyone before.

Despite the fact that this is the second time we've ever spoken, and the first real conversation we've ever had, I can't help myself.

I tell her about my parents. I tell her about Murray McBride. I tell her about my list and our adventures. And I tell her about Tiegan. Everything. I leave out nothing. So that when I finish talking, almost an hour later, Rachel has tears in her eyes.

"And you've been living with her heart ever since," she says.

"I have."

"And what's that like? To have your friend's heart?"

I take a deep breath, knowing there's a real chance I'm about ruin a beautiful thing with Rachel before it even gets started. But surprisingly, I want her to know.

"I was young when I got Tiegan's heart," I say. "But I still remember the feeling when I woke up, surprised to be alive. So much was the same— my mom, Collins, the hospital. But some things were different, too.

"My heart beats to a different rhythm. I had never noticed the rhythm of my heartbeat before. Not until it changed. I've become used to it, but every once in a while, I still feel it thump in my chest and know without a doubt that my original heart felt different."

"What do you mean, different?" Rachel asks. "Physically different?"

"I guess so," I say. I hadn't realized how difficult this would be to articulate. "At least at first. But as time went on, other differences arose. Sometimes I'd get an intuition, a gut feeling, foreign from anything I'd had before. There was never any doubt where they were coming from. There was only one possibility."

"These things, every bit as much as the physical things, have changed my life. These things remind me I'm not alone. That no matter where I go or what I do, Tiegan is with me."

Rachel hasn't run away screaming yet, so I take that as a sign that she hasn't decided I'm completely crazy. She actually looks like she's more interested than judgmental, which is different from what I've experienced with most people I've opened up to. Granted, I can count those people on two fingers.

Melanie from San Francisco, who accused me of "hearing voices" before she left me. And a pretty brunette from Tallahassee who I fell for so hard, I cancelled my next show after she told me she felt like she was sharing me with another woman. When I explained that I had no control over my heart, she politely asked me to leave and never come back.

Suffice to say, I learned my lesson early, and well.

"And that's why you don't want to get another heart." Rachel says, her voice soft.

I purse my lips, trying to figure out what to say. "That's why I *can't* get another heart."

She looks like she wants to say something but holds back. I wonder if she was going to say she admires me or if she thinks I'm ridiculous. I want desperately to know, but it's not to be. She takes a deep breath and sets her palms on the table, as if to reset the conversation. Although I still want to know what she's thinking about me, I ask about her past, then her family, then her profession.

After what feels like ten minutes, a waiter appears at the table and tells us the restaurant has closed. I awaken from the spell I've been under for the last few hours and realize there isn't a single soul left in the place other than a man mopping the floor and a woman putting chairs upside down onto tables.

We laugh and apologize, and then I catch her eye. In that brief moment, we share something that, at least to me, feels very meaningful. I follow her outside to her car, which is on the way to mine. She fishes her keys from her purse and turns to look at me with the same expression she had earlier, when I felt like she was holding something back.

"I had a great time," I say. "I hope I'm not being too forward, but I really, really like you and I'd love to go out again sometime. Like, sometime soon."

I'm looking to get a laugh, but her smile is brief and fleeting. She seems deep in thought. She's quiet for long enough that the moment gets awkward, and I think I might have really misinterpreted how much she enjoyed the night. I'm about to apologize when she says, "That stuff you said at the hospital—and then again tonight—about not being willing to undergo another heart transplant. Is that real? I mean, when it actually comes down to it and your heart is failing and you're going to die without another transplant, you wouldn't really turn it down, would you?"

And there it is. The speed with which I've fallen for Rachel has matched the speed with which we've gotten right to the heart of the matter, so to speak. The crux of the problem.

With every other relationship I've had, this has been the poison pill. It has been the beginning of the end. Or more often, just the end. But after tonight, after the most enjoyable three hours I can remember experiencing as an adult, I can't imagine not seeing Rachel again. So even though the truth hasn't changed—that I could never cut Tiegan out of my life—I don't come right out and say that.

"Look, I know my condition is getting worse, but I'm not going to die tomorrow, right? I just want to focus on today and deal with the future when it comes. And, hey," I say as I pull the hospital cell phone from my pocket and gesture to the bag on my shoulder. "I've got these, right? And the phone's not ringing. So there's nothing to worry about right now, nothing to decide right this second."

She considers my words for a long moment, then stretches onto her tiptoes and kisses my cheek. "I had a great time tonight, too. And yes, I'd like to see you again." She gives me that right-hook smile. "Like, sometime soon."

■　　■　　■　　■　　■

At 11:46 p.m., having just fallen asleep on an uneven hotel bed, I'm startled awake by the alarm on my cell phone. I follow the sound, fish through the pockets of the jacket I wore earlier in the night, and realize it's not the alarm on my phone after all. It's the ringtone of the phone Rachel gave me—the one designated for only one thing. If it had gone off a matter of minutes before, right when I was holding it up as proof that it hadn't yet rung, it would have been one of the most unbelievable coincidences of my life. I push the green icon with more than a little trepidation.

"Hello?"

The voice on the other end is succinct and professional, but unable to hide a high level of excitement. "Is this Jason Cashman?"

"It is."

"Mr. Cashman, I'm happy to tell you we've received a heart for transplant, that you are a match, and you are at the top of the list."

"Oh," I say, because I've never considered this conversation. "That's great."

"Surgery needs to begin within four hours, so the sooner you can get to the hospital, the better."

"Oh," I say again. When I realize the person on the phone is going to end the conversation so I can rush to the hospital, I finally clear the sleep from my mind. "Actually, I have a question," I say.

After a significant pause in which the other person is surely wondering why I'm wasting precious moments, she says, "Yes?"

"Who is the next person on the list?"

"Excuse me?"

"Sorry, I just mean, if I don't take this heart, who would get it?"

"Are you unable to make it to the hospital?" the woman asks. "It looks like you're in Lemon Grove. Is that right?"

"What? How—"

"The phone, Mr. Cashman," the woman says, her voice making her impatience clear. "The GPS is enabled."

"Oh, right." I hadn't thought of that. I'm not sure I like the idea of the hospital knowing my whereabouts. "So, who would get the heart if I can't make it in?" I ask again.

"Obviously, that's not something I can tell you," the woman says. "That's privileged information."

"Of course," I say. I should have known that, I suppose. But I just wanted to hear her say that Andy would get the heart. It would be nice to know for sure. "Actually," I say, "I'm afraid I can't make it there in under four hours. The heart will have to go to someone else."

After an even longer pause than the last time, the woman says, "Mr. Cashman, I want to make sure you understand this clearly. You are in need of a heart transplant. We've very recently received a donor that is a good match for you. You are at the top of the list. If you don't act now, you will lose this heart. Do you understand?"

"Yes," I say. "I'll lose the heart, but whoever is next in line will get it, right?"

"The next person who is deemed a good match, that's correct," the woman says. She speaks slowly, as if still trying to understand the question even while answering. "We would never let a donated heart go to waste."

"Excellent," I say, which sounds strange even to me, under the circumstances. "Please do that."

This time, there is no pause. The woman needs to get in touch with the next person—Andy—as soon as possible. "I need your verbal reply. Do you, Jason Cashman, understand that a heart is available for transplant, and do you decline—I say again, *decline*—the heart? And do you realize there is no guarantee another heart will become available that is deemed a likely match for you?"

"I do," I say, which sounds more matrimonial than I intended. But in a way, I am committing to something, I suppose.

"Very well," the woman says. "Thank you for your time and have a good day."

She hangs up before I can answer, and it's done.

I had a chance to extend my life by decades—and to cut Tiegan out of my life forever. And I turned it down.

I stare at the phone in the dark hotel room for a long time, unable to figure out exactly what I'm feeling.

Chapter Eight

Helping a kid with his wishes isn't quite as easy as I thought it would be, and that's a fact. For one, I had to get the Chevy out of the garage for the first time in a good, long while. Drove Jason around a bit. Contacted the Cubs. Still no idea what to do about his other wishes.

And all the while, neither of us knows if we're even going to wake up in the morning. How's that for a sorry pair?

—From the Journal of Murray McBride

Lemon Grove has changed a lot since I was here last, but Wet 'n Wild is still right where it has always been. Today I'm alone, but I was here a couple times with my mom, Tiegan, and Della. Before my condition worsened and I had my first go-round with an oxygen machine. After everything happened, I never came back.

So I suppose it's no surprise that I'm overwhelmed with longing and regret as I pull into the parking lot. I want those days back. Their innocence. Their happiness. I wish I'd held onto those days somehow, instead of taking them for granted. Before I knew it, they were gone. Things had changed. And they have never stopped changing. Some say that's life. But I don't accept that. Not that my acceptance matters.

Fortunately, it's September and school has started, so the park is empty. I don't think I could have handled seeing all those kids laughing and playing and letting time slip away right before their eyes.

Unfortunately, the place is locked up and completely deserted. It makes sense—why would anyone be here in the off-season? But it does mean I have to find another way to make Alexandra's "Water Park" wish come true.

I scan the area and notice a small, rundown Airstream trailer sitting on the edge of the property, outside the locked gates. A sign hanging from the door reads Office, so I take a long, energizing hit of oxygen, then leave the concentrator in the back seat.

When I approach the Airstream, I see a bald, bearded man through a window, sitting at a desk, punching his thick fingers at a keyboard. I knock, and he slowly gets up from his chair. When the door opens, his baggy eyes and drooping skin suggest one of two things: either the park isn't doing well financially or he has a massive hangover. Or both.

"Hello," I say cheerfully, which elicits a look of confusion. I tell him why I'm here and what I'm hoping to do, which deepens his look of confusion.

"It's September," he says. He leans out the door and looks around, as if to verify the fact.

"I realize it's a bit strange. But it's an unusual situation. My name's Jason, by the way."

He squints at me like he's trying to figure me out. Reluctantly it seems, he says, "Call me Badger."

I stifle a wise crack about his name and explain about Alexandra. How sweet she is. How she wants nothing more than to do things American kids do. How her time here might be very short. He seems receptive, until I mention the deportation hearing.

"Deportation?" he says. "She's getting deported?"

"I don't know," I say. "But she's lived here all her life."

"But she might get deported. That means she's an illegal."

I cringe. The thought that Alexandra could be illegal in any way seems ludicrous. And the way he says it makes it sound like it's more than her immigration status; he makes it sound like it's her personal identity. It's like that one word has the power to change everything about who she is.

The man in front of me transforms before my eyes. He leans forward, eyes bugging out of his head like he can't wait to turn in some little girl and have her tossed back to where she came from, even if she wouldn't recognize that place from Mars. He's never even met her.

I can tell I won't have any luck appealing to his softer side, so I go a different route. A very "American" route, I think bitterly, and I'm glad Alexandra isn't here to see this.

"How much?" I say.

"Excuse me?"

"How much to rent the entire park for one hour?"

"I'd have to turn on the water for the whole park?"

I think about what it is Alexandra really wants. "Maybe just a portion of it," I say. "Is it possible to have about a quarter of the park open?"

The man looks like he wants to spit, but I'm sure the need for money is putting up a good battle against his skepticism. Finally, he tells me a number that sounds ridiculously high. I counter, he re-counters, and soon we agree on a number that's still way too high.

"Tomorrow?" I say.

"Tomorrow," he says.

I shake the man's hand to solidify the deal—and only to solidify the deal. Something tells me he isn't the kind of person with whom I'd normally want to shake hands.

■   ■   ■   ■   ■

The thing about change that bothers me so much is that it doesn't just happen once in a while. I could handle a little bit of change. The problem is that it's happening every single second of every day of our entire lives. When we get old enough to realize things are ever-changing, so much has already changed. We've already lost so much.

So we start to hold onto moments as much as we can. To appreciate them. But it doesn't fix anything. Time still goes by, second by unstoppable second.

Sometimes I feel like a dog chasing its tail. I'll recognize a moment I want to hang onto. I'll try really hard to appreciate it. But even while I'm focusing on that moment, it's passing me by, along with another moment, and another, and another.

If only we could stop time. Call a time-out. *Hey! I've got an important moment here! Let's stop things so I can really appreciate it!*

But the next thing you know, not only is that moment gone but the next twenty years have passed by, too. And those who are gone are now further gone. And further still with every passing moment. Fading, and fading, and fading...

These thoughts are all too common in my brain. But as long as I'm awake and alive, they're going to happen. So I do the only thing that keeps them in the background: I busy myself with something else.

In this case, it's preparing for the next phone call I get on the hospital phone. It could come in six months or it could come tomorrow. Either way, I need to be ready.

So I bring out my cell phone and call Andy's mother. She starts crying as soon as I tell her who's calling. Andy is in surgery. So far, so good. It would have been beyond disappointing if he hadn't ended up being a match after all. His mom says she'll call me as soon as he's out of surgery, and she thanks me about a thousand times before hanging up.

It was an unqualified success, giving up that heart for Andy. And it gives me motivation to consult the stolen list for the next name. I'm still second from the top, of course, but obviously the person above me already received a heart, otherwise I wouldn't have received the call. So I take a blue pen and draw a line through that name as well as Andy's name, below mine. Immediately beneath Andy is another man's name: Gary Johnson.

The address listed is in Skokie and is followed by a large NOK, which means nothing to me. I'm hoping to check in on Alexandra later today, but I figure I'll have enough time to get to Skokie and back.

A half hour later, I find the street. It's old, potholed, and lined with houses that look like they could fall over on themselves at any minute.

The goal of these trips, if I'm completely honest with myself, is to discover why the person below me on the list should get the heart instead of me. It's not that I want to play God and decide who lives and who doesn't. It just helps me rationalize giving up a heart if I know something good about the person. And I'm pretty easily persuaded, of course, so it doesn't take much. If Gary Johnson lives in this neighborhood, he's obviously down on his luck even without needing a new heart. Maybe my passing on the next heart will be the first break he's had in a long time.

I double-check the house number and approach the door, careful not to fall on the three rotting wood steps that lead to it. After I knock, I have to wait a full minute before the door opens. A boy in his early teens answers. If Gary has a son, it's another good reason to give the heart.

"Is Gary home?" I ask awkwardly.

The kid's brow furrows deeply at the name. "Home? Nah."

"Okay." The kid's breathing increases as if my mention of Gary upsets him. "Do you know when he's expected back?" I say.

"Little over five years."

"Excuse me?"

"My dad's in prison. Armed robbery. Fifteen years. Done with almost ten. So, he'll be back in a little over five years."

Oh. Not what I was expecting. Although now I understand the NOK printed behind Gary's name on the wait list. Next of Kin. His actual address is a penitentiary somewhere.

The kid in front of me has a jaded way about him. The cutting tone of his answers are just aggressive enough to let me know he's on guard. Not somebody who can be taken advantage of. He's an adult in a kid's body.

"Where is he in prison?" I ask.

"Why? You gonna go see him?"

"I'm not sure," I say.

The kid scrutinizes me for a moment, then shrugs, as if I'm not worth being considered a threat. "Cook County," he says. "And hey, if you do see him, tell him he can just stay where he is. We don't need him here."

The door closes in my face, hard. And part of me thinks I should close the door on this idea. Who cares if the person on the list after me is a felon? This is all unnecessary anyway. The real reason I can't accept a new heart has nothing to do with Gary Johnson. It only has to do with Tiegan.

Still, when I get in my car, I find myself driving toward Cook County Correctional Facility.

■   ■   ■   ■   ■

The facility is what I expected. Cold concrete. Everything a colorless shade of gray. Depressing as I imagined it would be. Which is why I'm so surprised when I first see Gary Johnson. He's a large man with broad shoulders and a prodigious belly. As he walks through a door and sits in the seat across from me, separated by a glass partition, he would be imposing if it weren't for the huge smile that lights up every one of his features. Despite the fact that he's a felon, I can't help but be drawn to him immediately. We each pick up the phone on either side of the glass. He's the first to speak.

"I don't know who you are, but I sure am happy to see you," he says in a deep, rumbling voice. He giggles a little, as if he just said something funny. The giggle is several octaves above his normal speaking voice.

"Well I'm . . . happy to meet you too," I finally stammer. My lungs don't seem to be getting enough oxygen today, so I brought the concentrator with me. I take a long breath now, happy to have it. "My name is Jason Cashman, and I'm here for a pretty strange reason, actually."

"Strange? That's the best thing I've heard in weeks." He giggles again, and I can tell it's something he does after nearly everything he says. "So boring in here, Mr. Jason." Giggle. "Strange sounds better than boring." Giggle. "So, what is it?"

I glance at his chest but unlike me and my oxygen concentrator, there's nothing noticeable on the outside that would label him as needing a heart transplant. "I hear you have . . . cardiovascular problems."

I'm not sure why I feel weird talking about it. It's not like it's leprosy. And I have it every bit as much as he does. Even more, by the looks of it. Gary seems to get a kick out of my shyness as well, because his giggle is louder this time.

"Bum ticker," he says happily. "On my last go-round apparently. Been a good ride, though. Except for landing in here, of course." He looks around as if seeing his surroundings for the first time.

"About that," I say, and I shift in my chair. Likable or not, it would be easier to give my heart to someone I felt deserved it. "I know a lot of people are wrongly convicted. Was that the case with your armed robbery?"

"Nope." Giggle.

"No? So, you did it then?"

"Guilty as charged," he says, annunciating each word, almost like a song. "I walked right up to the man, pulled out the gun, and said, 'Gimme all your money!' Just like I'd seen in the movies, Mr. Jason."

"Oh." I can't hide the disappointment. I was really hoping to find another Andy.

"Yeah, I was young, dumb, messed up with the wrong people. But what else could I have done? They were the only people I knew."

I guess that's something. "Do you think you've changed?" I say. "It's not something you'd do again?"

"Again?" Giggle. "I never shoulda done it the first time. But it was ten years ago now, and a lot has changed since then. Got myself an education, for one."

"You did?"

"Sure did. Took me eight years, because I had to do all my high school courses over, too. Never was much of a student, the first time around. But now I'm the proud owner of a bachelor's degree in computer science. When I get out of here, I'm going to get a real job and make some real money. Get my boy out of that run-down house he's living in."

This changes everything. Gary certainly could have gone the other way and gotten himself deeper and deeper into whatever situation got him locked up. But instead, he put his time to use. He earned his high school diploma and a college degree, too.

"About your son," I say. "I met him before I came here."

Gary's smile gets even wider, if that's possible. "How is he? Isn't he a great kid?"

I think back on my brief encounter with Gary's son and have no idea what to say. *We don't need him here* certainly doesn't seem appropriate to share.

"He's doing okay," I say, because I can't get myself to say anything that might ruin Gary's apparent great mood. But he sees right through me. He shakes his head, and for once he doesn't giggle.

"He hates me," he says. "I know it. And I don't blame him."

I want to ask why, but I'm afraid of what other mistakes Gary might have made as a young man.

"Oh, I've never been evil," he says. "I never did anything to hurt him. But I never did much to show him I loved him, either. And then I disappeared. Got locked away. A boy needs his father around. I know that now." He leans back in his chair and tilts his head to the ceiling, but his eyes are closed. "I try not to focus on my regrets too much, Mr. Jason. But that's one thing I wish I could change. I wish I could make things right with my boy. But how can I do that? I got another five years in here and a bad ticker that won't last that long. And my boy won't even visit me."

For the first time, he looks sad. And there it is: my reason. I know this situation shouldn't give me pleasure, but I can't help but feel a little spark inside me.

I've found another Andy after all.

■　　　■　　　■　　　■　　　■

Back at Alexandra's house, a beat-up sedan of some sort sits in the driveway. I consider leaving my oxygen concentrator in the back seat, but the ache in my chest has become pretty much constant now. I probably just need to resign myself to having it with me at all times. Apparently, I didn't get to the top of that list for nothing.

When I knock on the door, a man a few years older than me opens it. His eyes, which are the same dark chestnut as Alexandra's, light up like we're old friends, and he invites me inside.

"I'm Juan," he says through an accent so thick I have to strain to make out the words. Fortunately, he speaks slowly so I can understand him. "I'm Alex's father. And you must be Mr. Cashman. Alex has told me all about you."

"Jason," I say, and I wonder if Alexandra even remembers my first name.

I shake Juan's hand just as Alexandra marches around a corner and into the room, her face buried in a three-ring binder. She doesn't even look up at us. Next to me, Juan rolls his eyes as if to say, *She's always like this.*

I smile, because I can tell the annoyance is fake. The pride in Juan's eyes is obvious. I've seen it before, I realize. In Della's eyes. Long ago. Whenever she'd look at Tiegan and say, "SBK."

"I can bring you water?" Juan asks.

I realize I'm lost in my thoughts again. Chasing my tail. "No, thank you."

"You have to see this, Mr. Cashman," Alexandra says. The way she says it makes my heart melt, but I can't figure out why. After a few moments, I place it. It's because of the nonchalance. The casual nature of the comment. Not even a "hello" or "good morning," It's almost as if I've been here the entire time and seeing me in her house is no surprise at all. In short, it makes me feel welcome.

Alexandra still doesn't look up from her binder, but she somehow grabs my sleeve with her free hand and pulls me toward the small table in the dining area. Juan smiles and shrugs, so I allow myself to be led to a chair, where I sit and take a deep breath of oxygen. Alexandra's eyes flick to the contraption, but she doesn't ask about it.

She moves to the other side of the table and plops down, almost missing the chair because her gaze is back on the binder. Finally, she sets it on the table, rotates it so it's right side up for me, and slides it toward me.

"Check it out," she says.

"What's this?" I sit a little taller and lean forward to read.

"My research."

I scan the first bit. "El Remate," I say. "That's the place you mentioned before, right?"

"It's where I was born. It's a little town on Lake Peten Itza in the northeast corner of the country, not far from Belize."

"So this is where you're from."

"No. I'm from America," she says defiantly. "It's true I was *born* in El Remate. But America is the only place I ever remember living. So I'm from Lemon Grove, just like you."

"Sorry," I say. "I know you're American."

Alexandra's stare lingers on me, but then she lets it go. She's not a "diabetic" and she is "American." I need to remember these things.

"I found a girl online who lives there," Alexandra says. "Not far from where my parents lived. I was trying to find a pen pal, but they don't even have a working postal service in Guatemala. Can you believe that?"

I shake my head because I think that's the reaction she's looking for.

"But that's fine. Email works better anyway. Except they don't have very reliable internet there, either. Zuri says she only has a strong enough signal to get online for a few minutes a day."

"Zuri?"

"The girl I found. The one from El Remate." Alexandra reaches over the table and flips the top page of the binder, revealing a photograph of a beautiful girl, probably a couple years older than Alexandra, with flowing black hair and large, piercing eyes. "We're email friends now," Alexandra says.

I flip through the pages in the binder, impressed by the amount of work Alexandra did in the short time I was away. She's printed off reams of information about Guatemala from a multitude of sources. Some from the government, some from NGOs working there, others from regular people who have volunteered there.

"Did you know that in El Remate, they don't have a dentist? Or a doctor's office of any kind. Technically, the whole country gets free health care from the government, but unless you live in a big city . . . " She shrugs, as if to say *Too bad.* "They have schools, but look at this." She flips to another page with a picture of a run-down, cement building with two dusty, outdated computers. "That's where Zuri emailed me from. How can they even learn there? And this," she says as she flips another page, "this is her house."

The structure on the paper before me is nothing more than a collection of sticks stood on end. It has a dirt floor, and clothes hang from ropes near the roof, which is also made of sticks shoved as closely together as possible. It's like so many pictures of poverty I've seen, except that Alexandra has actually communicated with the girl who lives there. And that changes everything. It has made it real to her. Not to mention this is the country she might get deported to.

"I asked Zuri if she knew where to find insulin in the village, but she didn't even know what I was talking about."

I try to think of something comforting to say but come up empty.

"I'm going to build them a new school. And I'm going to find teachers and everything."

I make an involuntary sound. Half chuckle, half chortle. Like I'm pretending to laugh at a particularly bad punch line. Alexandra freezes and glares at me. "What?" she says.

I feel like such a jerk. I'm supposed to be helping this kid with her wishes, and instead I'm mocking her efforts? Squashing her excitement before we even begin? What am I doing?

"It's just a lot, that's all. How are you going to do all that?"

"I can do anything," she says. "I'm an American."

When I fail to make myself look convinced, she shakes her head like she's trying to teach an infant. "Look," she says, flipping to another page, and I wonder how many pages of research this kid has done. Now that I really look at it, I can see the binder is practically full. "I made up this flyer that I'm going to post around town. And I'm going to give them out at street corners. You can help. I've already created the GoFundMe page so people can donate. Once we get enough money, I'll have Zuri put me in touch with people in the area who can do the building, and we'll get started. I can do it all remotely, from here. It'll change the lives of so many kids there."

The idea is crazy and her ambitions are nowhere near realistic, but what can I do? *Help poor people in El Remate* is on her list of wishes. So I toss my hands up as if I'm completely convinced. "Okay. Let's do it. When do we start?"

"I'll print out a bunch of copies of the flier and we can—"

"Alex," Juan says. He walks back into the room with ice water rattling in a glass jug, an apologetic look on his face. "We're low on ink for the printer. And, well, it's so expensive to replace."

"I'll grab some," I say quickly, hoping to cover Juan's discomfort. "I have to go out for some things anyway. I'll bring some back tomorrow."

"But then how can we hand out fliers *today*?" Alexandra says.

I hate to deflate her excitement. She's so motivated right now. "I think tomorrow actually works better. Tomorrow afternoon, even."

"Afternoon? Why? I want to get started right away. If it has to be tomorrow, it should definitely be in the morning."

"We've got other plans for the morning," I say.

Her eyes bulge again, and I can feel anticipation radiating from her. "We do?"

"Yep," I say. "You better invite all your friends, because tomorrow morning, we're doing wish number one."

Chapter Nine

Just did the first wish with the kid. He kissed a girl, all right. And definitely on the lips. I won't go into details because I'm trying to keep this journal clean. I'll just say that what happened was a little different than I expected and leave it at that.

—From the Journal of Murray McBride

I spend another night at a hotel on the outskirts of Lemon Grove. I don't know why, exactly. I'm sure my mother and Collins would be happy to have me. But I'm thirty years old. And if I'm honest about it, the fact that I've become a low-level celebrity magician makes crashing in my mom's basement less appealing, despite the fact that I've left the celebrity life behind me.

I also don't want her to have to see me like this. She had to deal with her son toting around an oxygen concentrator for long enough, and I don't think that's ever something a mother gets used to. The last thing she needs is to see me struggling for breath again, taking pull after pull from the oxygen machine to make sure I don't pass out.

But a stale blueberry muffin at the free continental breakfast is enough to convince me to leave the hotel. I can't even count the number of stale blueberry muffins I've had over the past twelve years, since leaving home. And soft apples and tasteless hard-boiled eggs.

So I go, finally, to my childhood home, but I leave the oxygen concentrator in the back seat. I feel naked without it. Vulnerable. It's like, without that thing nearby, I could black out at any moment. I just hope I can hang on long enough to get through this.

It feels strange to knock on the front door. I stand on the doorstep, waiting, unsure if I'm doing it right. Everything is so foreign. I haven't been here in a very long time.

The door opens and my mom is standing in front of me. Her eyes brighten, and she comes outside to hug me, as if the embrace couldn't possibly wait for me to take two steps to get inside.

"Good morning, Mom."

"Come in," she says. "Join us for coffee."

Her smile is wide, but also tight, as if she's ashamed at how excited she is to see her son. She has laugh lines around her eyes that I've never noticed before. It's good to see she's experienced laughter, even if the lines do show the passage of time.

In the dining room, I'm surprised to see Della sitting across from Collins. I shouldn't be surprised by it. She lives next door. And I have no idea how her situation might have changed over the last several years, but last I knew she had nobody. She and Tiegan had left her abusive husband, and then she lost Tiegan. It makes perfect sense for her to be here.

There are so many reasons for this group to be together: They experienced trauma together. They're connected by Tiegan—and by me. The only thing that doesn't make sense in this equation is me. I left. I turned my back on the trauma and tried to convince myself I was doing it for the right reasons. But was I? Or was I just trying to avoid the scene in front of me now? The discomfort. The pain.

I try to hide a strained deep breath as I grab a mug and pour a cup of coffee. But even something as simple as pouring coffee isn't normal. As many years as I've spent in this house, I've never had a cup of coffee here. It reminds me that when I lived here, I was very young and things were very different.

"What do you have going today, Jason?" Collins asks. His hands are wrapped around his coffee mug. He still has strong-looking hands, which reminds me of when I met him. He was sitting in front of a community center art class, where people painted his hands. Right up next to Murray, who sat there with a scowl on his face...

"Jason?" It's my mom, pulling me again from a memory.

"Sorry," I say. "There's a little girl I met at the church—"

"Wait," my mom says. "You went to church?"

"Not like that. I just wanted to talk to Father James." My mom nods, trying to hide her excitement that I was in a church for any reason. "Anyway, I ran into a little girl there. Well, it wasn't exactly coincidental. Father James set it up. And she's kind of like I was when I was young, except she's more mature for her age. I'm helping her with wishes."

I smile at Della, who nods in approval.

"Wishes?" my mom says, and I can't help but smile, too. If Alexandra were here, she'd understand why I have a tendency to repeat things.

The mention of the wishes does something to me. The change is immediate and dramatic. It's like a drug has been injected straight into my bloodstream. I breathe easier. My mind becomes clear. I'm focused. Determined. I forget all about chasing my tail.

I wonder if Murray felt this way.

"Yeah," I say, unable to hide my smile. "Five of them. Just like Tiegan and I had. We're starting on them today."

"Oh?" Collins says, taking a long sip of his coffee. He's comfortably in his routine and doesn't seem to recognize the change I just underwent. "What's the first wish?"

"We're going to a water park," I say.

Della, who has been watching me closely the entire time, does seem to understand what's happening to me. "Don't let us hold you back," she says. "You don't want to be late."

It's still two hours before Badger opens the water park for us, so I'm in no risk of being late. But Della's words suggest she knows the pull I'm feeling to be with Alexandra. How I feel lighter when I'm with her. Needed. Like giving her the wishes is worthwhile, purposeful.

Maybe it's intuition that only comes from tragic loss. Or maybe Della just needs to get rid of me and what I remind her of. It's hard to tell.

I finish my coffee and kiss my mom's cheek. "I'll let you all know how it goes."

"That would be great," my mom says, and she squeezes my shoulder, as if to hold me to it. I take a step toward the door, but Della's voice stops me. "Jason," she says. She pauses, as if she's considering her words very carefully.

"If you care about this girl, you should let her know you care about her."

■　　■　　■　　■　　■

"You know I care about you, right?"

Alexandra squishes her face together. "Okay. That's weird."

She looks at me over her binder of research, her finger marking a spot. She's wearing a red, white, and blue swimsuit under a sweatshirt with an American flag. I'm not sure if her fanny pack is underneath, but I've never seen her without it. "I mean, it's nice, but . . . "

"Forget it," I say. Of course, it's probably verbatim what I would have said to Murray. Actually, now that I think of it, it's a lot more respectful than what I would have said. "So who are we waiting on?"

Juan is in the kitchen, cooking some sort of breakfast that smells spicy and amazing. Alexandra keeps her finger on the spot in her binder and looks to the ceiling in thought.

"Um, Bella and Kate and Miley. And Sara and Tiffany are meeting us there."

That's a lot of kids. I'm not sure if their parents will be sending them with money for food or if that will fall to me. Maybe I should have been involved in the invitation process. Before I can ask, Juan, on his way in from the kitchen to set the table with plates and forks, stops and gives Alexandra a stern look.

"What about Camila and Juanita and Lourdes?" he says.

Alexandra's shoulders deflate. "I didn't invite them."

"Why not?" her father asks, and he stands a little taller.

Alexandra won't look him in the eye, but Juan isn't backing down. He waits for an answer. I think about the names of the girls invited: Bella, Kate, Miley, Sara, and Tiffany. Compared to the names of the girls not invited: Camila, Juanita, and Lourdes. And it breaks my heart that Alexandra's attempt to be American would lead her so far off course.

After several long, uncomfortable moments, I finally break the silence. "Do you like Camila and Juanita and Lourdes?"

"Yeah," Alexandra says. "They're all super-nice."

"Then I think you should invite them. Want to know why?"

"Sure," Alexandra says, her eyes downcast.

"Because this is America. And in America, you can be friends with anyone you want to be friends with. That's how it works here."

A smile creeps onto her face. Just like I thought. I hit the jackpot. "You're right," she says, and she closes the binder, grabs her phone, and starts texting her friends. Juan smiles at me as her fingers fly over the surface of the phone so fast I can barely see them. Soon, as if all her friends are attached by some magical hand that can gather them up in seconds, she sets her phone down and says, "They're all in. They'll meet us there, too."

"Good," I say. "Are you coming?" I ask Juan.

He shakes his head and says, "Work." His eyelids droop over his large brown eyes and I can't help but feel guilty about being a part of the festivities when he can't. "I know all the parents well. I told them they can trust you."

I hadn't even thought about that. Of course, parents would be hesitant to let their daughters go to a water park with only a stranger supervising. But never having had kids, things like that just aren't on my radar. Thankfully, Juan has better radar.

"Is there anything I need to know about your diabetes before we go?" I say to Alexandra. "Anything I might have to help with?"

"Nope," she says. "Just hold my fanny pack while I'm in the water, I guess."

"Easy enough," I say.

Out the window, a car pulls into the driveway and a bouncy girl in a one-piece swimsuit hops out. "Okay," I say. "Let's hit the water park."

. . . . .

Badger is waiting for us when we pull into the parking lot. Standing outside his beat-up Airstream, he looks just as hungover as the last time. No wonder he had to gouge me for the two-hour access to a quarter of his water park in September—he has a habit to fund.

I stand from the car and strap on my gear. I look like something out of a bad TV show. Oxygen concentrator on one shoulder, diabetic fanny pack around my waist. I guess my days of being cool are behind me.

Alexandra and I are followed by the three kids who met us at her house. Four others jump out of their various cars and run toward us. With a total of eight kids screeching and squealing in excitement, I've decided not to even try to remember names. As soon as they're all together, they run in circles in their swimsuits, beach towels flowing behind them like they're soaring on air.

Despite the clear, sunny day, I'm wearing jeans and a sweater, and I wish I'd brought a light jacket. I don't know how the kids are so unfazed by the cold. But they are, and as soon as Badger opens the gates, they tear into the park, straight to the nearest water slide.

Alexandra leads them up the first flight of stairs to a wide landing, where they turn and start up the next flight. They get to the third flight, with four still to go, when the group starts to slow. By the fifth flight, they're stopped on the landing.

I can hear snippets of conversation, but not enough to figure out what's going on. Just enough bits and pieces to realize something is wrong. So I walk to the first flight of steps, where their voices echo down to me.

" . . . too high. I don't think I can . . ."

"Yes, you can, Alexandra. It's not that scary, really. Just don't look down."

"Yeah, just don't look down."

"I don't know. I've never been this high before. I think I'm afraid of heights. What if I fall over the railing?"

"Why would you fall over? You'd have to jump over it."

A few moments of silence follow. It's killing me not to know what's going on. Then the voices start again.

"So are we going up, or what?"

"Guys, don't pressure her. She's scared."

"But there's nothing to be scared about. She's fine."

"Seriously. Don't pressure her. She doesn't have to do it if she doesn't want to."

I remain at the base of the stairs, paralyzed by indecision. Should I climb the stairs and help? I'm not sure my heart would allow that much exertion right now. Maybe I should yell encouragement up toward her? Or just stay quiet and let her figure it out for herself?

I don't know. The danger in doing nothing is that the wish might not end up like she was hoping it would. It wouldn't have the same impact on her that mine had on me. The entire idea could be ruined if she can't muster the courage to climb to the top. Or what if she does make the climb but is terrified the entire time and ends up hating it? If I don't know what she should do, how could she know? She's eleven-and-a-quarter years old.

Fortunately, my paralysis doesn't ruin things, because Alexandra's voice appears loud and clear down the stairwell. "It's okay. I can do it. I want to do it."

The girls' bare feet clink against the metal stairs as the caravan continues its way up. They move slowly at first, but as her friends words of encouragement increase in frequency and pitch, the girls move faster and faster up the stairs. Finally, they reach the top, and I hear the beautifully innocent voice of Alexandra.

"Wow," she says, and I picture her looking out at the view of Lemon Grove, with the skyscrapers of Chicago visible in the distance. "I can't believe I did it. This is so terrifying."

Fortunately, her voice is ecstatic. It's proud. And I feel my heart swell. I back up so I can see them, standing on the very top platform, gathered at the entrance to the waterslide. From this vantage point, I can see Alexandra's expression. She's as happy as I've ever seen her. For one second, from far below, I catch her eye. She's beaming. There's no sign of a thought about the cold air. Not a thought about her fear of heights. And best of all, not a thought about her diabetes or the deportation hearing.

That's the magic of wishes.

I walk to the base of the slide, where they'll end up after this crazy ride is over. At the top, they're laughing and screaming and having a dramatic discussion about who will go first.

Unsurprisingly, I see Alexandra approach the top of the slide and grab the railing. I pull my phone out and open the camera app. I flip to the video icon just in time to see her take off down the slide.

Her scream is half terror, half elation. Water droplets shoot up from her heels, an arc of water covering her face as she accelerates down the slide. Finally, the steep angle eases and she's slowed by a pool of deeper water, where she comes to a stop.

Through my camera, I see her blink water away with an enormous smile on her face. She quickly hops out of the water, then bounces and waves for the next girl to come. A moment later, one of the other kids splashes to a stop and hops out of the slide. Alexandra jumps at the girl with her arms wide open and they hug like they just won the World Series.

With each girl that joins, they do the same thing—open-armed hugs jumping in a circle of celebration. If I've ever seen such innocence, such pure, unrestrained happiness, I don't remember it. Growing up, my friends and I wouldn't have been caught dead acting like this.

The morning continues in the same way for nearly two hours. Once, about half-way through, Alexandra comes over looking a little worse for the wear. She grabs a fruit snack from the fanny pack and sits at a picnic table to eat it.

"Are you okay?" I say.

"Sugar's just a little low. I'm fine."

"Are you having fun?"

"It's absolutely the best," she says. She pops the rest of her snack into her mouth and heads right back to the others, obviously not wanting to miss a moment.

The girls, shivering in the cold, move from one slide to the next as one unit of very loud, preteen girls. It's like they're one organism. One hive of happiness. It makes my day to see it, and I document as much as I can for Juan.

With only ten minutes to go until our time is up, the girls decide to go back to the first and tallest waterslide. Back near the entrance, I notice Badger talking with an armed, uniformed man. It doesn't look like a police officer, but also not quite a security guard. Something about the way they look at the girls and talk out the sides of their mouths makes my stomach squirm. I walk toward them rather than waiting for them to come to me. Something tells me I don't want the girls to hear our conversation.

"Good morning," I say, as upbeat as I can.

"That's him," Badger says. He points to me like I'm in a lineup of suspects rather than standing two feet in front of him. "He's the guy."

The uniformed man looks at me in a way that is unmistakably annoyed. I was worried that he'd laugh at my backpack-fanny-pack get-up, but this is worse. I scan his uniform but can't find any sign of what organization he works for until I land on an identification tag on his shirt. It suddenly feels a lot colder out here when I see he's from Immigration and Customs Enforcement.

"This guy says you admitted to having an undocumented immigrant with you." the officer says.

Something switches inside me, and the cold I'd just been feeling turns boiling hot. Badger smirks at me like he thinks he's just orchestrated the greatest raid in Lemon Grove history.

"That's right," I say, and I point to the top of the slide. "There's an eleven year-old girl up there who's undocumented." I emphasize the words "eleven year-old girl" and glare at Badger when I say them. He stares back at me with unapologetic eyes. "But she's in the system and has a hearing scheduled."

The officer nods, as if he was expecting as much. "And the others?"

"No idea. I don't make a habit of going around, asking kids about their immigration status. I've found it to be a poor conversation starter."

The officer shakes his head, and I wonder if I'm getting myself in some kind of trouble. If it means protecting Alexandra, I'll happily go to jail. That realization hits me like a splash of cold water to the face. I hadn't realized it was true until this moment.

Fortunately, the officer's annoyance isn't with me, but with the park owner. "My job isn't to harass kids," he says to Badger. His next words come with a sharp edge. "No matter their skin color."

I want to express my gratitude to the man, but he turns on his heels and heads back to his car without another word. I avoid looking at Badger and go back to the base of the slide, where Alexandra is just stepping out of the water. In place of her excitement, she's squinting in the direction of the ICE agent, who's now pulling his car out of the parking lot.

"Who was that?" she asks.

"No one important." How can I possibly tell a little kid who has done nothing wrong that someone called the authorities to have her and her friends detained?

Water drips from her red, white, and blue swimming suit. I can't tell if the drips on her face are from the waterslide, sadness, or anger. Probably a mixture of all three.

When the last of the girls is down the slide, I make a big deal of checking the time before saying, "Okay. Time for ice cream!"

The distraction is enough for Alexandra's friends. But as they do their preteen screaming thing, Alexandra's face remains flat. The group of girls dance toward the exit, with Alexandra and I following a few steps behind.

Her sadness and anger are palpable. They're in her walk, her expression, even the energy surrounding her, which is usually so lighthearted. I put my arm around her shoulder, which is freezing cold, and pat her three times, like Murray might have. She doesn't react.

But just as I'm about to remove my hand, she leans in, puts her head against my side, and starts to cry.

Chapter Ten

I'm finding it hard to breathe tonight. And my knee hurts something fierce. Makes me wonder, what if I can't finish this whole wish business? What if I keel over and die after the kid only gets a wish or two? Would it be a good thing, all in all? Or would it be better for the kid if he'd never met this old-timer?

You'd think seeing Jason so happy after his first wish would make me sure I'm doing the right thing. But actually, it just makes me worry that I'm messing things up good.

—From the Journal of Murray McBride

A few years ago, I had a bad performance. It was in Los Angeles, I think. Or maybe Tokyo. Strange that I can't even remember what continent I was on, but I guess that's a pretty good illustration of what my life has been like. Wherever it was, that night was a disaster.

I had never been "found out" before. But complacency is a magician's worst enemy and that night, it caught up with me. A man in the second row, on the last seat to the far right of the stage, saw behind the curtain, so to speak. And he felt the need to interrupt my performance by standing up and yelling to the entire crowd that my assistant had not, in fact, been cut in half. From his perspective, he could see her intact the entire time.

I was embarrassed. I was ashamed. There was one thing I was supposed to be good at. One thing I was supposed to be able to do, and I couldn't do it. If only magic was real, I could have waved my wand and said "abra cadabra" and everything would have been fixed.

But those words don't have that kind of power. As proficient as I've become at performing magic, some things are beyond my abilities to fix.

I'm reminded of that now.

The ice cream place is on the way back to Alexandra's house, which is good because I'm ready for this first wish to be over. Everything was going so well. Alexandra overcame her fears, climbed to the top of the slide, and had a wonderful time. And then it all came crashing down.

I look into the rearview mirror many times on the drive there, and each time Alexandra is talking and laughing with her friends. But after each laugh, she lets her guard down just a little and I see the pain in her eyes. You'd have to be watching closely to see it, and none of her friends seem to. But I do.

The kids file out of the car and rush to the window, where they order their malts and ice cream cones. Alexandra and I go last so I can pay, and she stoically goes through the routine of pricking her finger and testing her blood sugar levels. Her expression is blank the entire time. She looks resigned, almost beaten. I try to make conversation to distract her from the injustice of having to concern herself with this when none of her friends have to. Also, to distract her from the way the wish ended.

"What's your favorite ice cream treat?"

"I always get a cone when we come here," she says. Her voice is normal, even if her eyes lack their normal sparkle. "Chocolate is my favorite, but I usually get vanilla."

"Really? Why? If chocolate is your favorite, why don't you get that?"

Alexandra squishes her lips together in thought. "If I got it all the time, it wouldn't be special. So I get vanilla, because that's good, too. But when it's a really, really, super-special day, then I get chocolate, and it makes it even better. Chocolate ice cream is only for the most amazing day ever."

"The most amazing day ever? Wow. I didn't realize chocolate had so much power."

"Yep."

We get to the counter and, sure enough, Alexandra orders a vanilla cone. I certainly can't order chocolate if she doesn't, so I get the same.

"How many times have you had chocolate ice cream cones?" I ask.

"As of today ... zero."

"What? You've never had a chocolate ice cream cone?"

"Nope. But I will someday. On the most amazing day ever."

I don't know whether to laugh or cry. She's built this thing up to monumental proportions and doesn't even know if she actually likes it. It's ridiculous. It's hilarious. And it's agonizing that she's never had a day that warrants chocolate ice cream.

I vow to give her a "chocolate ice cream day" someday—the most amazing day ever. But I quickly chide myself for even thinking such a thing. Have I already forgotten what just happened at the water park? How am I supposed to give her the most amazing day ever if I can't make a simple wish come true without having it end in tears?

When we rejoin her friends, Alexandra finds a seat at a picnic table right in the middle, and I stay off to the side and watch. They retell story after story of the amazing slides at the water park, and finish their ice cream in record time. As soon as the last one finishes, we pile back into the car and drive the rest of the way to Alexandra's house.

Once all the kids are out of the car, I back out of the driveway and promise myself I'll come back later. I try to think of a distraction from the fact that I couldn't give Alexandra a chocolate ice cream day, and the only one, unsurprisingly, is Rachel. So I decide to try my hand at making "sometime soon" be sooner rather than later. When I'm out of sight of the house, I pull over and text her.

—Hey. Sorry if this is too forward. I'm not good at the whole dating thing.—

Almost immediately there are little bubbles, telling me she's typing out an answer.

—Sorry if what's too forward? Are you proposing to me?—
—What? No! Sorry!—

—JK. Settle.—

—Oh. I knew that. How's this for a proposal: a walk through Harms Woods?—

—Sounds romantic.—

—Yeah, well. You know me.—

—Actually I don't. But I think I'd like to.—

My fingers tingle for the remainder of our texting, in which we agree to meet at the North Branch Trailhead at noon. It's only 11 a.m. now, but I have nothing to do and no expectations that I'll be able to think about anything else, so I grab take-out Chinese and eat it in the rental car in the Harms Woods parking lot.

I think about the list I stole and wonder if Rachel knows about it. I realize I need to come clean. Keeping secrets is no way to start a new relationship. I don't know how or when, but it's important that I tell her. If she's the kind of person I think she is, she'll understand that my intentions were good.

After an hour of scanning radio stations for decent music, I see Rachel pull into the parking lot in a newish Honda Civic. I reluctantly grab my oxygen concentrator as I get out of the rental car.

She leans in for a hug when we meet between our cars, and we start walking down a thin trail along the North Branch Chicago River. It's a beautiful autumn day with crisp, clean air and leaves just starting to turn at the tips.

"This is my favorite time of year," Rachel says. "I always take this week off work so I can spend time outside. I just can't get enough of it."

So she's been off work this week. That would mean she likely doesn't know about Andy Tart. Still, I should be the one to tell her. But before I can, she asks about my morning and even though I want to get my confession about the list out of the way, I can't help but launch into what happened at the water park. I briefly tell her about how much fun

Alexandra and her friends had, and how she overcame her fear of heights and had a great time, but then I skip to the part about the ICE agent and Alexandra's reaction.

"All she wants is to be an American. It's like that guy knew the most painful thing he could do to her and did it." I feel a flash of anger toward Badger but it quickly burns out. "I think Father James was wrong. I'm not the right person for this. I don't know anything about the prejudice Alexandra has to deal with. I mean, what am I trying to do? I don't even have a home."

"You have experience, though."

"What are you talking about?"

"Murray McBride?"

Hearing Murray's name has caused a lot of different reactions over the years. Sadness to start. Then love and appreciation. But when I consider the effort it must have taken him and the obstacles he had to overcome, and compare that to my situation, all I feel now is shame. "What about him?"

"He gave you five wishes. It's pretty apparent how much you appreciated it because you're doing the same for Alexandra. So the obvious question is, why would you stop now?"

I rub my forehead and stare at the ground, watching my feet glide over the dirt path. "With Murray and me, there wasn't anyone against us. There was my heart, but that wasn't another person. But with Alexandra and Juan, there are actual people who don't like them. Just because of what they look like and where they come from. And I don't know how to handle that."

Rachel's stare doesn't seem very understanding. "I would have thought a person like you—a person who has been through as much as you've been through—would have more courage."

Her words sting, but not as much as I would have thought. And I realize it's because I know they're not true. It's not that I lack courage.

When I think back on the fury I felt toward Badger, I know I'd take on the entire world for Alexandra, if that's what it required.

As if reading my thoughts, Rachel's voice becomes much softer. "What is it really?" she asks. "You've obviously developed a friendship with this kid. Why would you want to get out of this?"

I think about Alexandra's face as we left the water park. I had meant to give her something she wanted; to grant her first wish. And she'd ended up crying instead. I shake my head, trying to rid myself of the memory.

"What if I can't do what Murray did?" I say. "What if I try to do what he did for me, but in the end, I fail her?"

We walk in silence for a while as the sun shines overhead, casting a perfectly mirrored image of the sky against the surface of the meandering river. Rachel takes my hand, knocking the breath out of me.

"Did I ever tell you about my Uncle Don?"

"No," I say. "We just met, remember?"

"Oh, yeah. Weird. It seems like I've known you a long time."

I try to respond but find it difficult to speak through my smile.

"I lost my dad when I was in middle school," she says. "Which is a terrible time to lose a parent. Not that there's ever a good time."

"I'm sorry," I say, and I squeeze her hand a little.

"Thanks. Anyway, it was such a hard time for me, but then my mom's brother, my Uncle Don, came to live with us for a while. I can't explain how much he helped me during that time."

"What did he do?" I can't help but feel like Rachel is going to give me some great piece of wisdom for how to do better. Do more. Do . . . something.

"He didn't do anything."

"What do you mean?"

"He was just there. Somehow, his presence made things a little bit easier. It was like I had this giant, gaping void in my life, and although he could never completely fill it, his being around somehow made it smaller.

By not doing a single thing other than being there. His presence was enough."

We walk in silence for a long time, lost in thought. Maybe I can't accomplish everything I'd like with Alexandra. Maybe I can't prevent her from being deported. Maybe I won't even be able to give her five wishes. But now I know one thing I can do, even if it's the only thing I can do.

For a while, anyway, I can be present for her.

Chapter Eleven

Jason and I have been keeping in touch through my email machine. It's a hard way to communicate, especially since the kid doesn't use much punctuation, and he keeps putting down abbreviations that no one in his right mind would understand. We just see things so different, me and that kid. But maybe that's not all bad.

I guess that's something I should have learned earlier. I guess I'm not always right, much as I hate to admit it. Sometimes we should all see things through other people's eyes. Even a rambunctious kid's eyes, once in a while.

—From the Journal of Murray McBride

I keep the promise I made to myself and return to the Lopez's in the early afternoon. Alexandra seems like her normal self when I walk into the kitchen. It's as if the run-in with Badger never even happened. In a way, her recovery makes the entire thing more tragic. If Badger's actions were unusual, if Alexandra's reaction had been from shock that someone would do such a thing, her sadness might last longer. It would be difficult to see her sadness for a longer duration, but it would be a one-time thing.

The fact that she's able to get over it so quickly suggests it's something she has had plenty of experience with, something that flares up once in a while and can create moments of anger and sadness like she had this morning, but common enough that she's learned how to push it aside.

For me, it's more difficult. Now that I'm no longer with Rachel and back with the Lopez family, it reminds me of what happened. I realize I'm still fuming at Badger.

"Sit," Juan says. His white T-shirt is dirty from a day of work and a piece of mud drops to the floor as he gestures to the kitchen table. "I'll make some coffee."

He's gone before I can protest and a moment later Alexandra says, "Oh! I have to show you something. I'll be right back."

She scampers up the stairs and I'm left by myself until Juan reenters with two steaming cups of coffee. He sets one down in front of me and takes the chair opposite me. He's grinning ear to ear—and why not? His daughter just got her first wish—until he sees my expression.

"What's wrong?" he asks.

I look toward the stairs Alexandra climbed to her room, afraid she'll overhear. Of course, she was there when it happened. She's the one who has lived with this sort of thing for . . . her entire life, probably. There's no need to try to protect her. So I tell Juan about Badger and the ICE agent, and Alexandra's reaction.

"She seems fine to me now," Juan says. "She said she had the best time at the park."

"That's great," I say. "But I just can't get over what Badger did. Why did he think it was okay to try to get little kids arrested just because they were different than him?"

Juan clicks his tongue disapprovingly. "You're too quick to jump to conclusions."

"What do you mean?" I say, surprised that he's not agreeing with me. "As soon as he heard me mention the deportation hearing, he got angry."

"When things like this happen, I think it helps most to think from the other person's eyes." Juan sips his coffee with perfect calm.

"His eyes seemed pretty racist, if you ask me."

"Maybe," Juan says. "Maybe not."

"You heard what I said, right? About the ICE agent and everything?" I try to keep my voice level, but I find myself getting angry for him. If he's not going to be as mad about this as he should be, someone has to do it.

He takes another long sip of coffee, his eyes turned to the ceiling in thought. "The man is afraid."

"Just because—"

"He's afraid for his future," Juan says, cutting me off with a stern look I imagine Alexandra sees every now and then. It's enough to make me shut up and listen.

"He probably believes immigrants are taking jobs from his friends and family, and that soon his job will also be in jeopardy. He worries he won't be able to pay his bills, that he'll be kicked out of his house, he'll lose his water park. He'll be left homeless, while all these people who don't look like him or sound like him take what used to be his."

"Why does it matter if they look and sound like him?" I say. I think it's the unanswerable question, but Juan just smiles.

"There's comfort in familiarity," he says. "Familiarity of language—can you imagine suddenly not being able to understand what people are saying around you? I remember very strongly how that felt. And familiarity of culture—it would be hard to live with different holidays and customs than you've grown up with. And yes, familiarity of looks. It might be a human weakness, but it's no coincidence that most people feel most comfortable around people that look like them."

This conversation isn't going how I thought it would. I figured Juan, of all people, would commiserate with me and fume with me about Badger's actions. I certainly didn't expect him to understand the man's point of view.

"How can you be so . . . I don't know, calm about it?"

"I've been through all the phases," Juan says. "There is a place for anger, and a time, don't get me wrong. Sometimes anger is required to make a change. But it can't be your normal. It will eat you up from inside. One day, after many, many angry days, I knew I had to find another way."

Alexandra bounces back down the stairs, interrupting our conversation. Her hair is wet from the shower, but she's in dry, clean clothes. All red, white, and blue, unsurprisingly, with her fanny pack in place. And she carries her three-ring binder, which she tosses onto the table and opens.

"One hundred fliers," she says, eyeing her work before passing it to me. "I figure we give out what we can, and post what we can't on streetlights and in coffee shops and stuff. If enough people see them, we'll have enough money to start construction by the end of the week."

The fliers are impressive. They're beautifully designed with fancy lettering and a colorful picture of a small village nestled in a lush, tropical forest. The GoFundMe page is prominently displayed, making the call to action clear. But it's funny how little she understands about how the real world works and how long things can take.

"These are great," I say. "But don't worry if it takes a little time. First, we'll have to hope people donate, but even then, we'll have to contact people in El Remate—and not just your pen pal. We'll have to somehow figure out who can design the building, who can do the labor, and how much we'll pay them. There are lots of details with this kind of thing."

Alexandra looks at me, shocked. At first I think it's because she can't believe how many details might be involved in her plan, but then she walks toward an adjacent room and says, "Follow me."

Juan smiles like he knows what I'm in for, but I sure don't. So I take a deep breath from the oxygen concentrator, then dutifully trail behind Alexandra as she enters a small room with a computer on a desk and sits in front of it. There's no other chair in the room, so I take a knee next to her as she opens a file.

"Look," she says. "Here's a list of who's going to do what."

Her list is surprisingly thorough. She has jobs listed in a vertical row: cement, carpentry, safety, even architecture. And to the right, corresponding with each job, several names are listed.

"Who are all these people?" I ask.

"People from El Remate that are looking for work," Alexandra says, as if it's obvious. "And a few from nearby villages. Zuri put the word out and tons of people wanted to help. The guy in charge of safety even went to college in the U.S. and got a degree before he got deported. And they all only want about five dollars a day for work. And look at this." She taps a few keys and another screen comes up. It's a donation page with a number very large and prominent in the middle of the screen. The number shocks me.

"You already have five hundred and twenty dollars? How?"

"I don't know. Mostly an anonymous donation of five hundred dollars. I've been sending out emails and posting on social media. But do you know how far five hundred dollars can go in Guatemala? We can have a team of people working for weeks. It's going even faster than I thought. Now I need to get some supplies ordered, but I'm still working on that."

She continues scrolling, clicking, and scheming while I wrap my mind around all she's done. "This is real," I finally say. "I mean, this could actually work. You could do some really big things for that town."

She stops typing for a moment and looks at me with confusion in her eyes. "I know. That was the plan, remember? It's my fifth wish."

"Well, yeah but . . . I guess I'm just impressed by how much you've done."

Alexandra shrugs and turns back to the computer. "I just figured there was no reason to wait around." She blinks a few extra times while staring at the screen, then says, "The hearing is coming up soon."

■　　　■　　　■　　　■　　　■

The hearing.

It's easy to forget when I'm watching Alexandra plummet down a water slide, screeching with glee, that she might not live here in two weeks. Every time I think about it I get a renewed sense of urgency to make her American wishes come true.

It's already 3 p.m., and I have a meeting set up in Chicago for six o'clock. So I drive Alexandra to downtown Lemon Grove, where we stand on the corner of Main and First, handing out fliers to disinterested people passing by. The reactions we get are discouraging. Most people take the paper while ignoring what we're saying and avoiding eye contact. Many decline to take the flier at all. Some even glare at us for disturbing their walk.

I get it. I'm not a fan of people seeking signatures for ballot initiatives or trying to rope me into some scam. But this is different. This is about Alexandra's wishes. So I force myself to extend a flier to every single person that comes by, even though I'm out of breath and extremely uncomfortable doing it.

Alexandra, on the other hand, has no such issues. I don't know where her energy comes from, but she gives out twice as many fliers as I do, and the people seem happy to take them from her. The benefits of being a cute kid, I guess.

After a couple hours, we're down to a half dozen fliers, so Alexandra suggests we take them into the shops along Main Street. Most shop owners are happy to allow her space on their bulletin boards and, before long, Alexandra is pinning her final flier and wiping her hands off in an exaggerated way.

I give her a high five, every bit as eager as she is to see if donations start to flow. After seeing the work she's put in and how far she's already come, I can't help but let my imagination run wild with possibilities.

"Want to go back to my house and help me research where to get building materials?" she asks.

"Actually, you seem to be doing a great job without me, and I have a meeting to get to in Chicago. Think you'll be okay doing it yourself for now?"

"Of course," she says, as if the answer should be obvious.

I drop her off in front of her house, watch to make sure she gets in the front door—she turns and waves with that giant smile of hers—and then point my car toward Chicago.

I haven't often made the drive from Lemon Grove to Chicago. Mostly because I haven't been in Lemon Grove. But each time I do, I'm cast back to that night, twenty years ago, riding in the front seat of Murray's old Chevy, Tiegan stowed away in the back. Even today, I get tingles thinking about how exciting it was.

Today, the tingles of excitement have as much to do with the present as the past. I'm not just looking back today. I'm looking forward. The drive to Wrigleyville is uneventful. I park near Wrigley Field and walk to the gate. I explain my reasons for being here to the security guard, who relays the message via walkie-talkie before leading me inside the stadium.

"Would you like a wheelchair?" he asks.

At first I'm insulted. He thinks I can't walk through the stadium without help? But my second reaction is temptation. My chest is squeezing, I'm having a hard time getting enough air, and the thought of having someone push me around rather than exerting myself doesn't sound all bad. In the end, my pride wins out. I decline the wheelchair and take a deep breath from the oxygen concentrator.

I follow the guard through hallways, up an elevator, and into an office with a view out onto the playing surface. The office is empty, and I walk straight to the tall windows and stare at the field.

The ivy covering the outfield wall is red now, its leaves turning with the rest of the foliage in Chicago. When I was here as a kid, it was green. Bright, vivid green. I remember that. The only red was on the grass of the outfield, and that was from my blood. But I only know that because I was told. I don't remember anything past watching the ball fly over the fence, which is still one of the best moments of my life. Courtesy of Mr. Murray McBride.

The security guard's voice startles me out of my memories.

"You can have a seat, if you'd like," he says. "Mr. Gonzalez will be with you in a moment."

I sit in the padded chair across from the desk and read the placard on the desk: Javier Gonzalez, Director of Baseball Operations. A minute later, a tall, lean man with shoulders the size of small boulders enters and I stand at attention. He's wearing a blue suit, bright white shirt, and a smile that lights up his face. Even if I had never seen Javier Gonzalez before, I'd know immediately that this man is a star. I might be considered a star in the world of magicians—at least able to fill theaters pretty regularly. But Javier's star is like a supernova. I'm a dwarf star.

"Jason," he says as he shakes my hand.

My hand is lost in his, completely enveloped. The fact that he knows my name makes me feel special, even if it is only because the security guard reminded him.

"Mr. Gonzalez, thank you for meeting me so late in the day."

"It's Javier," he says, waving me off. "Please, have a seat."

I sit. With his muscular frame, square jaw, and perfect suit, he's the kind of person people follow. His accent, which has smoothed since I last saw him, comes off as dignified and almost exotic. I'd follow him even if he hadn't had such a long, successful career with the Cubs.

"I have to ask," I say. "Do you remember me? From when I was sick twenty years ago?"

Javier swivels in his leather-bound chair and looks toward the ceiling. "I remember the World Series, so clearly," he says. "I remember my wedding day and the birth of my son. But visiting you in the hospital . . . " His voice trails off and he shakes his head. "I remember that like it was yesterday." He shrugs. "Maybe it was the time in my life. My age. Or that I once had a baseball card of Murray McBride, back in Cuba, where we had no baseball cards. I don't know. But something about that time . . . " Again his voice trails off, and he taps his temple as if to say those memories are lodged deep in his brain.

I know the feeling.

"But I didn't know you would still have health problems," he says, motioning to my oxygen concentrator. "Are you unwell?"

"Yeah," I say, trying to muster as much nonchalance as possible. "A heart transplant only lasts so long."

Javier looks at my chest with a scowl on his face. "So," he says after a moment. He folds is hands together and leans forward onto the desk. "What can I help you with? Whatever the Cubs family can do for you, we're happy to help. Another visit to Wrigley? For another kid, perhaps?"

"You're very perceptive," I say. "There is another kid. A little Guatemalan girl." I catch myself right away. "I mean, an American girl, but she was born in Guatemala."

Javier nods. "This girl," he says. "She and I are the same. I come from Cuba, where we are not allowed to go to the United States. She comes from Guatemala, where she is not allowed to go to the United States. And yet, here we both are."

"Yes," I say. "Unfortunately, her immigration status is . . . uncertain."

Javier's low growl suggests he knows more about this type of thing than I do. Certainly, he has more experience with it. "When would you like to bring her? And how can we make her visit the very best?"

"Actually, I don't think she wants to come to Wrigley."

"Oh," Javier says, "then what does she want?"

"I was hoping you might have some contacts with the Nationals."

"The Nationals?" Javier stands up and turns toward the large windows overlooking the playing surface. "I have always hated the Nationals. They are my bitter rival. Why would a Chicago girl like the Nationals?"

Javier's reaction surprises me until I remember a clip that went viral several years ago. A Cubs pitcher hitting a National batter with a four-seam fastball . . . the batter charging the mound . . . Javier coming in from his shortstop position to protect his pitcher and landing on the thirty-day disabled list with a fracture of some sort.

If I had remembered that earlier, I never would have come to ask for his help. Well, that's actually not true. When I think of Alexandra, I realize I would have come anyway.

"I don't think she does like the Nationals," I say. "I don't think she even likes baseball actually. But we're working on her five wishes, just like Murray did with me, and I think we can do three in one trip to D.C., if I can figure out how to make this one thing happen."

"She has wishes?" Javier says.

"Yes. And a deportation hearing coming up very soon."

"Now you are speaking my language," Javier says. "That is bigger than a baseball rivalry. For this, I have friends in the Nationals organization. What does the girl want?"

"She'd like to sing the National Anthem before a game. Very soon, if possible."

Javier raises his eyebrows as if impressed. "The girl can sing, then?"

"I actually have no idea," I say, and I toss my hands up. "She wants to do it anyway."

"She is very brave, this girl. To go in front of many thousands of people and do something she might not be good at doing."

"Yeah," I say. "She's...unique. She's pretty determined to be an American."

"An American? This is why she wants to sing the National Anthem before a Nationals game?"

I nod. "Her wishes are all about being American. And I guess she sees this as a very American thing to do, so she wants to do it."

Javier strokes his chin before abruptly sitting at his desk and sliding a notepad across to me. "This must happen," he says. "I will make sure of it." He sets a pen on top of the notepad. "Please write your email address on this paper. I will contact you by the end of the day tomorrow to let you know of my success."

"Thanks, Javier." I stand to leave. Javier is already picking up the phone. He punches at the numbers, so I start to move out of the room to let him get to work. But he calls my name just before I get to the door.

I turn back and see him holding his hand over the phone. "Murray was a special man," he says. "And you were a special kid. I'm happy you're alive." He flashes me his movie-star smile. "Now you can do for another what Murray did for you. I want you to know, I think it is beautiful."

And with that, he turns his attention back to his telephone call.

Chapter Twelve

Jason was having a bad day today, and it breaks my heart to see it. Every night I pray these days, I ask the Good Lord to heal Jason's heart. So far, no dice. I just don't understand why a grumpy, old codger like me gets to hang around this joint while a kid like him has a heart that doesn't work.

It hurts me to see him struggle to breathe. It hurts me to hear him talk about dying. Mostly, it hurts me to see the hopelessness he sometimes feels.

—From the Journal of Murray McBride

The drive back to Lemon Grove can't go fast enough. I can't wait to get back and tell Alexandra about my meeting with Javier. Javier Gonzalez, the All-Star. It's crazy that I can call the Cubs and get a meeting with one of their legendary players, now running things from his plush front-office position. Again, it's all thanks to Murray.

I'm just starting to realize how much work goes into making a kid's wishes come true. There's more legwork than I realized when I was the recipient of the work. But I'm starting to understand what Murray said about how my wishes kept him alive. Throwing myself into doing something for someone I've come to care about turns out to be the best medicine for the emptiness I have inside me. Or maybe it's the emptiness I *had*. I'm not entirely sure.

My heart even feels better. Not physically, of course. The pain in my chest still flares up more frequently than I would like, even though I have the oxygen with me constantly and I use it often. But I can tell by the way it's beating that I'm doing the right thing. That Tiegan approves.

Somehow, Alexandra has already learned what it took me so long to figure out. She's thrown herself into her fifth wish completely. I'm excited to see how her plans are coming along. What she's already accomplished for that small village in Guatemala is truly amazing.

As I pull into the driveway and approach the front door of the Lopez home, I'm starting to think of it as my own home. I don't live here, of course, but there is no place I look forward to going more. And although I love my mom, Collins, and Della, at this moment there's no one in the world I enjoy more. Although there is a certain transplant coordinator who's growing on me.

I have a bounce in my step when I get to the door. But something about Juan's expression when I first see him gives me pause. "Is everything okay?" I ask as he opens the door so I can enter. I'm hoping he's just upset that I interrupted their dinner or something, but Juan doesn't seem like the kind who would be upset by something like that.

He shrugs and motions toward the computer room. "Alexandra is in there. She's . . . well, maybe you should just go talk to her."

I hurry into the room and see Alexandra sitting at the computer, but not looking at it. In fact, the screen is dark and she has her head down, leaning against her crossed arms like she's taking a nap. But when I walk in I notice she's not sleeping. Her eyes are open, and full of tears.

"What's wrong?" I ask, taking a knee so I can meet her at eye level. "Is it something with the donations? Or a problem finding supplies in Guatemala?" She doesn't answer, so I move a strand of hair off her face and tuck it behind her ear. I pat her shoulder three times, feeling a bit awkward as I think of how Murray might console me. "Whatever it is, I'm sure we can figure it out."

She blinks and looks at me, and it's almost like she's just realizing I'm here. She sits up tall, hits a button on the keyboard, and points to the computer screen, which is now lit up. "Look," she says.

It's a newspaper article. She scrolls to the top so I can read from the beginning. The headline reads "Diabetes Crisis in Guatemala." I don't have to read much to get the gist of what's in the article.

"Look, Alexandra. We don't even know if they'll make you go."

She ignores me and scrolls further down the article. "You didn't get to this part. It's about a girl who died because she didn't know that the insulin she got was different than her usual kind. It was a seventy-thirty mix. You can't just take whatever kind of insulin you can find and expect everything to be the same. I need Lantus for my long acting and Humalog for my short acting, not some seventy-thirty mix."

I'm impressed by the smart-sounding words she's using, but even more than that, I'm horrified about what she's saying. Like a lot of people, I've heard tragic stories from all around the world, but there has always been a degree of separation between me and those tragedies, making it easy to feel a moment of compassion or empathy and then get on with the rest of my day.

But in a short amount of time, I've grown really fond of this kid. She's so real. So unlike all the people I've read about in newspaper articles or heard about on the radio or TV news. Alexandra isn't some random person I've never met dealing with some horror I can conveniently stop thinking about. The separation is gone. She's right here in front of me. And in a matter of days, this person, right here, who I care for, could be faced with the horrors in that newspaper article.

"Do you know what scares me the most?" she says. "It's not the different kinds of insulin, even though that's really scary. What scares me the most is the thought of getting sick. Like, throwing up and stuff. Because then you can't eat to get your sugars back up, and then you have to go to a hospital if you don't want to die, and I won't have access to a hospital."

I try desperately to think of something to say, but I come up with nothing. I wish she'd stop, but she continues.

"And I'm going to start puberty pretty soon, and that can cause lots of complications for diabetes, too. And stress does, too, and I'll be super-stressed. And now I might not even be able to get the right kinds of insulin."

Everything she says scares me, but when she talks about insulin, it's the most terrifying. I can't get Father James's voice out of my head, telling me she could be dead in twenty-four hours without insulin.

Like Murray and his pill.

There's nothing to say to her. Nothing that can change the truth. Nothing I say or do can protect her. That's out of my hands. I'm completely powerless to help.

Part of me wants to tell her about my meeting with Javier and the possibility of going to Washington D.C., and maybe even singing the National Anthem before a game. But that seems inconsequential now. What she's facing is real and it's terrible and it can't be hidden by slapping a Band-Aid on it.

So instead, I close my eyes and listen to my heart. I listen closely for Tiegan's voice. I try to channel her spirt and her wisdom. Her kindness. I think of what she would do, if she were here.

When Juan comes in the room to check on Alexandra's crying, I wrap my arms around them both. We stand in a huddle for a long time and I bend low, so our foreheads all touch. And with every fiber of my being, I try to be strong for my new friends.

Chapter Thirteen

Saw Father James again today. Well, I see him every day, but I saw him again outside of mass. To hear him tell it, life is nothing but a great big mystery, and so is the afterlife. It's harder to get a straight answer out of him than it was to hit a slider on the outside corner, that's what.

I just want to know that what I'm doing matters somehow. Cause I know the kid might die. And what good will these wishes be for him then? I try not to, but sometimes I just can't help but wonder, what's the point of it all?

—From the Journal of Murray McBride

It's early in the morning and in the driver's seat of the rental car, I stuff the last bite of a stale hotel muffin into my mouth. I park the car across the street from St. Joseph's Church and retrieve a bundle of flowers from the back seat, along with my oxygen concentrator. I never heard Murray talk about a love of flowers, but it would feel strange to come empty-handed.

I enter the church grounds, but instead of going through the large, wooden doors, I curve around the old building and take a grass path to the back and into the cemetery. My mom brought me here a few times when I was a kid, but I haven't been back in years. Things have changed, unsurprisingly. The trees are taller and the sunlight filters onto the grass differently. It's disorienting, and it takes me several minutes to find his gravestone.

Murray Everet McBride
Born 1898 - Died 1998
Loving father, grandfather, and husband

I place the bouquet on the hard granite, leaning it up against his engraved name. I'm not sure why I came out here today. Maybe I'm looking for inspiration. A way forward.

Until I saw the fear on Alexandra's face, I didn't fully understand that she and her father could actually be deported. Not just theoretically, but for real. I've heard stories and read newspaper articles about deportations, but it happened far away and I didn't know those people. It wasn't in Lemon Grove. And it certainly didn't concern a little kid named Alexandra who just wants to live the life she's known her entire eleven-and-a-quarter years.

"Hey, Murray," I say. Only the air and the rock and the trees are listening, but maybe Murray can hear me somehow, too, even after all these years. So many years. I hate how time takes people away a little more each day.

"I wish you were here, I could use your help." I chuckle a bit, remembering our escapades together. "I know I never would have admitted it when you were alive, but you knew a lot more than me about this kind of thing." The words take me back to the time we spent together. The support he gave me. The wisdom he shared. "You knew a lot more about everything," I say.

I lean over and touch the ground next to the gravestone to make sure it's dry, then sit and wrap my elbows around my knees. I sit like that for several minutes before the real reason I came here, even if I didn't know it until this moment, appears. It's Father James, with his flowing robes trailing behind him like a cape as he walks through the morning sunshine.

When he reaches me, he says nothing. He adjusts his robes as he takes a seat on the ground a few feet away. He leans his back against a large tree trunk and exhales as if the effort takes a lot out of him.

We sit in silence for a long time without even saying hello. Father James has done enough of this kind of thing to know that I'll talk when I'm ready. It takes longer than I expect to realize why I'm here and what it is I want to ask. Finally, I look at the granite of Murray's grave and speak.

"Did he ever think it was hopeless?" I ask.

Father James picks up a small leaf from the ground and twirls it between his fingers. "Until the moment he died, I believe a large part of Murray thought the situation was hopeless. He thought he had failed to grant you all your five wishes, and he thought he had failed to save you."

"How could he have saved me? There was nothing he could have done for my heart."

Father James seems to be studying the dates on the gravestone. "When we love someone, what we can and can't do becomes irrelevant. We no longer think in those terms. Would we stop trying to find water in the desert if a loved one was dying of thirst? No. When we love someone, we no longer have a choice. *Can* or *can't* doesn't even play into it."

"So, what? We just flail around hopelessly? Trying to achieve something that we don't actually have any control over? Praying for a stroke of luck? Or a terrible accident that benefits us?"

I say the last part bitterly and immediately wonder if I've gone too far. If maybe my questions have offended his faith. He looks to the sky, but whether he's asking God for guidance or just watching the sun shine through the leaves, I don't know.

"What happened to you was so fortunate, and yet so tragic. But that was God's doing." He sees me squirm and says, "Or fate, or destiny, or karma, or random chance. I'm not telling you what to believe. My point is, it was out of your control. Or Murray's, or Tiegan's, or anyone else's. But I believe Murray learned to focus on what matters, and that is what we can control."

"What do we control?" I ask. "Sometimes it feels like I can't control anything."

"We control the way we live our lives. The things we think about and work toward on a daily basis. The amount of joy we spread among other people just as lost and struggling and sometimes as hopeless as we are."

I don't like the answer, and I think he can tell. He shifts his weight forward, no longer leaning against the tree. "What is it you hope to accomplish with Alexandra?"

"I don't want her to be deported, for one," I say. "Although I don't know how I can stop that from happening. And I want to help her get her five wishes, which is stupid because they're just a consolation prize."

"What do you mean by that?"

"I mean, what's going to happen? Even if I do somehow figure out a way to make each of her wishes come true. So what? She gets a few fun experiences before they ship her off to a country she doesn't even know, where she lives for a little while before something goes wrong, she can't get her insulin, and she dies? What, I'm just hoping to give her some good times before that happens?"

I hadn't recognized my level of frustration until this all came spilling out. But seeing Alexandra deal with the realities she might have to face makes everything feel hopeless. Which is why I came here, I realize now. To see if Father James has an antidote to hopelessness.

"I asked you what you hope to accomplish with Alexandra, but your answer has nothing to do with the girl."

"How could it not—"

"Your answer was about a theoretical future. Something that may or may not come to pass. I'm not asking about that. I'm asking about the girl." He emphasizes every word, as if that emphasis is the only way to get through to me. "What do you hope to accomplish with Alexandra?"

I try to step back from my frustration and hopelessness to find the answer. It takes a few moments, but when it comes, it seems obvious. "I just want her to be happy."

"Exactly," Father James says, as if I've stumbled upon the secret of life. "You wish for her to have joy. That's why the wishes matter, Jason. It's not about preventing some theoretical future. It's not about changing something that is out of your control. It's about creating joy for someone you hold dear. That is all. Nothing more. And that's enough. That, in itself, is so very worthwhile."

Father James reaches over to me and pats my knee softly. Then he stands, adjusts his robes, and leaves me with my thoughts.

Chapter Fourteen

One bad thing about what I'm doing with Jason, it reminds me of my failings as a father. And there were plenty, I see that now. Being away all the time, working too much. Ah, who am I kidding? No one's going to read this, so who am I trying to impress?

I was a bad father because I was a bad father. No excuses. I guess I'm trying to make up for that now, even if it is too little too late.

—From the Journal of Murray McBride

Father James, as I had hoped, has rejuvenated me, at least a little. The idea of spreading joy resonates with me. When I think about Tiegan and the lasting impact she had on me, that's exactly what I remember: whenever she was around, there was joy. She radiated it. When I was with her, I couldn't help but feel it, too.

I'm not sure I can be the kind of person capable of spreading joy like that, but as long as Tiegan's heart is in my chest, I figure I have a fighting chance. So I'll fight to make it happen with Alexandra.

My phone rings, but I don't recognize the caller ID, so I let it go to voicemail. A minute later, a ding tells me that there is, indeed, a voicemail. I can't help but smile when I hear the booming voice of another person I'd like to give joy to: Gary Johnson.

Mr. Jason. I have a letter for my son. I just wrote it and thought maybe you'd take it to him. Come on by the Marriot if you're willing.

It takes me a moment to realize that "Come on by the Marriot" doesn't mean he's out on parole. As soon as I understand, I turn my car straight for the prison.

When I get there, the walls are no less gray, no less concrete, and no less depressing than the first time I was here, but knowing that I'll be seeing Gary puts a bounce in my step. It's strange that I consider him a friend after just one meeting. He's a felon, after all, imprisoned for armed robbery—which he joyfully admits to. But when I see his jolly face again as he sits and picks up the phone, my heart gets a little boost.

It could really use a boost. Each breath is harder than the last, it seems. The squeezing never stops now. It forces me to stop and consider, again, what I'm doing. If my heart is giving me this much trouble, dropping dead at any moment seems more possible than it has in a very long time. Should I really be passing up another chance at a heart, if it comes?

But then, like always, I think of Tiegan, and I realize I don't have a choice.

Gary sits on the other side of the plexiglass and breathes heavily into the phone, but I don't know if it's the result of his heart issues or his obesity. Either way, it's like a tornado in my ear. "Mr. Jason!" he booms, followed by his characteristic giggle. "You got my message."

"I did."

"I don't know if I wrote the right things," Gary says. He slips a sealed envelope under the thin slot beneath the plexiglass partition. "But it's kind of personal, if you know what I mean." Giggle.

I put the envelope into the inside pocket of my jacket. "I promise to deliver it perfectly sealed. And I'm sure whatever you wrote is great, as long as it came from your heart."

Gary's laugh is very different from his normal giggle. It's booming and thunderous and draws stares from everyone nearby. "My heart might need a little help," he says, then points at my chest. "We're both a little defective in that area, aren't we?"

I stifle a flare of anger. Gary doesn't know about Tiegan. He has no way of understanding how his words might upset me. So I force a smile. "I'll get the note to him today," I say.

■　　■　　■　　■　　■

On the way to Gary's home—well, his family's home anyway—I make a quick call to Andy's mom. She picks up right away and is happy to pass along the good news. Andy's recovery is going as well as possible. He's in good spirits and gaining energy every day. Most importantly, his body seems to be accepting the new heart. All good news that makes me feel even better about my decision.

Gary's son doesn't answer the door this time. Instead, it's a tiny woman with her hair stacked on top of her head. If this is Gary's wife, seeing the two of them together would be a sight to see. She couldn't be more than half his size. "I'll get Aaron," she says and rushes back into the house.

Her brusque greeting suggests there's some disapproval of anything having to do with Gary. I have no interest in getting involved in a family drama. Well, not *another* family drama. So when Aaron comes to the door, I don't ask about his mother, assuming that's who the woman is. I just hold up the envelope Gary gave me.

Aaron's response makes me glad I didn't ask about the woman. His head jerks to look behind him, making sure the coast is clear. Then he joins me on the front step and closes the door behind him.

"That's from my dad?" He takes it from me and holds it softly, as if he's afraid of what might be inside.

"It is. He seemed very excited for you to read it."

Aaron doesn't waste any time. Or maybe he's just afraid to bring the letter back inside the house. I get the feeling he doesn't want his mother to know any more than she has to. Either way, he tears it open and scans the letter, his eyes darting back and forth over the lines. His brow crinkles and he starts over, reading it again from the beginning. Finally, he lowers the letter, still holding it by his side.

"My dad's a loser," he says.

It's not the reaction I was expecting.

"Why do you say that?" I ask.

"He's a jailbird. A felon. I don't want to have anything to do with him."

I hear the anger in his voice, but he hasn't torn up the note, and he didn't tell me to leave and never come back. "I actually found him to be a good man," I say. I put my hands up to stop Aaron's interruption. "I know he's made mistakes—"

"Mistakes?" Aaron says, forcing his interruption through my feeble attempts. "You call leaving your family for fifteen years a mistake? It's no mistake. It's betrayal."

"Fair enough," I say. "But he's sorry. He's repentant. And he's trying." Aaron looks like he swallowed a bug, but I press on. "Did you know he earned his college degree in prison?"

Aaron lifts the letter with a flick, as if to say Gary mentioned it in its pages. "Doesn't change anything," he says. "He still left his family."

There's a difference, I think, between someone who chooses to leave his family and someone who makes a mistake and is forced from his family. But I don't think Aaron would appreciate the distinction, and maybe it doesn't matter anyway. "He'd love to see you," I say.

"Yeah, I know," Aaron says, as he flicks the letter again. "Don't know why, though. There's nothing he can do to fix what's already done."

"Maybe," I say. "But what can it hurt to give him a chance?"

Aaron checks behind him again, inside the house, and I realize I can't comprehend the forces he's dealing with, coming at him from opposing directions. But to his credit, he takes a deep breath and says, "Fine. But not today."

"No problem," I say, relieved to hear him agree.

"My mom's working tomorrow afternoon. Let's do it then."

That should work, I think. The Master Hearing is tomorrow morning, and I think Juan would like me to be there for it. But the afternoon is open. Aaron looks me in the eyes for the first time, and I'm surprised at how much vulnerability I see there.

"I'm only fourteen," he says. "Can you drive me?"

Chapter Fifteen

Sometimes the kid can get under my skin, if I'm honest about it. He doesn't understand what it means to be polite and civil. Or maybe he just comes from a different time. Maybe I shouldn't judge him so harshly. After all, one thing I've learned over a hundred years is that no one likes when other people judge them.

—From the Journal of Murray McBride

I wake up the next morning, sick of this hotel. It's strange, I've lived most of the last twenty years in hotels. You'd think I'd be used to it. You'd think I'd feel at home. But that was when I didn't have anyone in my life. I thought I needed to focus every ounce of my time and energy on the all-encompassing goal of raising a million dollars for the homeless. I was convinced that distractions of any kind—even from well-meaning family and friends—could only get in the way.

But now, somehow, my life has expanded. I've had coffee with my mother, if only briefly. I have what could be something special with Rachel. And, of course, I have Alexandra and Juan. Maybe I could even throw Father James into the mix, and Gary Johnson. The list is longer than I realized.

I call Juan to see if he wants some company before the hearing. I figure it's probably a stressful time for him and Alexandra, and sure enough, he accepts gratefully. When I get there, I tell him I'll just stay for a little while. When it's time for them to get ready, I'll get out of their hair and meet them at the courthouse before the hearing starts, at 11 a.m.

"You will stay with us," he says, and next to him, Alexandra nods hard. "Here in this house. Not just today. From now on. Until you find a proper home."

"I couldn't do that," I say. "It's your family—"

"You are part of our family," he says. "And besides, you can't be alone. I've seen how much you use your machine. You need people around you."

It's embarrassing to be seen as weak, but I can't argue with the truth of what Juan said. Being alone is dangerous for me.

Juan is persuasive, and Alexandra doesn't give me a choice. On some level, I must want to stay as well because I allow them to convince me to check out of the hotel I've been staying at, bring my two suitcases into their home, and settle into the half-finished basement, insisting it will just be for a few days.

When I've finished finding places for my stuff, I come back upstairs. Juan and Alexandra are at the top of the steps, looking like they've been anxiously awaiting me. Juan hands me a cup of steaming coffee, and Alexandra is so excited she spins a circle on the scratched-up hardwood floor.

"Would you like me to come to your hearing?" I say. "I'm happy to, but I can stay here, too, if you'd rather not have people watching."

Juan squints at my words, like he's trying to decipher them. "I want you to come," he says. "We don't know what will happen."

"I wouldn't worry about it," I say. "I'm sure your lawyer has a plan. We just have to hope it works."

The confusion in Juan's eyes deepens. "No, we don't have a lawyer."

"Wait. You don't have a lawyer? You're representing yourself?"

This is worse than I thought. I had no idea he was planning to defend them. Juan trying to convince an immigration judge that he and Alexandra should be able to stay in America doesn't seem like the wisest course of action. I can't help but wonder if his thick accent will hurt him.

"Actually, I was hoping you would help us," Juan says.

I don't know how to respond. I have no legal experience whatsoever. I don't see how I could do them any good, and who knows, maybe I'd do or say something that could ruin everything. I could never live with myself if I was the reason Juan and Alexandra were deported.

"I don't think you understand—"

"There is nothing to misunderstand," Juan says, breaking into what was going to be a very firm *I'm sorry, but I can't help you.* "I cannot do this. And I cannot afford a lawyer. And since we aren't citizens, we don't get one for free. I was lucky they let me out of jail, but paying the bond took all the money, so I cannot pay a lawyer. You have perfect English. And, forgive me, you have white skin. I would feel much better if you were the one speaking to the judge on our behalf."

Somehow, I've gotten myself stuck. If this had happened a week ago, or even yesterday, I could have tried to figure out a way to find someone else. There have to be public defenders who specialize in immigration law. Some probably even do pro bono work. But with the trial only two hours away, it looks like, for now anyway, it falls to me.

Father James was right: it turns out I am the only one who can do this. We just didn't know "this" meant representing Juan and Alexandra in court.

Without much time, and without any real idea of where to start or what I'm looking for, I scour the internet for information about the immigration and deportation process. The first thing I look up is representation. Juan is right. Since no one in the family is a legal U.S. citizen, they aren't entitled to free legal defense—not even from an overworked, underpaid public defender. The more I read, the more I realize the lack of professional help could put Juan and Alexandra at a huge disadvantage.

I'm able to learn a little about the process, the most important thing being that the first step is a Master Calendar Hearing, which is what we're about to go to. Hopefully, things get cleared up there and they are allowed to stay. If necessary, there's a Merit Hearing, in which we would have a chance to make a more complete argument of our case.

For this first hearing, there's simply not enough time to plan a true legal defense. I bookmark several websites to come back to later and memorize a few important sounding phrases, but for today, I'll simply tell the judge their story and hope mercy—and common sense—prevail.

An hour before we need to leave for the hearing, I sit at the dining room table with them, all of us staring at the Notice to Appear spread out in front of us.

"Okay," I say, taking a deep breath and trying to wrap my mind around everything. "How did this all start?"

Juan shrugs sheepishly at the Notice to Appear. "My car is not very reliable." He seems embarrassed, almost ashamed. "But I have no choice. It is the only way to get to work."

"What kind of work do you do?" I ask.

"I work at a farm. Planting, picking, that sort of thing."

I remember now; Father James had mentioned it when he first told me about Juan. It's the reason they wouldn't be able to live in a city in Guatemala, where medical care would be more reliable. What good would medical care be if they starved to death because they had no money?

"And what's that have to do with your car?" I ask.

"It broke down on the way to work a couple of weeks ago. I pulled over to the side of the road to try to fix it, and a policeman showed up. At first, he was helpful, but then he noticed a taillight was broken—it was smashed somehow. I woke up one morning and it was just like that. But since I was driving with only one brake light, the policeman asked for my driver's license. But I don't have one, because I'm undocumented." Juan's embarrassment turns to something like sadness. "I was arrested for driving without a license. Because of that, they found out I am undocumented, so they said I might be deported."

A silence hangs over us as I try to take in everything he said. "Wow," I finally manage. "So a series of unfortunate events that you had no control over, and only happened because you were trying to get to work to support your daughter, led to this entire debacle."

"Yes," Juan says. "I guess so."

"And you haven't broken any other laws since you've lived here? None at all?"

Juan shrugs. "Not since I crossed the border. But I had to do that. When we found out Alex had diabetes, we couldn't stay in Guatemala. The doctor said people usually have some time after they are diagnosed when their body still makes a little insulin. So we needed to be in America by the time her body stopped making it completely, or she might not have survived. Anyone who loved his family would have done the same."

Immediately, my spirits lift. I can't imagine there's any way the courts will deport someone who has been living here for so long, following every law, working hard to support his family. Especially when an eleven-year-old girl is involved.

"Okay," I say. I glance at the paperwork on the table. "Let's go to this Master Calendar Hearing. We should be able to clear things up."

■   ■   ■   ■   ■

The courtroom is in Lemon Grove, thankfully, so it's a quick drive. When we walk in, the pillars and stone inscriptions are intimidating, and I'm not even the one on trial.

I'm happy to see Rachel sitting in the back row. She called this morning and offered to help any way she could, but I told her we shouldn't need any help, if there's any justice in the world. But I'm still happy she came.

The Immigration Judge looks down at us from his bench after calling Juan's and Alexandra's names. The few people seated in the gallery watch our every move. I'm a legal citizen and haven't done anything wrong and still, I feel guilty. I can't imagine what Juan and Alexandra are feeling. Judging by their posture and blank stares, they're even more intimidated than I am.

So I try to stand up tall, for their sakes, but a shooting pain in my chest makes that impossible. I guess I'll go the opposite route and hope the judge sees my oxygen concentrator, feels sympathy, and allows that sympathy to extend to Juan and Alexandra.

We walk into a thin row between two wooden railings and sit. The judge is skinny and breathes loudly through his nose. "Are you represented by an attorney?" he says.

I stand back up and try to look and sound more confident than I am. I'd love to be able to pull out some sort of magic trick, but I've never been so nervous performing in my life.

"No, your honor. Not an attorney. But I'm a family friend, here to help them through the process."

"Very well." He glances at the papers in front of him. "Do you argue against the ruling that the immigration status of the defendants makes them eligible for removal?"

"No, your honor," I say, and I look at the notes I took while researching on the internet earlier. "But I believe there are two things that warrant—"

"—And, with their immigration status making them eligible for removal, do your clients agree to voluntary removal?"

"No, your honor," I say, flustered. I take a breath to dive back into my argument, but it catches in my throat as I'm stabbed with an intense pain in my chest. I try to keep the agony inside, but some combination of a grunt and a moan sneaks out before I can stop it. For a brief moment, the courtroom is silent. All eyes are on me. Some appear curious, some annoyed, most simply look confused.

I struggle to keep my face blank as the pain stabs at me, but it's difficult. I feel the muscles around my eyes squeeze, overcoming my attempts to hide it. And then, as quickly as the pain came on, it's gone.

I realize Juan has grabbed my hand. I try to reassure him with a nod and a gentle squeeze, then I clear my throat and try to act like nothing happened. "As I was saying, I believe there are two things that warrant legal or discretionary relief."

I make sure to use the exact phrase I read in my research. *Legal or discretionary relief* sounds impressive. At least to me. The judge, however, rolls his eyes like he knows he's dealing with an amateur.

"That's not the purpose of this hearing," he says, his words clipped. "The Master Calendar Hearing is to determine whether the defendants are eligible for removal. As you have stipulated, these defendants are. Therefore the removal process will continue with the Merit Hearing, after which a judgment on removal will be rendered." The judge glances at a computer screen on his podium, looking down through bifocals on his nose. "That hearing will take place next Thursday at 8 a.m."

The slam of the gavel announces in no uncertain way that our time is up. Juan and Alexandra turn their eyes from the judge to me, looking for answers. I try to look unconcerned and purse my lips into a smile.

"Don't worry. Nothing has been decided," I say. "We have to come back for another hearing in a little more than a week. Their eyes droop and I wonder if they knew the process could drag out.

Juan, with tears in his eyes, grabs my shoulder. "Thank you," he says. "Thank you for your help. I don't know what we'd do without you."

His gratitude, combined with the fact that I did absolutely nothing of value for them during the hearing, is more than I can handle. "I'll see you back at the house," I say, and quickly make my way out of the courtroom.

■　　　■　　　■　　　■　　　■

Still in the courthouse, I cross the threshold and turn into the hallway. I know I should be worried about what happened with my heart in the courtroom—and on some level I am. But any concern about that is overshadowed by an all-consuming feeling of failure.

I feel tears threatening to break free so I look for a place to hide. There's an alcove I can dart into just ahead and I stride toward it. As soon as I duck in, I cover my eyes and take a few deep breaths, trying to convince myself everything will be okay for Alexandra and Juan.

I'm learning, more quickly than I had hoped, that I'm no Murray McBride. Somehow, through sheer strength of will, he made my wishes come true. He saved me in so many ways. And all I've done is exposed

Alexandra to prejudice at the water park and shown complete incompetence in the courtroom.

A light knock on the entrance to the little alcove startles me. It's not like I'm in a separate room, but I'm definitely out of the way—and I think it's obvious that it's intentional. I'm annoyed that someone would invade my privacy, until I see Rachel poke her head in. There's a small bench attached to the wall, and she sits on it, then pats the spot next to her.

"That judge was pretty abrupt," she says. "I'm sorry."

"Yeah, well. I'm sure someone who knew what he was doing would have done better than I did in there."

"I don't know. It didn't seem like there was much to be done. It sounds like the next hearing is the big one."

A dull ache builds in my chest. The kind that's been happening more frequently. The kind that tells me the doctors know what they're talking about in regards to my heart—my physical one—whether I choose to believe it or not.

"It doesn't matter that you don't have a law degree," Rachel says, misinterpreting my silence. "They just need someone to tell the judge their story. And you're the perfect person to do that."

"No," I say, thinking about what just happened in the courtroom—and what almost happened to me. "The perfect person would be reliable. I can't even be sure I'll be able to stay on my feet."

"What's that mean?"

I lean my elbows onto my knees. If it was anyone else, I'd play it down, pretend it's not happening. But I can't lie to Rachel.

"It's getting worse," I say. "Just now, I almost passed out again. And it was painful. Much more painful than ever before."

"It's okay," she says. "We'll figure it out. You're still on the top of the list."

"But you know I can't do that."

Now is the time to tell her. It's time to come clean about the list. I thought it would be so easy, but now that the moment is here, I'm not sure how to say it.

Neither of us speaks for a long moment.

"I should probably apologize," she says.

"For what?"

"For the last couple minutes. I've been deceptive. But I really was hoping something had changed."

"What do you mean? How have you been deceptive?"

"I know about the list, Jason."

If my heart still has a regular beat, it's thrown out of pace. Why didn't I tell her when I had the chance? I'd planned to tell her at Harms Woods. But I got distracted because we spoke about so many other things, and I forgot. Then, of course, she went back to work where, obviously, she learned about Andy right away.

I can't think of anything to say.

"I know why you stole the list," she says. "And I know why you gave that heart to Andy. He's a great kid, and he's recovering well, you should know. His body seems to be accepting the heart."

"That's good," I say. It seems like everything I say is incredibly inept.

"I know that, ethically, I probably have a responsibility to tell someone you stole the list. But I'm not going to."

"You're not?"

"No. I even admire what you've done, if I'm being honest. It was selfless, in a way. But the fact that you stole a list you weren't supposed to have? Or even that you gave Andy the heart? Those things aren't the problem."

"What is?" I ask.

When she doesn't answer right away, part of me holds onto the crazy hope she'll pretend this conversation never happened and go back to acting as if she doesn't know I took the list. But that's not what happens.

"I know this isn't a good time for this," she finally says. "But I don't think it makes sense for us to continue like this."

"What do you mean?" Adrenaline pulses through my heart and into my veins. "Please tell me you're not breaking up with me."

Rachel looks straight ahead, like she doesn't trust herself to meet my eyes. "Jason, you know I like you. It's so frustrating to finally meet a guy I really like. A genuinely nice guy. There's a serious lack of good guys out there."

"I sense a 'but' coming," I say, thinking if I can keep things light, maybe nothing bad will come of it.

"You already know the problem," she says, and when she finally looks at me, I wish she hadn't. "I know it sounds insensitive. Cruel, even, considering the timing. But how can I let myself fall for someone who isn't going to be here in a year? I'm not going to set myself up to get hurt like that."

"Rachel," I say. But she isn't finished.

"It's like you want to die. Like you're convinced the only way you can do what's right is to sacrifice yourself. Well, I don't believe that. And as long as you do, there's no future for us. Because no matter how great we might be together, it doesn't matter, if you're not here."

"Rachel, please—"

"You know what the hardest part for me is?" she asks. "It's that you're manufacturing this. You're constructing reasons to allow yourself to die. And it doesn't have to be that way. I just wish you could see that."

I want to contradict her. To tell her that I will be around in a year. And five years. And twenty years. But I can't. And even if I did, she wouldn't believe it. She saw how quickly I turned down the last heart.

"I just have one question before I go," she says. "This unwillingness to get another heart. This need to keep Tiegan as a part of you. Is it really for her? Or is it for you?"

It feels like a slap in the face. But before I can think of something to say—something that might correct her misconception or change her mind about leaving me—she stands and kisses my forehead.

"If you ever change your mind, call me," she says. "I'd love to see you . . . if you'll be around for a while."

When she walks away, my world is completely ruined.

Chapter Sixteen

I just can't stop thinking about Jenny. I'm finally realizing I never will. And thank the Good Lord for that, because that's all that's left of her, is my thinking of her. So I'll think about her as often and as hard as I can, and that's a fact.

Father James tells me death is a part of life and Jenny's passing doesn't mean I should stop living my own life. He may be a man of God, but he's got no idea what he's asking.

Still, there's the boy now. Who knows? Maybe he'll make sticking around this place a little bit easier.

—From the Journal of Murray McBride

Over the last twenty years, I've tried many times to get into Murray's head. To really understand what he felt, why he sought out a little kid and decided to turn his life upside down to help. But I'm not sure I ever really understood until now. Because now, I can truly see what it is to have one thing—and only one thing—that makes life worth living. With Rachel gone, Alexandra's wishes are all I have left.

So I try to focus on that. To move on from the heartbreak I feel over Rachel. But I can't shake the question she asked me. The entire night, as I curl up under the threadbare blanket in the basement of Alexandra's house, I can't get it out of my mind.

Why is it so important that I keep Tiegan's heart? Is it really because I feel like part of her is still alive, and by keeping her heart I'm actually keeping her alive? Or do I understand that she's gone and the only reason

I'm afraid to let go of her heart is because of the comfort I get from knowing it was hers? Because I couldn't live without her guidance? Am I just protecting myself from the guilt I'd feel if I cast her heart aside? Which begs the question: do I deserve that protection?

I sleep terribly, tossing and turning all night. When my alarm goes off, I feel like I haven't even slept. I drag myself up the stairs, put on a pot of coffee, and get online. I look up every immigration lawyer I can find within a hundred miles and send them all a message, asking if they would consider a pro bono case. With any luck, I'll find Juan and Alexandra a real lawyer to help with their case, and I can go back to focusing on the wishes.

Speaking of wishes, while I'm sending the emails, one comes into my in-box from Javier. Fortunately, it's good news, for a change.

Javier Gonzalez has come through, and come through big-time. The Washington Nationals have a three-game home stand starting today, and the person scheduled to sing the National Anthem before tonight's game had to bow out—some pop star with a sore throat. The spot is ours if we want it, Javier tells me in an email. We just have to let him know soon so he can confirm with the Nationals, and then get ourselves to Washington D.C. as quickly as possible.

"Javier Gonzalez," I say when he answers the phone, because I've always thought of him as being both names, the same way David Copperfield is both names. I was fortunate enough to meet David Copperfield a few times in my performing days, and he was never David or even Mr. Copperfield. He was always David Copperfield to me.

"Jason Cashman," Javier replies. "You received my email?"

"I sure did," I'm surprised by how excited I sound, despite my lingering feelings about Rachel and the hearing. My voice even cracks a little, and not from sorrow. "This is amazing. Thank you."

"So I should confirm it with the Nationals?" Javier says.

"Definitely."

After a pause, during which I hear typing on the other end of the line, Javier says, "Done. Oh, but one little thing."

"Anything," I say. "What is it?"

When I say "anything," I'm thinking along the lines of a fee. Maybe I'll have to pay a few hundred bucks for the privilege. But Javier says, "The girl. Do you know yet if she can sing? I told the Nationals I didn't think she would want to sing a very difficult song in front of thousands of people unless she can sing at least a little bit." It's quiet on the line for a long moment, before Javier says, "Right?"

"Yeah," I say. I have absolutely no idea if Alexandra can sing, other than in the shower, like she said. And she didn't instill much confidence that she was very good at that, either. But it's one of her wishes, so I'm going with that assumption. "I can't wait for you to hear her. She's an amazing kid."

I ease my guilt a little bit by rationalizing that neither of those things are lies. I am excited for Javier to hear her sing—as well as everyone else in the stadium. And she's definitely an amazing kid. But an amazing kid that can hold a tune? No idea.

"Great," Javier says. "The Nationals just wanted me to make sure." It's quiet for another long moment and I wonder if Javier is trying to decide whether to believe me. But then I hear him clear his throat, as if he's uncomfortable. "Actually, there is one other thing I wanted to ask."

"Sure. What is it?"

"This trip to Washington D.C. Who will be going?"

I realize I haven't talked to Juan about the details yet, but I assume he won't be able to take off work. If it was yesterday, I would have invited Rachel. But now? "I think it's just me and Alexandra," I say. "We'll have to hit the road right away. Why?"

Another uncomfortable pause. "I just wondered if . . . maybe I could come along?"

I have no idea what to say. Not because I don't want Javier to join us, I'm just shocked that he would want to. "Of course," I manage to say.

"Wonderful. In that case, I will take care of our transportation, and I will get us there in time. We will leave shortly after noon."

"That will get us there in time?" I've never driven from Chicago to Washington D.C. but it must be a ten-hour drive. And we'll lose an hour.

"Yes. Certainly in time. I'll pick you up at the girl's house." After a moment of silence, he says, "It's just that I like this idea of giving the girl wishes. What's her name again?"

"Alexandra," I say, chuckling.

"Yes. You see, I'm also Latino. I also can't go back to my home, which you said might be the girl's situation soon. I feel I should try to help, if I can."

Javier has already helped so much. How many kids—American or not—get the chance to sing the National Anthem in front of thousands of people? And Javier is making it happen. But if he's still willing, there is one more thing he could do that I can't. I've made a career out of performing, but I wouldn't say I'm famous. Magicians aren't on the same level as professional athletes when it comes to celebrity status. And if I have a real celebrity asking how to help . . .

"Have you ever talked to your congressman before?" I ask.

"Of course. Why do you ask?"

I'm not sure exactly how this could work, but maybe Javier has a little magic up his sleeve. "I just have a couple questions about voting."

"About voting?"

"Yeah," I say. "I happen to know someone who wants to cast a vote."

■　　　■　　　■　　　■　　　■

It's a good thing I woke up early, and that Javier apparently is an early riser as well. It's only eight o'clock when I get off the phone with him, and I'm going to need every minute to be ready by noon. The first thing on my to-do list is to talk to Juan about this D.C. trip. Since we're hoping to leave in a matter of hours, that means I need to visit him at work.

So I creep upstairs, careful not to wake Alexandra, and sneak out of the house, trying not to make a sound. I get in the car and start driving west. I follow the directions my phone gives me, and eventually it gets me there, but not for a good thirty-five minutes. Finally, I see a sign for South Barrington, and the small farm that is Juan's employer.

I pull into a dirt parking lot and grab my oxygen concentrator. There's no doubt I'll need it here. I'm not sure how much walking I'll have to do, but the fields seem to go on forever.

I head to the main office, wondering why Juan lives so far from where he works. It likely has something to do with Alexandra. Maybe he wants her to have access to the beautiful Harms Woods area, or the amenities that come with living in the suburbs, or maybe the schools. Whatever the reason, it makes for a long commute in what has proved itself to be an unreliable car.

There's a man at a desk when I enter the office, and he scowls when I tell him I'm here to see Juan Lopez.

"He do something wrong?" the man asks.

"No, not at all. I just need to talk with him about some logistics. I'm living with him now, actually."

The man's eyes bulge, but he recovers enough to point at a field to the north. "He should be out there. Picking rock."

I'm no farmer, but I can't figure out why anyone would pick rock. Corn or beans maybe, but rock?

I walk through the field for ten minutes. After a while, I put the nasal cannula in and use the concentrator for every breath I take. I still feel like I shouldn't be doing this, the way my chest is feeling, and I'm relieved to finally see Juan, bent over next to a wheelbarrow filled with basketball-sized boulders. He lifts another half-buried rock from the earth, grunting from the effort, and drops it into the wheelbarrow. He's wiping the sweat off his face with a handkerchief when he notices me. Immediately, his tired face breaks into a smile.

"Mr. Cashman," he says. "What are you doing here?"

"Definitely not the same thing as you," I say, looking incredulously at the wheelbarrow full of dirt-covered boulders. "That looks like hard work."

Juan shrugs. "It's a good job. I'm happy to have it. And they even provide health insurance. Most farmworkers don't get that. It's more valuable than the money I make."

"That's understandable," I say. "Speaking of Alexandra, I'm wondering what you think about my taking her to Washington D.C. for a couple of her wishes."

"Washington D.C.? That's very far away."

"That's why I'm asking," I say. "If you don't want her to, or if you think it's too dangerous because of her diabetes, we don't have to go. And it's possible we might even fly in a helicopter or something," I say, remembering how confident Javier was that we'll arrive in time, despite the tight schedule.

I really hope he says it's okay, but I'll also understand if he doesn't. Unlike Murray, I'd never do this without permission. Fortunately, Juan is quick to answer.

"No, no. Alex will be fine. She knows what to do. But what about you?" he says, gesturing to the oxygen concentrator.

"I'll be okay," I say, although I have no idea if I actually will be. My biggest fear right now is that my health will fail me and Alexandra's wishes will be ruined as a result.

"Good," Juan says. He doesn't look convinced, but he lets it go. "As for me," he says, gazing back toward the main office. "I don't think I will be able to come, if that's okay. I don't get vacation days this time of year."

"No problem," I say. "We'll only be gone one night, and we'll get hotel rooms that are joined together by a door, in case Alexandra needs anything."

Juan looks to his feet, covered in dirt from the field. "It will be very expensive."

"You don't have to worry about that," I say. "We'll have some help from someone who has plenty of money."

Juan doesn't respond to that. I wonder if he feels a responsibility to pay since it's Alexandra's wishes. Maybe it's a hit to his pride. But what he says has nothing to do with money.

"It is a risk," he says. "For Alex, even though I am confident she can handle it. And for you, with your sick heart." When his eyes meet mine, they're decisive and firm. "But it is for Alexandra's wishes. For that, it's worth the risk."

.   .   .   .   .

It's still a few hours before Javier arrives for me and Alexandra. I'm excited—and also unsure how we'll make it in time for Alexandra to sing the National Anthem—but I'm also glad we're not leaving until noon. It gives me the chance to get one more thing done before we go.

I drive to Aaron's house and find him waiting outside his front door, shifting his weight back and forth nervously.

He hops in the car and looks straight ahead. To a man of lesser experience, his lack of conversation could come off as rude. But I've been in his seat, so scared about the idea of kissing Mindy Applegate that I couldn't have formed a word, much less a sentence.

"I think you're making the right choice," I say. "It's going to go well. Trust me."

He nods slightly. "I have to be home in an hour," he says, still looking forward. "Before my mom gets back."

So his mother doesn't know what he's doing. I'm not sure I approve of the secrecy, but it's not a simple calculus. It seems obvious that Gary genuinely wants to improve his relationship with his son, and if I can help facilitate that, I should. But it's equally as obvious that Aaron's mother thinks it's best for him to have nothing to do with his father—and for all I know, she might be right. Which puts me in a tough position.

Once again, I understand Murray a little better. He, too, faced a difficult calculus in his attempts to do the right thing. My wish was in Chicago, and at that point in my life, making that wish come true was extremely important. But my dad wouldn't let him take me. The decision to stick his neck out, break the rules, and act on what his conscience was telling him couldn't have been an easy one.

Aaron and I drive to the prison in silence. When we park and get out, I realize I didn't hear him breathe the entire ride.

Aaron follows behind me as we go under an arch at the entrance to the prison, make our way through the metal detector, and find the room where Gary is waiting. As soon as Gary sees us, he bounces to his feet faster than a man his size with a bad heart should be able to. The effort makes his eyebrows lift high onto his forehead. He leans over slightly and puts a hand to his heart.

I know exactly what he's going through, but all I can do is hope his heart is able to recover in time for this reunion with his son. Aaron, for his part, seems confused by the episode, which makes me wonder if he knows about his father's heart condition. I understand wanting to keep something like that hidden. As soon as people know about it, it becomes your identity. The guy with the heart problem. The sick guy. The helpless one. I imagine that's not how a father would want to be seen by his son.

Fortunately, Gary stands straight and shakes his head like a dog trying to dry itself. He closes the gap between us, his arms outstretched to his son for a hug. Aaron takes a step backward, which isn't totally unreasonable. A large man who he hasn't seen for years comes at him as if he might smother him? I might back away in that situation, too. But before it gets too awkward, Aaron extends his hand and Gary, looking only slightly disappointed, shakes it firmly.

"I'm so happy to see you, son," he says. When Aaron doesn't say anything, Gary motions toward the small table where he was sitting when we arrived, and the two of them move to it. I stay where I am so they can have some privacy. Just before they reach the table, Gary turns back to me with a huge smile on his face. He gives me a big thumbs-up, then sits across from Aaron.

While they catch up, I wander over to a vending machine and look at the candy bars and bags of chips. I'm not hungry, but it feels weird to have my hands empty and nothing to do while Aaron and Gary talk. Still, I don't buy anything. There's a table in front of a TV in the corner and even though it's playing *Judge Judy* reruns, I take a seat and pull out my phone.

I sit up straighter when I see a new email from one of the immigration lawyers I reached out to. I try to keep my hopes in check, but it's impossible. If Juan and Alexandra can get some professional representation, their chances of winning the right to stay in the country would increase exponentially.

My hand's shaking so much that I miss the link three times before I finally manage to open the email. I bring my phone close to my eyes and read.

Dear Mr. Cashman,

Thank you for your email. Although we wish we could take on every person in need as a client, I'm afraid we just don't have the ability to do so. In these difficult times, our staff is completely booked and unable to take on new immigration cases. We sincerely wish you the best of luck in your search.

I return my phone to my pocket and force myself to swallow. I hadn't realized how tense I was while reading, or how disappointed I am in the answer. But it's only one law firm. Hopefully others will have time available.

I look over to Gary and Aaron and wonder how things are going with their reunion.

It doesn't take long to deduce the answer. Gary's voice raises over the others in the room. "Now, that's not fair," he says.

"You wouldn't even know," Aaron yells. He stands from the table, knocking the chair onto the floor. "You haven't even been there!"

Gary's eyes flick around the room as he answers with a hushed voice, trying to reign the situation back in. But it's too late.

"You can just stay here, for all I care," Aaron says. "I don't care if you never get out."

He storms out of the room, leaving Gary in his under-sized chair, running a hand through his hair. He stares straight ahead as if he's replaying the conversation in his mind, trying to figure out where things went wrong. I'm tempted to comfort him somehow, but I don't know where Aaron is going, and I have a responsibility to get him home. So I head out the door as fast as I'm able, ignoring the squeezing in my chest, and catch a glimpse of Aaron as he pushes through the building exit and runs into the bright sunlight.

By the time I catch up with him, he's at the car. It's locked, so he's standing beside the passenger-side door, staring into it, as if that might unlock the door. My steps are tentative and slow.

"What happened?" I ask gently.

"Nothing happened. He's just a loser. Like I told you, he's an inmate, not a father."

I'm not sure what to say to him and besides, it's strange to be standing outside the car, trying to talk to him while he continues staring in at the passenger seat. So I go around to the other side, lower myself into the driver's seat, and unlock the doors. When he sits down, I put the key in the ignition, but after a moment of contemplation, I remove my hand without turning it.

"I have issues with my dad, too," I say.

Aaron shakes his head, as if he doesn't want to hear it. But I think it's important that he does, so I continue. "He was around. He even did some things that were in my best interest. But then I survived something I wasn't supposed to survive, and I don't think he saw that coming. Ever since then, he's never had any interest in a close relationship." Aaron stays silent. I take it as permission to continue. "Maybe it's a self-preservation thing for him, knowing that I'll probably die before him. I don't know."

For a long time, Aaron doesn't speak. Just when I'm about to start the car and drive in likely silence the whole way back, he says, "Did he ever hit you?"

"No," I say. "He was never abusive. He just didn't seem to care. But as a kid, that's what I needed. Just to know he cared. I don't know, maybe that's still true."

"My dad never hit me, either," Aaron says.

"I would have been shocked if he had. He strikes me as a kind man."

"Lots of my friends get beat up by their dads. The ones who are around, anyway. Most aren't."

Aaron's words remind me that he lives in a very different world than I grew up in. Sure, I had challenges to face, but I had a mother who doted on me, a friend I could share my secrets with, and even an old man helping make my wishes come true. I don't know what Aaron has. Which makes it even more important to help him reconcile with his father.

"I can't claim to know how hard your life is," I say, and Aaron nods as if to verify the truth of the statement. I wait until he looks at me, and when he does, I try to sound as authentic as I feel. "But I do know I'd give a lot to have a dad like you have. A dad who, for all his faults and all his mistakes, loves his son and wants to be there for him. Wants to guide him and help him avoid the mistakes he made so his son can live a better life, have a better future."

Aaron's eyes moisten, but before he allows himself to cry, he shifts his gaze out the window. He's silent the entire drive back to his house, with a crinkle in his brow suggesting a depth of thought. When I pull the car in front of his house and shift into park, he looks at me for the first time since we left the prison.

"I'll go back," he says. "I won't make any promises, but I'll go back."

I want to tell him how proud I am of his maturity, but I can't find the right words to say to a teenage boy. So instead, I extend my hand toward him. When he shakes it, I say, "You won't regret it."

. . . . .

When I return to the Lopez house, Alexandra slides into the room in her slippers. They have ears flapping on each side and look like Easter bunnies.

"I have good news," she says and waves me into the computer room. She bounces into the chair and punches at the keys until she gets to the GoFundMe home page. I do a double-take at the number on the screen.

"How in the world do we have seven thousand dollars?"

"Seven thousand one hundred eight dollars," Alexandra says.

"Yeah. What did you do?"

"It's what *we* did, remember? All those fliers? We did it together. This is *our* wish."

A warm sensation slides into my chest. Maybe this is what Murray meant. Maybe this is the beginning of finding meaning.

I turn my attention back to the computer screen. I can't believe what she's done. Seven thousand dollars. I can only imagine how far that can go in a country like Guatemala, how much she can help the community of El Remate. "Wow," I say.

"You seem surprised. You shouldn't be. I told you Americans are the most generous people in the world. I wouldn't be surprised if we get twenty thousand by the time we're done."

She turns her attention back to the computer and starts writing an email. I watch for a minute, amazed at her organization. She has nine different people on the email thread and appears to be coordinating the people who will purchase and transport the materials with the people who will design and construct the building.

Once again, I'm baffled by what this kid has pulled off. It's a little embarrassing to think about how tech savvy I thought I was when I was her age, when all I did was play video games and write illogical emails. This kid is changing the world.

"Is there anything you need my help with?" I say.

Without looking up, Alexandra says, "Does it look like I need help?"

No. No it doesn't.

I figure I should shower before we leave, so I grab some clean clothes out of my suitcase in the basement, then come back upstairs and head into the bathroom. After living on my own for so long in hotel after hotel after hotel, it's strange to be in someone else's home. The crinkled tube of Crest toothpaste makes me feel like an intruder. The half-closed mirror, not quite hiding deodorant and perfume and a bottle of ibuprofen—it all makes me feel like I shouldn't be here. A nomad like me has no business invading a normal family's life.

But then I see the Post-it Note. It's on the floor next to the shower, as if it were stuck to the shower curtain before losing its adhesive and fluttering to the rug. The distinctive large, rounded penmanship of a middle-school girl covers the entire surface.

Make it a great day, Mr. Cashman! We're so happy you're here!

I wonder when Alexandra put it there. I imagine her waiting until bedtime, after I've brushed my teeth, then sneaking into the bathroom and sticking the note where she knew I'd see it in the morning.

I can't identify the ache in my chest because there's so much all mixed up together. The wave of gratitude toward Alexandra is strong and genuine. The kid unknowingly helped me during a moment of need. Or maybe not unknowingly. Maybe she has so much empathy she imagined I might feel like an intruder and took steps to help me. Which leads to the other part of the ache.

When I was her age, I thought only of myself. Sure, some might argue I had good reason. I was facing the very real possibility of not surviving until my eleventh birthday. Of course I would be self-centered. Some might even say I should be.

But Alexandra isn't, and she's facing something just as real and potentially just as terrible as I was. The only difference is, she's not focusing on herself. She's doing the most good, for the most people, while she still has the chance.

I fold the Post-it Note and put it in my pocket for safe keeping. I take my time showering and shaving, thinking it might be nice for Alexandra to have some time without me in her space. But then I remember I'm using the only bathroom in the house. I finish quickly, nicking my jaw with my razor. I put a small bit of toilet paper on the wound to stop the bleeding, which makes Alexandra laugh when I walk back into the computer room.

"I'm going to have to start shaving my legs soon," she says.

I try to think of something to say to that. *Congratulations? I'm sorry? It's great that you're growing up?* Nope, none of those responses sound remotely appropriate. Not to mention, she said puberty can cause changes and complications with her diabetes. So I'm happy to be able to change the subject when, out the window, I see a long, black stretch limousine pull to a stop at the curb in front of the house.

I know right away what it is and I can't help but shake my head. I already knew that being a successful magician didn't put me in the same world as superstar athletes, but now I realize I'm not even in the same universe.

Alexandra and I watch with our noses against the window as the driver—in a full uniform and hat—jumps out of the car, jogs around to the back door, and opens it like there's a king inside.

Judging by Alexandra's voice when Javier steps out of the limo wearing a perfectly tailored suit, he might as well be a king. "Who is that?" she asks, awe dripping from her voice.

I shake my head and chuckle. "If I'm not mistaken, I think that's our ride."

There's a knock on the door, and when Alexandra answers, we see Javier in his three-piece suit and perfectly styled hair. Alexandra introduces herself without a trace of intimidation, which Javier seems to get a kick out of.

"You are ready?" he says. "We have a tight schedule."

"We're ready," Alexandra and I say at the same time.

We hurry outside in a rush of excitement. Halfway to the car, Alexandra stops. She looks disappointed and I can't figure out why.

"Are you forgetting something?" she says.

"Oh!"

In all the excitement, I forgot to bring my oxygen concentrator. It's a good thing I have someone responsible around. Without the oxygen, I don't think I'd have much chance of staying upright very long. I go back in for it, then lock the front door on the way out and accept Alexandra's eye roll. Once we're all in the car, Javier turns to Alexandra.

"Is this car okay for you?"

"It's amazing," she says. "Mr. Cashman is really good at granting wishes."

"Is that right?" Javier arches his eyebrows at me. I know his meaning is *I thought I was the one who brought the limo,* but all I can think is that

Alexandra thinks I'm good at granting wishes. And this whole time I've thought the water park was a disaster.

"Well," Javier says, oblivious to my thoughts. "Let's go to Washington D.C."

Chapter Seventeen

My whole life, I've tried to do right. Haven't always succeeded, and that's a fact. But I've tried. Another thing I've done my whole life is follow the law, right down to the letter. I never jaywalked or ran red lights—not intentionally anyway. Only seems right for a man to be law-abiding. And those two things—trying to do right and being law-abiding—never conflicted. But they will tonight, when I pick up Jason from his house and take him to Chicago, against his father's wishes.

This here feels like a turning point in my life. Who woulda thought I'd have a turning point in my life at a hundred years old?

—From the Journal of Murray McBride

The limo pulls away from Alexandra's house, makes a few turns out of the neighborhood, and merges onto the highway. I happen to know we should be heading east, but we seem to be going northwest.

"Do we have to stop somewhere first?" I ask.

"Something like that," Javier says with a conniving smile. "I think you will approve."

Alexandra stares out the window with large, excited eyes. Fifteen minutes later, I see what "something like that" means when we pull into a small regional airport. I had thought maybe he organized a helicopter ride to get us there on time. Actually, this is even better. On the tarmac, there is only one plane. With a large Cubs "C" painted on the side.

"Are you serious?" I say.

"I figure, the Cubs have a plane. We have a trip to make. . . . " Javier shrugs as if it only makes sense.

The limo pulls up next to the plane, and we all exit the car—I make sure to bring my oxygen this time—and climb the steps into the cabin. The inside is less like a plane and more like a small apartment. There's a large, rectangular table in the middle with six leather-bound chairs surrounding it. Further back are more comfortable-looking chairs with large TVs set up in two of the corners.

Alexandra goes straight to the long table and studies the items sitting on it. First is an official Cubs jersey with Javier's name and number embroidered, and his autograph scrawled across the back. Next to that is a clear case holding a baseball, also with Javier's autograph.

"Wow," I say. "You've really gone above and beyond here. Thanks, Javier."

"I have help," he says. "Now, let's go to Washington."

"We can't," Alexandra says. "Not yet."

Javier and I look at her like she's crazy, but Alexandra seems very sure of herself. She eyes the jersey and baseball on the table while she says, "How much range does this plane have before it has to refuel?"

Javier's brow crinkles. "I don't know. Several hundred miles, I guess."

"Good," Alexandra says. "Because we need to go to Dallas."

"What?" Javier and I say together.

"I've filed a flight plan to Washington D.C.," Javier says. "That's where your wishes are, right?"

"Yes," Alexandra says, still studying the items on the table. "But flight plans can be changed, can't they? We really need to make a quick stop first."

"In Dallas?" I say, not following her logic at all.

"Yep. Fort Worth, actually."

"What for?" Javier asks.

"I have a meeting there. Kind of."

Javier seems baffled—and why wouldn't he be? As a Major League All-Star who made millions of dollars a year, then as a front-office executive making decisions about the direction of the team, Javier has spent that last twenty years being looked up to, admired, and most of all, deferred to. And here's an eleven year-old girl giving him orders about what to do with the charter jet he's been generous enough to supply?

It's because of Javier's generosity that I say, "Look Alexandra, we can't just ask Javier to fly us to Dallas without a reason. Can you at least tell us why?"

"It has to do with my fifth wish," she says. "Helping poor people in El Remate."

That's all Javier needs to hear. He claps his hands and speaks with the authority I've come to expect from him. "We are here to make wishes come true," he says. "If Dallas is where you need to go, then Dallas is where we will go."

■　　　■　　　■　　　■　　　■

For the entire flight to Dallas, Alexandra punches away at her computer. Except for when she rotates her fanny pack, pricks her finger, and tests her blood sugar. She pulls out a fruit snack, eats it, and turns her attention back to her computer, as if it's the most normal thing in the world. Of course, for her, it is completely normal. Every single day, a dozen times a day, she performs her ritual without fail.

I sit nearby and try to wrap my mind around how she must constantly be thinking about her diabetes. She can never let a day go by without testing, never forget her insulin, never allow herself more than a few moments when the condition isn't somewhere in the back of her mind. Her life, quite literally, depends on it.

It makes me think about her future and what I can do to help with the upcoming hearing.

The biggest thing is to find them a lawyer who will work pro bono, since non-residents aren't entitled to free representation. Maybe I should have done more before now, but this trip came about so fast. And besides, we have time. The trial isn't for another week. This trip needs to happen today.

I decide to find time this evening, after the baseball game, to follow up with the immigration lawyers I've already reached out to. Maybe I'll go online and search for lawyers I might have missed who might take on a case for free. If it comes to it, I could also talk to Javier about the possibility of paying for a lawyer, but I don't want to do that if there's a chance someone will take the case pro bono. He's already done so much.

Next, my thoughts predictably venture to a subject I'd rather avoid: Rachel. I wonder where she is, what she's doing now, and most of all, who she's with. Rather than allowing my imagination to make me crazy, I stand abruptly and head to the bathroom. I splash water on my face for a few minutes, but it's not long enough to completely clear my mind.

My thoughts are interrupted when the plane touches down at a small airport outside Fort Worth.

"How long do you need here?" Javier asks Alexandra. "The opening to sing the national anthem is for tonight's game. Should I cancel the singing wish? Tell them we can't make it today? I'm not sure if it will be easy to reschedule."

"Well, this shouldn't take long," Alexandra says. "If it only takes ten minutes, can we still make it on time?"

Javier looks to the ceiling of the plane as if he's calculating in his head. "I think yes," he says.

"Great, then let's hurry."

On the way out, Alexandra grabs the jersey and ball from the table. I see Javier start to object—to say she should leave them here so she doesn't lose them. I'm sure they're worth a ton of money to baseball fans. But before he gets any words out, Alexandra is out the door, down the steps, and into the waiting car.

It's another limo, and I wonder if Javier ever travels in any other kind of car. Alexandra gives the driver an address, and he puts it into his navigation system. Fifteen minutes later, we pull in front of an office building attached to a warehouse.

"Okay, is everyone ready?" she says.

Javier looks confused. "Ready for what?" he says.

"Oh, right. I haven't explained. This is a sales negotiation, and you guys are my bargaining chips." She looks at me and says, "Well, mostly Javier, but Mr. Cashman can do a magic trick or something. That might help."

A magic trick? I wonder if she realizes that magic is illusion and distraction, not actual conjuring of rabbits. I can't just "do a magic trick" with no tools or props. But I'm so taken aback by the way she's talking—like an adult businessman rather than an eleven-year-old kid—that I can't think of anything to say.

Alexandra hops out of the car and heads toward the building, carrying the baseball jersey and ball. At least she's being careful not to let them out of her sight. I put in the nose cannula, assuring me a steady stream of oxygen while we're here, and grab the cumbersome oxygen concentrator. Then Javier and I catch up to Alexandra just as she enters the foyer of the building and approaches a woman behind a desk.

"I'm here to see Patrick Ramsey," Alexandra says.

The woman eyes her suspiciously. "Do you have an appointment?"

"No, not technically. But I think he'll want to take this meeting." Alexandra looks at me briefly, then turns meaningfully to Javier. The woman stares at Javier for a long moment, as if trying to place him.

"Just a moment," she says. "I'll see if Mr. Ramsey is available."

We stand there for an awkward moment, none of us with any idea what we're doing, except Alexandra. "Where did you learn to talk like that?" I ask, keeping my voice down. "*I think he'll want to take this meeting?*"

Alexandra beams at me through crooked front teeth. "I've seen every episode of Shark Tank," she says. "Just wait. That's not even the best I have. There's a lot more where that came from."

The woman speaks quietly into the phone, her eyes darting to us, then away, and back again. Finally, she puts the phone down and says, "You're in luck. Mr. Ramsey says he has five minutes. You can go back."

She points to a hallway and Alexandra starts down it. I look at the woman and shrug, trying to convey that my dismay equals hers. Alexandra goes to the end of the hall, taps on a door, and pushes it open. Javier and I follow like lost puppies.

"Mr. Ramsey," Alexandra says, approaching a large desk and shaking hands with the man behind it. "Thank you for seeing us on such short notice."

The man looks like a typical blue-collar manager: collared, button-down shirt tucked into his jeans, and the no-nonsense look of a man who gets things done. "Sure," Mr. Ramsey says, sounding very unsure. "What can I help you with?"

"I'm Alexandra Lopez. We corresponded through email?"

Mr. Ramsey does a terrible job hiding his surprise. "I'm sorry," he says. "I thought you were older."

Alexandra nods and says, "I'm here to talk about your price for delivering the steel to El Remate."

"Like I said in the email," Mr. Ramsey says, recovering, "the cost of getting materials to that little village is high. Guatemala City is a long ways from that place."

"It's called El Remate," she says. "And that's true. But like I said in the email, you could fly into Belize City. It's much closer to El Remate."

"Yes," Mr. Ramsey says, looking tired of the conversation already. "But like *I* said in the email, then I'd have to worry about the border crossing and the fees associated with transporting that much steel between countries."

"True again," Alexandra says, not backing down. "And in that email, you gave me the new quote for that situation. But I'm here to negotiate different terms to the agreement."

The kid really has watched Shark Tank. She turns and looks meaningfully toward Javier, who hasn't caught onto what Alexandra is doing. Mr. Ramsey, who has been forced to deal with the tornado of a girl in front of him, looks to Javier for the first time. He squints, as if trying to decide something. Then his eyes bulge to twice their normal size.

"Are you . . ." He looks like someone who has bit into a very hot pepper.

"I read your bio on the company website," Alexandra says. "Born and raised in Chicago. 'Ultimate Cubs fan.' Well, Ultimate Cubs fan, meet Javier Gonzalez, Cubs All-Star shortstop."

The man is frozen in place, staring at Javier and possibly having a stroke. Finally, he comes around the desk and shakes Javier's hand, still looking up at him like he can't believe he's real.

"That home run you hit in Game Six of the Series," Mr. Ramsey says. "I've never screamed so loud in my life. My wife ran downstairs, thinking I'd stepped on a nail."

One look at Javier's smile, and I can tell he's enjoying himself.

"Thank you," he says. "That was a fun time."

"Fun? The final out was one of the greatest moments of my life," Mr. Ramsey says.

Alexandra steps in. I'd swear she's timing the momentum of the situation. Mark Cuban would be impressed.

"One visit from Javier Gonzalez to your office," she says. Then she lays the jersey on the desk and sets the ball next to it. "One autographed Javier Gonzalez jersey. And one autographed Javier Gonzalez baseball. In exchange, you deliver the steel through Belize City at the originally quoted amount."

Mr. Ramsey hesitates. His scowl makes it obvious he doesn't find the agreement to his liking.

Javier speaks in his deep baritone, the epitome of politeness. "It would mean a lot to the kids of that village," he says. "And it would mean a lot to me. Consider it a personal favor?"

It only takes a second. "Done," Mr. Ramsey says. He rushes to the desk and picks up the jersey, holding it up so he can see it better. "This is amazing," he says.

I'm sure he'd love to sit and chat with Javier about the biggest moments of his Cubs career, but Alexandra is all business. She extends her hand toward Mr. Ramsey and says, "So we have a deal?"

Mr. Ramsey takes the jersey in one hand and shakes Alexandra's hand with the other. "We have a deal."

"Good," Alexandra says. "Now, if you'll excuse us, we have a baseball game to get to."

Chapter Eighteen

I kidnapped the kid last night. At least, that's what Father James calls it. It's not actually kidnapping though. Jason wanted to come. Apparently Tiegan did, too.

I've always been a fan of adventure. Sure, it's been decades since I've had one myself, but that doesn't mean I'm not a fan. Just means I'm old. But look at me now. Having an adventure with a couple ten-year-old kids.

Sometimes you just never know what the Good Lord is going to throw at you next.

—From the Journal of Murray McBride

Back in the Cubs plane, we all gather around the table and the atmosphere has become even more excited than it was before, if that's possible. Alexandra sticks her chest out like a conquering hero.

Javier adds to the festive atmosphere by popping a bottle of champagne—and, of course, sparking apple juice for Alexandra. For a moment, I think I catch a glimpse of what it's like to be a World Series champion. It takes some willpower not to take the bottle and spray it around the airplane.

The celebratory mood is dampened a little later when Alexandra comes out of the bathroom saying she feels tired and needs insulin. She injects a bolus into her abdomen and curls into a leather chair.

It could just be the effects of her diabetes, but I've never seen her so lethargic. So soon after the high from her successful meeting, I can't figure out why she's sprawled in her seat with her head tilted like she's too tired to lift it. I go to her and touch her forearm.

"Hey, everything okay?"

She shrugs and turns her gaze out the window at big, puffy clouds below us.

"Are you feeling sick? Should I call your dad or something?"

"No," she says, still looking at the clouds. "It's not that."

"Then what's wrong?"

She looks at me with big, pleading eyes, looking completely vulnerable. Then she reaches into her pocket and removes her cell phone. She swipes at the screen a few times, then holds it out to me.

At the top, I recognize several names from the water park. The rest of the screen is filled with text messages. I only read two of them:

Yeah, and maybe next time Alex won't slow us down by being so scared!!!
Seriously! She was so like, "I'm gonna die!!!"

The texts take me by surprise. The girls seemed to get along so well at the water park, and now they're talking behind each other's backs? But then I realize, it's not even behind Alexandra's back. She's on the text thread. I don't know whether to chalk it up to a failed attempt at humor or if it's an example of the cruelty of kids. Either way, they've hurt Alexandra.

For the last hour, she's seemed like such an adult, speaking more like a businessman than a little girl. It's hard to believe that someone who can do what she has done would still be vulnerable to being bullied by kids.

But I guess that's what she is: a kid. No matter what she's capable of, she's still an eleven and-a-quarter year-old girl.

She falls asleep a few minutes after I return her phone to her and doesn't wake up until we touch down at a small airport just outside Washington D.C. The rest does her a world of good. As soon as she wakes up and remembers where she is, she bounces out of the chair like she's never felt better. Like the text messages never even happened.

Just like before, a limo is waiting for us and we pile out of the plane feeling like we could take on the world. For the first time in days, my chest doesn't even hurt.

And there's more waiting for us than just a limo. Standing at the back of the limo is one of the last people I expected to see in Washington D.C.

Rachel.

When I see her at the back door of the limo, I press my nose to the airplane window and squint, trying to figure out if my eyes are deceiving me. But no, they're not. It's her, and I'm as happy to see her as I am confused.

In a moment of vanity, I yank out the nasal cannula, then grab the oxygen concentrator and rush out of the plane. But when I get to Rachel, I realize I don't know how to greet her. With a hug? A kiss? A handshake? In the end, I don't have to make that decision. She reaches out and wraps me in an embrace that I could live in, if given the choice. After a moment that goes by way too fast, she kisses my cheek and pulls away.

"I'm sorry," she says, but she doesn't explain what she's sorry about.

I try to ask, but don't know how to do it. She shifts uncomfortably from one foot to the other, glances at Javier and Alexandra, who are watching us while pretending not to watch us, and finally shakes her head, as if she's been ridiculous.

"The truth is, I missed you more than I thought I would. I actually couldn't stop thinking about you. You, and Alexandra, and what you're doing for her, and how you made me feel when I was with you." She pauses again, as if recognizing a last chance to back out. "I don't want you to die, Jason," she says, putting her hand on my cheek. "But no matter what happens, no matter what you decide, I want whatever time I can have with you. I just want to be with you."

There is so much I want to say to her, but because of the detour, we're behind schedule. The first pitch of the baseball game—a 7:10 start between the Washington Nationals and the St. Louis Cardinals—is only an hour away. And we still have to fight game-day traffic to get to the stadium. So instead of trying to think of what to say, I kiss Rachel with all the passion I have in me, trying to say everything I'm feeling right now with the kiss.

"We have to hurry," I say, out of breath.

"I know. I heard. I talked to Javier on the phone."

"You talked to Javier?" I say. "How?"

"Your phone," Alexandra says, obviously satisfied with her cunning.

"How did you get my phone?"

"When you were in the bathroom."

"But, my password..."

"Yeah, about that. 'One, two, three, four' probably isn't the best choice."

Javier slaps my shoulder when he hears his name. He ends a call on his phone and puts it in an inside pocket of his suit coat. "How else did you think she knew to come here? Magic?" He grins his GQ grin. "I spoke with the Nationals people and let them know we're on our way and will arrive in time. They know it'll be close. We have to hurry."

We do. Or at least, the limo driver does. Or, at least, I assume he does. I'm too busy flying over the moon about the fact that I'm holding Rachel's hand to have any comprehension of time. Or anything else, for that matter.

When we pull up to the stadium, pregame festivities are in full swing, and it takes so long to weave our way through all the people that by the time we pull into a small parking area inside the stadium, Alexandra has only ten minutes until it's time for her to sing.

"You should put this in," Rachel says, picking up the nasal cannula from the oxygen concentrator. Reluctantly, but knowing she's right, I obey. Then I turn to Alexandra.

"Are you ready for this?" I ask.

She answers by singing, "*Oh, say can you see?*" through a giant smile.

She doesn't sound terrible. She's no pop diva or opera star, but she's not bad for a kid. It eases my mind a little. With everything else that's been going on, I haven't had much time to consider how this will go. I wonder if it's the same for Alexandra, especially since she's been working so hard on the Guatemala stuff. Maybe it's better that way. Instead of ruminating and getting more and more nervous, she'll just go out there, sing, and be done before she has time to be scared.

A representative from the Nationals meets us at the car and calls Alexandra "Ms. Lopez."

Alexandra blushes as the man leads us all through some hallways, past several offices, and finally to a tunnel with bright sunlight at the end. As we walk toward the light, chatter and cheers from the crowd mingle with the perfect green of the infield grass under a bright, sunny sky.

"Wow," Alexandra says, and for the first time her steps slow. But she seems to realize she's committed to do this, so she keeps walking, as if on autopilot.

The Nationals representative keeps looking at his watch. He lifts a microphone of some sort from the lapel of his shirt and speaks quietly into it. A static-filled reply comes, and he nods to Alexandra.

"One minute," he says. "You'll be announced over the P.A. system, then just go out there and do your thing."

Alexandra's head bobs up and down several times, which I take for a bad sign, as far as nerves go. Way too soon, a booming voice echoes throughout the entire stadium. "Fans, will you please draw your attention to the home plate area . . . "

Javier sticks his hand up for a high-five, which Alexandra stares at for several long, confused seconds before she slaps her hand against his. I lean down to her height and look out at the field with her.

"What do you think? Are you okay?"

Alexandra takes a deep breath. "I'm in America," she says. "I can do anything."

With that, she stands tall and walks down the remaining portion of the tunnel and into the sunlight. I don't know about Alexandra, but my nerves are on the thinnest of edges. I breathe in a huge burst of oxygen, squeeze Rachel's hand, and feel a little better.

The applause from the crowd is muted. No one knows a singer named Alexandra Lopez. But when they realize it's a middle-school-aged kid, the cheers get louder. From where I am, I can see the home plate area and a small swath of the stadium behind Alexandra. But then the Nationals representative motions us forward and Javier, Rachel, and I step out of the tunnel and onto the warning track along the first base line.

As soon as I'm out from under the confines of the tunnel, the whole world changes. It's like when the curtain opens on a magic show and thousands of people are revealed for the first time. Except instead of being three or four thousand, this is forty-four thousand. And the stadium dwarfs any theater I ever performed in.

Alexandra looks tiny as she approaches the microphone at home plate. She keeps looking back toward me, but I don't know what I can do. She's on her own, on an island out there. I give her a thumbs-up when she looks over again. She's biting her bottom lip hard.

"And now," booms the voice, covering every inch of the stadium. "Please stand and remove your headgear for the singing of our national anthem."

The wave of silence that covers the stadium is smothering. If it were me up there, I'd turn around, cover my head, and run back through the tunnel. But Alexandra is not me. So she steps up to the microphone, takes a deep breath, and starts to sing, acapella.

Oh, say can you see, by the dawn's early light?

The kid has amazed me many times already. From her perseverance in the face of prejudice, to conquering her fear of heights, to what she's accomplished in such a short time for the village of El Remate, but I'm not sure I've ever been as proud of her as I am right now, as she belts out the American national anthem.

Her face is beaming. Her eyes are closed. Her voice isn't perfect, but somehow that makes the whole thing even better. She's just like everyone else. A shower singer. A kid living out a wish.

An American.

I fight the lump in my throat as she sings about the "rockets' red glare." Everyone knows it's a tough line to sing, with that octave jump. I've heard many singers of the anthem struggle with it, some of them completely missing the mark. But Alexandra drills it. It's not a shower-singing voice anymore. She's pouring everything she has into it, and it's beautiful.

I look to Javier, who is standing next to me and looking every bit as proud as I am. His right hand covers his heart and a blissful look covers his sharp features. I remove my hand from Rachel's and wrap my arm around her shoulder while I stare at her beauty.

But then something happens. Two things simultaneously, actually, but strangely the first thing I register is a change in Rachel's expression. She flinches, almost as if something hit her. In the very next moment, I realize the other change.

The stadium is nearly silent.

I look back to Alexandra and see fear on every inch of her face. Her chin leans toward the microphone, as if she's expecting to sing again at any moment. But nothing comes out. And it hits me like a sledgehammer—she's forgotten the words.

The few voices in the crowd singing along fade away, and now there isn't a sound in the stadium.

A loud, scared exhalation hits the microphone and echoes throughout the upper deck. The noise seems to knock Alexandra out of her trance and she momentarily recovers. She starts over from where she was, repeating the last line she sang.

And the rockets' red glare! The bombs bursting in air. Gave...the rockets' red glare...

She stops again. She can't get past that line. For some reason, her mind simply will not come up with the remaining lyrics, instead repeating the same line over and over. She stops singing again, and stands as still as a statue. If a pin were to drop in the stadium, it would be the loudest sound in it.

Gave proof through the night! I think. *Gave proof through the night!*

Someone in the crowd yells the words to her, trying to help her out. But Alexandra is too panicked to hear. She stares at the microphone, paralyzed. It's the most painful silence I've ever heard, punctuated only by a random cough that echoes from the upper deck.

Alexandra looks to the ground and presses her palms against her eyes. Wiping tears, I realize. And that's all it takes to make me move. I have to get her out of there. I have to bring her back through the tunnel, where it's safe.

I pull out the nasal cannula and try to jog at first, without thinking. But without the oxygen I'm barely able to walk. When I get into the view of all forty-four thousand fans, I try to stride confidently, hoping it will look natural.

I get to Alexandra and put my hand on her back. With her face in her hands, she doesn't know I'm approaching and jumps at my touch. In a split second of eye contact, I see so much. Disappointment. Anger at herself. And most of all, fear. Debilitating fear.

"Let's go," I whisper.

I put my hand on her shoulder and try to steer her back toward the tunnel. To safety. I'm shocked when her feet don't move. When I look at her, she shakes her head defiantly. And I realize, to my extreme horror, that she isn't going to leave this job unfinished.

The amount of stage fright that crashes over me is something I've never felt before. I've performed hundreds of times, but I've always had a plan. I've always been confident in my abilities. I've never been stranded in front of this many people without a clue how to proceed, without any idea if my heart will allow me to finish.

But it's important that Alexandra doesn't know any of that. So I force a smile and a small nod, then face the microphone, shoulder to shoulder with her. I look at her out of the side of my eye and take a deep breath.

And the rockets' red glare!

The words waver as they come out of my mouth. They're off-key or out of tune or something. And they don't harmonize with Alexandra's voice at all. We're like two preschoolers singing a song we barely know. Somehow, in my desperation to help Alexandra, I forgot just how terrible I am at singing.

But it's too late now, so together, both recognizing how awful we sound, we continue belting out the anthem.

The bombs bursting in air,
Gave proof through the night,
That our flag was still there!

We've made it through the tricky spot. With me singing next to her, Alexandra didn't even hesitate to find the words. But in the moment of pause as we both take a breath, I think maybe we should quit while we're ahead. We sound awful. Absolutely terrible. The song we're singing can barely even be considered *The Star-Spangled Banner*, that's how badly we're butchering it, with our off-key voices wavering up and down.

But Alexandra doesn't seem to understand that. The huge smile is back on her face, and I can tell by the depth of her in-breath that she's going to sing the next lines with all the energy she has in her.

So I limp in with her. I sing.

Oh say does that star-spangled
Banner yet wave?

The amazing thing is, Alexandra and I aren't the only ones singing. A large part of the crowd is singing with us, and it actually helps keep us in tune. And over the last line of the song, the entire stadium joins in, full-voiced, singing along with the little girl at home plate.

O'er the land of the free,
And the home of the brave?

The ovation that breaks out is unlike anything I've ever heard. If there's a single fan not on his feet, clapping with all he has and cheering us on, I can't find him.

Alexandra spins a circle, soaking in the ovation. She still has tears in her eyes, but she doesn't hide her face now. The booming voice over the speakers fills the entire stadium again.

"Alexandra Lopez, everybody!"

And as the volume of the cheers spikes yet again, Alexandra bows, blows kisses to the crowd, then lifts her hands high over her head and pumps her fists in triumph.

■　　■　　■　　■　　■

Alexandra's performance makes her a star at the baseball game. On our way to our seats, which end up being in the fifth row directly behind home plate, Alexandra gets one standing ovation after another. As one section of fans realizes who she is, they stand and cheer. As soon as the next section sees her, they stand, too. It's like the stadium is doing "the wave" for her.

In typical Alexandra fashion, she eats it up. With my limited amount of celebrity status—which really only reached as far as the walls of whatever theater I was performing in that particular night—I always felt a little like an imposter. They were cheering for the magic, not for me personally. Whenever someone would make clear they were cheering for me personally—by saying, "I love you, Prospero," or asking for my autograph—I always felt a little awkward.

Not Alexandra. She has the gracious bow down to a tee. And the little wave of thanks? It's like she's been doing it her entire life in preparation for this moment. Rachel gives me a look of bemusement at one of Alexandra's deeper, more flamboyant bows to the crowd.

Of course, fame is a strange thing in our society today. The desire to see the mighty fall is intense, so I'm happy this particular game isn't nationally televised. She can enjoy her fifteen minutes of fame and be done with it, which is the best thing for her whether she realizes it or not.

It turns out, fifteen minutes is just about right. After the top of the second inning, Alexandra turns to me in her $300 seat and says she's bored and ready to go. Javier can't seem to get through his head the idea that someone might want to leave a baseball game early. Especially seven-and-a-half innings early. So he tells me he'll stay, gives me free rein with the limo, and agrees to meet us at the Hilton for a late dinner afterwards.

"Jason," he says, pulling me aside. "I called my congressman, like you asked. He was out of the office, so I wasn't able to speak to him. But the person I spoke with said there is a vote today. Just ceremonial, he said, not for a real bill. But it has to do with immigration and is scheduled for some time this afternoon. He didn't know any more. But maybe Alexandra could watch? Maybe that would be good enough for the wish?"

"Maybe," I say. "Thanks, Javier. You've been amazing."

He smiles his picture-perfect smile as Alexandra, Rachel, and I pack up our few belongings, excuse ourselves, and walk past confused people who shift in their seats to let us by. I wrap the nasal cannula around my head and into my nose, then we head up the stadium seats to another round of raucous applause.

Halfway up, I have to stop for a deep breath. It's embarrassing, but it would be a lot worse if Alexandra didn't take the opportunity to twirl a couple circles and wave to the crowd. She does a good job keeping the attention off me.

You'd have to be right next to her to see the difference, but I am right next to her, so I see it. As soon as she finishes her last twirl, I see the slightest discomfort in her smile. I think maybe she's already getting tired of the attention, but then she takes my hand and stretches her chin up toward me as if she has something to say.

"Can we walk a little?" she asks when I lean my ear toward her.

I played enough video games with Murray to know what that means, so I lead Alexandra toward the stadium exit in silence. When she continues to give Rachel sideways glances, I realize they don't know each other as well. Alexandra's hesitation is obvious enough that Rachel, perceptive as always, says, "I'm just going to check out the souvenir shop. I'll meet up with you guys soon."

She heads one way, and Alexandra and I make our way out of the stadium and to Potomac Avenue, where we find a little walkway along the Anacostia River. Because of my heart, our pace is so slow we barely cover any ground. After several long minutes, in which I give Alexandra as much time as she needs, she finally speaks.

"Do you ever wonder why you're in the situation you're in while others are in a very different situation?"

"All the time," I say. And for the first time, I think about the conversations Murray and I had, from his perspective. All I'd been focused on at the time were my own thoughts and feelings, my own fears, my own questions. I never once stopped to wonder how our video game conversations affected Murray. But I wonder now, because Alexandra's question cuts to the core of what I've dealt with for twenty years—why Tiegan died while I lived.

"It doesn't make any sense, does it?" Alexandra says. "I mean, what did I do to deserve being born in Guatemala instead of Illinois? And then what did I do to deserve surviving our journey to the U.S. when so many others didn't? Even my own mother. I didn't do anything to deserve either thing. So why did it happen like that? Who decides?"

"I don't know," I say, amidst a sudden wave of sympathy for Murray. The questions I asked him—does it hurt to die, and why was I cursed with a bad heart—were no more answerable than what Alexandra is asking me.

She looks at me sideways, trying to hide the fact that she's looking at my chest. "Do you ever feel bad? About having your friend's heart?"

"Every day," I say. And a large part of me wants to leave it at that. It's the truth, after all. Every single day I ask why. I wish I could give the heart back to her. I wish Tiegan could have lived. But when I think back on how Murray answered my questions, or at least how he made me feel, I know I need to do better than what I've said. I need to at least try. "If everyone felt bad about everything they had, the world would miss out on one of the most important, most powerful, most beneficial feelings humans have."

"What's that?" Alexandra asks, looking like she's searching for a lifeline.

"Gratitude," I say.

Alexandra nods like she understands. Several paces on, she says, "I wish I had more gratitude. But I have so much fear instead. And . . . I don't know what it's called. When I want those people in Guatemala to have a better life, because I have a good life here, even though I don't deserve it any more than they do."

"I think you're talking about another important, powerful, and beneficial human emotion. And like gratitude, it's one most people don't have enough of."

"And what's that one?"

"Empathy," I say.

She nods again, in the same way as before. "Gratitude and empathy," she says. "Instead of fear and guilt. It's sounds good." After several more steps, she says, "Does it ever get less hard?"

I want so badly to answer, but no matter how hard I try, I can't get myself to tell her the lie she's looking to hear.

Chapter Nineteen

I just got done talking with Jason about dying, and I feel more tired than usual. The hand that kid's been dealt. It's not fair, that's what. I wish there was more I could do for him. But the only thing I can do is work on this here list with him, so that's what I'll focus on.

Don't know how he's ever going to hit a home run at Wrigley, and become a superhero? What am I thinking, trying to help with something like that? If he's going to get his wishes, something pretty unexpected is going to have to happen.

—From the Journal of Murray McBride

After our discussion, I see a change in Alexandra. She's not as light as before. Her steps are heavier, her words are heavier. Even her shoulders seem to slump under some unseen weight.

I know what the weight is: my words. My lack of reassurance. But I always appreciated Murray's honesty when he was answering my questions even if it wasn't what I wanted to hear, and I want to do the same for her.

I consider leading us back to the baseball stadium, but I know Alexandra has no interest in that, so we keep walking and wrap around toward the National Mall. I figure we've taken care of two wishes: the water park and the national anthem. By the end of the day, if all goes well, we could have four of the five done, and the fifth—helping the people of El Remate—well underway. So I make plans to take care of number four— tour Washington D.C.—and lead her toward the Washington Monument.

By the time we get to the base of the monument, Alexandra seems to have forgotten about our discussion. It's nice to see her resilience, the resilience of kids. Instead of ruminating about her survivor's guilt, Alexandra is overwhelmed by what she's seeing.

It makes me wonder about her life. I know so little about it. But now I remember that she has never been out of Lemon Grove. It seems crazy, but who knows? Juan can't make much money with his job, and as adept at managing her diabetes as Alexandra is now, she couldn't have been so responsible a few years ago.

"Look, Mr. Cashman," Alexandra says, pulling on my sleeve. "People can actually go inside."

"I know," I say. "Believe it or not, there's an elevator in there. You can go all the way to the top."

Alexandra laughs at that. "Sure," she says, in a sarcastic tone.

"I'm serious. Look, that's where you buy tickets."

I lead her to the ticket booth, but there's a sign that says "Sold Out For The Day." Inside, a television in the corner plays the regional telecast of the Nationals game we were just at and a woman behind the counter answers questions from tourists, mostly repeating over and over that the sign is correct and there really are no more tickets to the top remaining.

"Sorry," I tell Alexandra. "I should have planned this better. Ordered some tickets before we left town."

"It's okay," Alexandra says. "Just seeing it from here is enough. I might still be a little afraid of heights, anyway. Oh, look!" she says.

She points to the TV with the baseball game on. With every pitch, if we look beyond the batter to the seats directly behind home plate, we can see Javier with three empty seats next to him.

"Wait, what?" the woman behind the ticket counter says. She's staring at Alexandra, but then she looks at the television and back again. "You're not the kid . . . yeah! And you're the guy! From the game. The national anthem people."

I'm embarrassed to be recognized for that, considering how terribly we carried the tune, and I feel my face getting hot. Alexandra has the opposite reaction. She stands up tall and informs the woman that it was our first time singing the anthem in front of people. As if that hadn't been obvious.

"Amazing," the woman says. "Hey, what do you guys think about taking the elevator up to the top of the monument?"

"What? Really?" Alexandra can't control her excitement. "That would be super-duper fun."

To the dismay of several people nearby, the woman hands us two tickets, good for five minutes from now.

"They're my own, personal tickets," she says. "But my friends will understand. They're running late anyway."

I thank her very much and take the tickets. We go straight to the base of the monument, enter through the security gates, and before we know it, find ourselves in the elevator, streaking toward the top.

Alexandra grabs my sleeve tightly, gripping harder and harder with every second we ascend. When we finally get to the top and the doors open, she jumps out of the elevator, goes straight to a window, and presses her nose up against the glass. Apparently, she's completely conquered her fear of heights. At least, when there's a window in place.

Watching her gives me that feeling in my chest I've been getting a lot since I met her. A mixture of happiness and fear. Something in my heart tells me to focus on the moment, so I try to do that. I join her and point out the things I recognize. The Capitol Building, the White House, and from a different window, the Lincoln Memorial.

"Who are all those people?" she asks, pointing to a large crowd on the National Mall.

"I don't know." I squint at the stage set up in front of all the people and read the banner: *Immigrant and Refugee Music Festival*. "Looks like it's a concert," I say. "Want to check it out?"

I expect Alexandra to jump at the chance to go somewhere that might make her feel welcome, but she hesitates. "Do you think they'll have any ICE officers there?"

That feeling in my chest turns cold, and I realize, not for the first time, the challenges that come with being an undocumented immigrant. Whereas I can take for granted that no one is going to detain me—maybe even deport me—for no apparent reason, Alexandra doesn't have that luxury.

"Don't worry," I say. "Stick with me and it'll be fine. I promise."

After a few more minutes of gazing at the city from above, we finally take the elevator back down and wander straight into the crowd. Reggae music blares from giant speakers. Looking around, I realize I've never been surrounded by such a diverse crowd. All around me, people with black and brown skin of every shade dance and sing and smile.

Alexandra dances her way into the crowd, bobbing her head to the music as she spins occasional circles. I notice when she discretely eats a fruit snack from her fanny pack, but she joins right back in with the smiling and dancing. And the people seem really happy to see a kid her age joining their group, cutting loose with such wild abandon. Somehow, we find ourselves closer and closer to the stage, until we're dancing right below it. Well, Alexandra is dancing. I'm trying to manage the constant ache in my chest while maneuvering the oxygen concentrator through the crowd.

Alexandra is twirling and bouncing to a song I don't recognize. A mixture of rock and reggae now. When the singer sees her, he waves at her, beckoning her to join him onstage. I don't know if he recognizes her from the baseball game or if he just thinks the crowd would like to see a cute kid up there. I try to get closer to her, in case she needs me to help her decline the invitation.

But Alexandra has no such hesitation. Apparently, she's getting used to this fame thing. Before I can suggest we move back, she grabs onto the stage and starts pulling herself up. When she gets stuck, she looks back at me, full of excitement and struggle. I shrug my shoulders a bit, then take hold of her feet and push with the little strength I have right now while the singer wraps his hands around her wrists and pulls.

When she gets all the way up, Alexandra continues flailing her arms and legs, even though she doesn't seem to be keeping with the beat of the song. But it doesn't matter. The singer is loving it. The band is loving it. The entire crowd is loving it. When the song ends, I have a feeling the roar is more for the dancing kid than for the song.

The singer bends over and talks with Alexandra while they wait for the cheering to settle down. The crowd is pretty riled up, so it goes on for almost a full minute. Alexandra fills most of that minute by talking into the guy's ear. I try unsuccessfully to read her lips, but it doesn't matter. I can tell by her posture and gestures that she's telling the man all about forgetting the words to the National Anthem. Finally the crowd quiets a little and the man speaks into the microphone with a distinct Jamaican accent.

"I'd like to introduce to you Alexandra Lopez." The crowd roars again. "Earlier today, she had her first musical performance at the Nationals baseball game. And now, before Congresswoman Marquez leads our march to the Capitol Building for the ceremonial vote, I've asked Alexandra to sing her song one more time." He opens his arms to the crowd and yells, "Would you like to hear it?"

The crowd roars again and the singer gives the microphone to Alexandra. She doesn't miss a beat as she begins singing the National Anthem in a voice every bit as passionate as our earlier rendition.

The crowd loves it. And Alexandra makes her way through the entire song without forgetting a word. When she finishes, the singer takes one of her hands, and a woman, I'm assuming it's the congresswoman the singer mentioned, takes the other, and they lead her off the stage and toward the Capitol. I squeeze through the hoard of people and stay with them the best I can, but my pace is slow and it's difficult to keep them in sight.

For a moment, I wonder what would happen if I lost Alexandra. How would I find her? What if something happens to her when I'm supposed to be responsible for her? The thought creates a wave of panic, which sticks in my chest and makes me lose my breath. I have to lean over, hands on my knees, and inhale through the nasal cannula as deeply as I can. Still,

I can't seem to catch my breath. My chest aches, right where my heart is, and I can't seem to move. My vision starts to swirl in waves. There couldn't be a worse time for this to happen.

The fact that the pain won't go away scares me. Not for my own sake, but if I pass out, what will happen to Alexandra? She's far ahead now, with a group of people who don't know who she is or how to return her to those who are supposed to be watching her.

After several more excruciating seconds, the squeezing releases, I get a full breath, and I can see straight again.

It's another reminder of the condition of my heart—of Tiegan's heart. I don't want to think about it, but lately I haven't had much choice. I just need it to hold on long enough to finish Alexandra's wishes and get through the trial next week. Whatever happens after that, I'll be okay with. But I have to hold on until then.

As I continue toward the Capitol, I call Rachel, who answers right away.

"Hi," she says. "How'd the talk go?"

"Okay." I'd almost forgotten why we'd separated from Rachel. "But Alexandra has found herself another adoring crowd. She's headed to the Capital with them now. Can you meet us there?"

I decide not to let on how concerned I am about my heart almost giving out, and about not having Alexandra in sight. Rachel agrees to meet on the front steps of the Capitol Building.

It's a short walk for both of us, and I see Rachel across the street before she sees me. I catch up to her as quick as I'm physically able and touch her elbow. Every time she looks at me, I can't believe how lucky I am to be with her.

"Hey," I say, and I kiss her cheek.

She smiles, but freezes when she looks toward the Capitol. I follow her gaze and understand why. On an enormous screen set up by the front steps, Alexandra's grinning face is projected with the singer and the congresswoman, raising their hands together for the crowd.

"Is that for real?" Rachel says.

The congresswoman speaks into a microphone. "Thank you for joining us today. The music has been wonderful, the dancing has been fantastic, and now it's time to vote." The crowd goes crazy for several long moments before the woman speaks again. "This may only be a ceremonial vote, but it is not insignificant. It tells our leadership in no uncertain terms that we, a nation of immigrants, want to be a welcoming nation to those who are just coming to our great country now."

During this round of cheers, the congresswoman reaches out to Alexandra and pulls her close. "Joining me now is the young immigrant we just heard sing the National Anthem. *Her* National Anthem. And now, this girl, Alexandra Lopez, who wants nothing more than to vote like a true American, will get that opportunity. She will cast my vote on the floor of the United States House of Representatives."

Well, this changes my plans a bit. As much as Javier has done for us, apparently Alexandra is going to take care of the "Vote" wish all by herself.

Before I can maneuver my way to the front of the mass of people, the congresswoman turns around and walks into the Capitol with Alexandra by her side. Fortunately, the giant screen that focused on Alexandra and the congresswoman outside the building has flipped to a long shot of the inside of the House of Representatives. Alexandra is out of sight, and all I can do is take Rachel's hand and watch.

But then in the corner of the shot, Alexandra and the congresswoman enter and take a seat. A loud screeching sound makes the crowd groan before the audio from inside the building is piped out to us. A bill is being read to the members of congress, although I don't pay much attention to the reading. I'm too busy watching the image of Alexandra talk to one lawmaker after another as they come over and shake her hand.

Rachel and I finally make our way to the front of the crowd and approach the entrance of the Capitol. A policeman is there barring everyone's entrance, and he holds out his hands to indicate that we're not about to get by.

I point to the projection on the big screen. "We're supposed to be with that girl," I say. "I'm supposed to be taking care of her."

The officer looks skeptical at first, but he must see the panic in my eyes because after a moment of scrutinizing me, he sighs and says, "I'll have to pat you both down."

I spread my arms, and he does a thorough check for weapons. Once he's satisfied that I'm not a threat, he does the same to Rachel, then waves us through to the metal detector. I look at my oxygen concentrator, then back to the security guard. He seems annoyed, but opens a small gate next to the metal detector and lets us pass through.

We rush to the floor of the House of Representatives as the names of the members are called out one by one. Many representatives appear to be absent, which reminds me that this is just a ceremonial vote. But the room is still impressive, with its giant columns and marble floors. And many members of Congress are here, making it feel very official and dignified.

I spot Alexandra and Congresswoman Marquez sitting off to the side. And just in time, too. When the name Olivia Marquez is called, the little girl who wants to be an American stands and bellows out for everyone to hear, "Ay!"

There's no pause in the vote. No standing ovation or round of applause. But Alexandra doesn't seem to care at all. She continues standing, her shoulders thrust back, pride emanating from her.

At first, her excitement and pride seem overboard. But then I remember what she said when we were making the list. Voting, she said, is the most American thing she could possibly think of. I find my own shoulders straightening as I watch her live out her American dream.

I take Rachel's hand and absorb everything. All these powerful people, dressed in their perfectly pleated outfits, standing beneath the domed ceiling and thick, gothic pillars. And a little girl in the middle of it, getting her wish. Feeling as American as a kid can feel.

It's easy, in times like these, to forget all your troubles and just enjoy the moment. I remember that feeling when I skipped back to Murray's car after I kissed Mindy Applegate. And although it's fogged by what came next, I can still feel the elation of watching the baseball soar over the wall at Wrigley Field.

But remembering those moments is always bittersweet. There was the elation, definitely. But then there was what came next. That's the problem with flying too high—sooner or later, gravity finds you.

When my cell phone vibrates in my pocket, it sounds like an alarm. Like a wake-up call. And I'm reminded, when I see Juan's name on the caller ID, that this foray we've had outside of real life was never something that could go on forever. We were always destined to come back down to earth. I had just hoped we could have a softer landing than I had all those years ago.

But I know before I even hear his voice that it's not meant to be.

"Hello?" I say into the phone.

Juan's voice is heavy and thick with tears. "I'm sorry, Mr. Cashman," he says. "I'm so sorry."

I'm terrified to ask what he's sorry about, so I wait him out. After a few sniffles on the other end, Juan's voice returns.

"I was arrested again," he says. "There was traffic from an accident. I was speeding because I was going to be late to work."

He starts sobbing, so I don't think he hears when I ask if he's okay. It's like it takes everything he has to force the next words out. "The prosecutor asked them to move the hearing up because of the arrest. They won't let me go until then."

When he's not able to continue, I give him a moment to collect himself. Finally, I ask, "When is it, Juan? When is the Merit Hearing?"

He starts several times but is unable to speak. Finally, as I fight the urge to yell at him to tell me, he sniffles and says, "Tomorrow. It's tomorrow morning, Mr. Cashman."

He breaks down again, now finished with his mandate to tell me the news. Neither of us speaks. I hold the phone to my ear and try to stay calm.

"What's wrong, Jason?" It's Rachel squeezing my hand, a look of deep concern on her beautiful features.

"Bad news," I say.

When I look at Alexandra—shaking hands now that the vote has concluded, accepting congratulations, smiling wide—it breaks my heart. But not nearly as much as when her eyes find mine.

She sees the phone pressed to my ear; the expression on my face. And all the joy slowly drains from her smile.

Chapter Twenty

Everything was going so well. The Cubs came through, and then Jason came through. The kid actually hit a home run in a major league baseball stadium. With some adjustments, of course, but those didn't matter. The smile on his face could have lit up an entire baseball stadium at midnight.

And then it all came crashing down. And I'm left here sitting on my duff, powerless to do anything to help him, wondering if everything I've done has just made things worse.

—From the Journal of Murray McBride

The flight back to Illinois takes place in near silence. The drone of the engines, which earlier in the day reminded us we were on a private jet flying off to make wishes come true, now sounds like the audio manifestation of sadness.

From across the aisle, I watch Alexandra sit with her forehead against the window. Rachel is holding her hand silently. I can't tell if Alexandra is scheming and planning, or simply trying not to cry in front of us. Javier watches her intently, without his usual energy.

As we near Chicago, my phone vibrates. I have a new email. I reluctantly pull my hand from Rachel's and check the message. It's from another immigration lawyer. They'd be happy to meet with us . . . a week from Tuesday.

This is all happening so fast. It's far too late to get real help. We're on our own in this.

When we land, we all transfer into the limo and drive off. For the entire ride, the only sound is the hum of the tires against pavement. When the car pulls in front of Alexandra's house, she bolts out of the car and sprints to the front door. She disappears into the house, leaving me and Rachel with Javier.

"I'm sorry she didn't express it, but I know how grateful she is for what you've done," I say. "Trust me, I can promise you that."

Javier waves it off. He's still looking at the front door of the small house. "She's a good kid, isn't she?"

"She's the best kind of kid."

He doesn't remove his gaze from the house as he shakes his head, as if understanding that there are things beyond even his control. "You'll let me know if you need me at the trial?"

"It would be great to have you there. Eight o'clock tomorrow."

Javier extends his hand, and I shake it. "Then I'll be there," he says. "Thank you."

I follow Javier's gaze to the house and realize how terrified I am to go in. At the moment, I want nothing more than to go back to my old life, when things were simpler. When my only goal was to raise a million dollars for the homeless.

Sure, Tiegan and Murray were always on my mind. And yes, a deeply rooted pain went along with every show I performed. But my goal was simple; my path was clear. And I slowly, but perceptively, moved toward it one step at a time.

I take out my cell phone and look again, desperate with the hope that maybe another lawyer's office responded to say they can meet us tonight.

But, of course, it's not to be. It looks like we'll have no help. And if Juan was arrested and the hearing moved up, I don't see any way this can work out. I don't see how we can possibly win.

Feeling more tired than I have in a very long time, I lift myself out of the limo, take Rachel's hand, and enter the Lopez house. I hear Alexandra's footsteps upstairs in her bedroom. I consider going to her, but I don't know what I'd say.

The only way I can possibly help is with the trial. They have no lawyer, no professional assisting them, nobody preparing their arguments for them. Juan is in jail, and Alexandra, as amazing as she is, is eleven and a quarter years old. Somehow, unbelievably, this has fallen to me. Someone with no qualifications at all.

"I'll help you," Rachel says, squeezing my hand. "However I can, whatever you need. If I can help, I'll help."

I wrap her in a hug that I wish could last forever. I wish we could be transported to some other world where there are no problems, no responsibilities. Where we can just be together.

But that's not the world we live in.

"Thank you," I say. "I'm afraid it's going to be a long night."

■　　■　　■　　■　　■

It is.

We work for hours, searching for any relevant law, any informative article. By three in the morning, my eyes will barely stay open. I slap my cheeks hard enough to hurt and take another long sip of cold coffee. Forcing my eyes open as wide as possible, I stare at the computer screen. Rachel replaces my coffee with a fresh, hot cup, and sits next to me.

"I don't think we can go with Deferred Action," I say.

"Really? I think Alexandra is the perfect candidate. Brought here as a child through no fault of her own, doing well in school."

"Maybe a few years ago, but look at this article. It's about a girl with a serious disease. She'll definitely die if she's deported, and she's been staying in America under Deferred Action for Childhood Arrivals. Just read. It looks like things have changed."

I point to the computer screen and read along with Rachel.

Without any public announcement, the United States Citizenship and Immigration Services eliminated a "deferred action" program that had allowed immigrants like her to avoid deportation while they or their relatives were undergoing lifesaving medical treatment.

I shake my head for what feels like the hundredth time tonight. "If that poor girl can't even stay for lifesaving medical treatment, what chance does Alexandra have?"

"Okay, so maybe we don't go the DACA route," Rachel says. "What about the thing you said earlier? About the authorities not deporting people who have lived here for a long time and followed the law?"

"Ten years is the number they give," I say. "Alexandra has been here since she was two. That's only nine years. And even if they'd make an exception for that, it's only if your criminal record is clean. Juan has been arrested twice now."

"Yeah, but just for driving without a license," Rachel says. "Because he needed to get to work. I can't imagine they'd hold that against him."

"I wish that was true. But the more I read, the more it seems like we, as a country, just don't care about people if they weren't born within our borders."

"What do you mean?"

"Look at this one," I say.

Rachel stands behind me so she can see the computer screen. She puts her hands on my shoulders and massages out some knots. It takes all I have not to collapse into a puddle at her feet. But I want her to hear this. I point to another article I've brought up.

"We take people who try to get into the U.S. because they'll likely be killed if they stay where they are, and we block them at the border. We don't even let them claim asylum and we send them to these camps that not only aren't in the United States, they're nowhere near the place these people have to show up for their trials. Like, hundreds of miles away, and the only way to get there is to walk through territory run by drug cartels. The cartels pretty much run the camps, too. It's like we *want* innocent people to be murdered."

"That's terrible," Rachel says, leaning closer to read over my shoulder.

I'm so fatigued it's difficult to regulate my emotions; rage is threatening to break lose at any minute. "I agree with a strong immigration policy," I say. "But it's another thing entirely to sentence families to death like this. And make no mistake about it, that's exactly what we're doing. I don't see how anyone who values human life could support this."

Rachel rubs her eyes with her palms. "Jason, why are you reading this? It has nothing to do with Juan and Alexandra's case."

I know she's right. This article is about people attempting to cross the southern border of the United States. If Juan and Alexandra lose tomorrow, they'll be sent to Guatemala, not Mexico. But it's all related. After all, it wasn't that long ago Juan and Alexandra were in the exact same place as the people trying to cross the border into safety. And I can't help but think, if our government will knowingly send innocent people into situations they likely won't survive, what hope do Juan and Alexandra have of finding leniency tomorrow?

"I'm just scared for them," I say. "We can be so cruel, as a nation. And people like Juan and Alexandra? They're the ones who suffer the consequences."

Rachel runs her hands through her hair and rubs her face. "Maybe we should get some sleep."

I shake my head hard. "We're not ready yet. The trial is in five hours."

"Exactly. And you need to be at your best. You need to be rested." She puts her hand on my cheek. I want nothing more than to melt into it and sleep for days. "All you can do is tell them about Juan and Alexandra," she says. "Who they are, as people. I know you were hoping for more, but you're as ready as you can be."

◆　　◆　　◆　　◆　　◆

The time has come.

The courtroom is just as intimidating as last time. Maybe more so, knowing that the stakes are so high for Juan and Alexandra. As the trial before ours ends and our turn begins, the situation feels dramatic, but also forgotten, somehow. It seems like it should resemble the climactic scene of a movie. A courtroom drama in which every reporter in the city is outside, or pushing their way in, microphones extended, firing questions at us as we hide our eyes and duck into the safety of the courthouse.

But there are no reporters. There is no fanfare whatsoever. It's obvious the rest of the world doesn't care what happens here today.

But I care.

I walk toward the front of the courtroom, hand-in-hand with both Rachel and Alexandra, who's wearing bright red, white, and blue—as always, as well as her fanny pack. But in place of her normal T-shirts and shorts, she's wearing a blue dress with red-and-white stripes. It looks like it was made for a Fourth of July party. The judge will probably think it's a ploy. A way to use the kid in the room to gain up some sympathy for the family. If only he could get to know Alexandra before he rules on the rest of her life.

I guess that's my job today. Just like Rachel said.

Juan is waiting for us in the same seats as last time. It's jarring to see him in orange prison clothes. This for a man who was just trying to drive to his job.

The judge shuffles some papers around, then says, "This is the Merit Hearing for the Lopez family. Juan and Alexandra. It has been previously determined that both have legal grounds for removal. Today, we will determine whether they will face deportation to . . . " After a long pause, the judge says, "Guatemala City, Guatemala."

The way he says it feels like a slap to the face. He could have said Key West, Florida, or Honolulu, Hawaii, and it wouldn't have sounded any different. It's like he has no idea what living there could mean for Alexandra. He could have said Timbuktu. I really don't think he understands.

But Alexandra understands. As she sits in the same spot she did for the last hearing, her face tells me exactly how well she understands.

"The defendants may make a statement, if they so choose," the judge says.

I take a deep pull from my oxygen concentrator, rise to stand, and try to speak with a strong voice. "Thank you. Your honor, today we ask for Cancellation of Removal for the Lopez family, based on a combination of factors. First, that no crime involving moral turpitude was committed. It's true, Mr. Lopez was caught driving without a license, but he was simply trying to get to his job, so he could support himself and his daughter. There was no violence. No malicious intent.

"Second, Juan and Alexandra Lopez have lived in the United States for nine years and three months, since Alexandra was two years old. I ask the court to consider leniency because that is so close to the ten years required for Cancellation of Removal.

"And finally, we ask the court to consider Alexandra's type-one diabetes as extreme and unusual hardship, because of how unreliable it can be to find insulin in rural Guatemala, where the family would have to live in order for Juan to support them."

After a long pause in which the judge types something into his computer, he looks up at us over his glasses. "Would the defense like to call anyone to speak on the defendants' behalf?" He asks in a drone that suggests he's done this more times than he'd like.

My chest squeezes in that new way—more painful and breathtaking than before. But it's Tiegan's heart. I know she'll pull through. I clear my throat, which echoes through the silent courtroom, and try to stand tall.

"Yes, your honor," I say. "I'd like to call Juan Lopez."

"Very well," the judge says, and motions Juan to a small podium with a seat behind it. Alexandra touches his arm, but Juan doesn't seem to notice. He stands slowly, strides to the podium slowly, and sits in the chair behind it, slowly. He looks terrified to make a wrong move, understanding well the possible consequences for him and Alexandra.

I feel like an imposter as I approach the other side of the podium. I'm no lawyer. But I'm the only chance they have, so I turn my attention to Juan, who trembles in his chair. "Could you please tell us your name?"

"Juan Carlos Lopez," he says, his voice shaking.

"And where do you live?"

"1716 Forty-fourth Street in Lemon Grove."

"How long have you lived in Lemon Grove?" I ask.

"A little over nine years." Juan smoothes a wrinkle from his shirt. "Since Alexandra, my daughter, was two years old."

"And where did you come from?"

"Guatemala. A small town called El Remate."

"And why did you leave your home to come to the United States?"

Juan sits up tall. "When Alexandra was diagnosed with diabetes, my wife, Maria, and I agreed we had to try to get her to America. There, she could get the treatment she needed much more easily. More reliably."

I sneak a glance at the judge to gauge his reaction, but he's giving nothing away.

"How did the journey to the United States go?" I ask.

"Very badly," Juan says, and his gaze turns inward. "It was very hard. Very hot. And we never had enough food or clean water. What we had, we gave to Alexandra first. In the end, my wife became sick. She died on the side of a road in Mexico."

The simple fact, put so matter-of-factly, is forceful enough to render the courtroom silent. I let his words hang in the air for a long time.

"But you and Alexandra kept on?"

"Yes," Juan says. "I buried my wife near an agave field, and Alexandra and I continued our journey. It would make no sense to turn back then. Not when we were so close to our goal. I didn't want Maria to have died in vain."

"And since you arrived, nearly ten years ago, what has your life been like?"

Juan takes a deep breath, as if moving from one chapter to the next. "Amazing," he says. "It has been everything we hoped for. Alexandra has learned to manage her diabetes, which is most important. I found work for a farming company shortly after we arrived in this country. They even have benefits, so I can afford Alex's insulin. I work hard, so we're no longer poor. We have friends. America has saved me and my daughter."

I say the next words as gently as I can. "I'm afraid I need to ask you about your recent arrest. Is that okay?" Juan nods and shifts in his seat, as if in preparation for an attack. "What happened yesterday to land you in jail?"

Juan swallows hard. I told him to look at the judge during this part, but after a quick glance, Juan looks away. I curse under my breath. No matter how innocent he might be, the gesture looks like one of guilt.

"I was on my way to work, but there was an accident, so traffic was very slow. By the time I was past the traffic, I was almost late. My boss, he doesn't like people to be late. Sometimes he fires them. So I drove fast to get there. Too fast."

I lean toward him, hoping to give him some comfort. "And you were pulled over?"

"Yes," Juan says. "And I had no license, because I don't have documentation. So he took me to jail and now I am here."

I close my eyes for a long moment, trying to feel Tiegan within me, asking her to guide my actions, my words.

"Before I let you go," I say, coming close to the podium. "Will you tell us why you think you should be able to stay in the United States?"

Juan shifts in his chair and nods. "We've tried hard, ever since we arrived in this country, to do the right thing. It's our home now. The only home we've known for almost ten years. For my daughter, it's the only home she's ever known. And if we have to go back to Guatemala . . . " His voice trails off before he takes a deep breath, steeling himself. "I don't even want to think about what might happen if Alex can't get her medicine."

I let his words hang in the air for a long moment, looking to the judge and back to Juan again. "Thank you," I say.

As I'm walking back to the bench where Alexandra is, a suited lawyer bounces up from his seat and heads straight toward Juan, as if he's on a mission.

"Mr. Lopez, I'm Marshall Lamont, and I represent the United States of America in this trial. I'd like to ask you one question."

"Okay," Juan says, looking at his lap.

"Do you deny that you crossed the border into the United States illegally?"

"No. But like I said, we had—"

"And in the last three months, you've been arrested twice for driving without a license, is that right?"

"Yes, but I was just trying to get to work so I could—"

"I understand," Lamont says, in a way that oozes condescension. "Which is great, except that here in the United States, we can't read people's minds about why they do something. So we have no choice but to go by their actions. And your actions, as you have readily admitted here in open court, were illegal."

Juan has nothing to say to that, and the lawyer decides it's a good way to end his cross-examination. When Juan sits next to Alexandra, he has tears in his eyes.

■   ■   ■   ■   ■

I call Javier to the stand next. I have no idea if the judge knows who Javier is or not, but he definitely sits up a little taller in his leather chair when Javier approaches the podium in his three-piece suit and a giant, sparkling World Series ring on his finger.

After quick introductions and formalities, I ask Javier the one question he's here to answer.

"Based on your experience with the Lopez family, why do you think they should be allowed to stay in the United States."

"I am from Cuba," he says. "I was not supposed to be here anymore than this family. And yet now I am a hero to millions of little boys and girls. Now, the United States not only welcomes me but claims me as its own. And that is fine. That is great. But I haven't done anything more than Juan, who has worked hard in this country for almost ten years, and I especially haven't done more than Alexandra, who every single day reminds us what it means to be an American. I have been allowed to stay in this country and become a citizen. It only seems right that this family should be able to do the same."

When I sit down, I almost lunge for the oxygen concentrator and take a long, saving breath. The judge asks if Lamont would like to cross-examine, but the lawyer declines. It's a smart move. No one in his right mind would want to go up against an American hero like Javier Gonzalez. So next, trying to take as much time as possible between words so I don't get out of breath, I call Alexandra to the stand.

My chest tightens as she walks up to the podium. It hurts to see her have to defend herself like this. She should be running around outside, playing with friends. Suddenly, I feel better about making her wishes come true. It's impossible to know what's going to happen with this trial, but no matter what, no one can take those experiences away from her.

"Thank you for being here," I say to her, although I know she would rather be anywhere else.

Alexandra shrugs. "It's part of the process, which means it's an American thing to do."

I smile. That wasn't an answer we talked about. "We've heard a lot about your family today. About why those who know you think you should be able to stay. But now I'd like to talk about what could happen if you don't get to stay." Alexandra purses her lips and smooths the legs of her pants. "You spent some time researching the health-care system in Guatemala. Can you tell me what you found?"

Alexandra takes a deep breath, as if preparing herself for something unpleasant. "Technically, Guatemala has free health care for all its citizens, and in the bigger cities, that actually works pretty well. But outside the cities, it's really hard for people to get the medicines they need. For me, I need insulin because I have diabetes."

"How long could you survive without insulin?" I ask.

"Not very long. If I didn't have any I'd probably get ketoacidosis and die in less than a day."

I'm taken aback when the judge leans toward Alexandra and asks a question. "And you think there's a chance that could happen to you," he says. "If you're forced to go to Guatemala?"

"I think it would just be a matter of time," Alexandra says. "Even if I'm able to get the insulin I need, and it's the kind of insulin I know how to manage my diabetes with, other things could happen. Like, what if the power went out and I couldn't keep it refrigerated? It's hot there, it would ruin the insulin. And then what?" She shrugs. "I'd die."

There's more I want to ask her. About her dreams in America. What she wants to do when she grows up. But two things stop me. First, I realize the scary picture she's painted might be more powerful than happier things. And second, I'm short of breath. It's like when I was a kid all over again. My heart squeezes in my chest, and I struggle for breath. I couldn't ask another question if I wanted to.

I give the judge a moment, but he doesn't ask another question, either. He just sits with a slight scowl on his face, thinking.

"That's all, your honor," I manage to say.

Again, Lamont declines to cross-examine. Now, all we have to do is wait.

The judge leaves the courtroom. I have no idea how long he'll deliberate in his chambers before announcing his verdict, but I hope it's not long. This anticipation isn't good for my heart.

"Do you think this is normal?" I ask Rachel when the judge has gone. She hugs me, and I try to focus on the feel of her for as long as possible. When she finally pulls away, I feel less whole, as if part of me was removed when her touch was removed. But I force myself to focus on the moment and the task at hand. "I was thinking he'd just let us know right now what his decision is."

"I think this is normal," she says, but I can't tell if she knows what she's talking about or if she's just trying to make me feel better. "Maybe it means it's a hard decision. He wants to take some time to think about it."

"Is that good or bad?"

"I wish I knew," she says.

It turns out the judge didn't have to think about it for too long. Just a few moments later, the bailiff says, "All rise," and the judge reenters the courtroom with his decision.

Chapter Twenty-One

Well, I guess this is the end. I'm headed down to Chicago, finally able to see Jason in the hospital. I don't rightly know what's going to happen to him, but I don't expect to make it back here, myself. Sometimes a man just knows when he's on his last leg. It sounds like Jason is on his last leg, too.

Me? I've been on mine for quite some time now. Even though I'm excited to see Jenny again, I have to admit, I sure am going to miss this place.

—From the Journal of Murray McBride

"After serious consideration, I have come to a conclusion on the Cancellation of Removal request of Juan and Alexandra Lopez."

We all sit, rigid as two-by-fours, as the judge continues.

"It is possible for a person or people who cross the border illegally to, over the course of time, prove themselves worthy of staying in the United States. Our law even gives a time frame for such situations—ten years. The Lopez family, however close, does not meet that requirement."

"Oh, no," Alexandra whispers next to me.

"And while it's also true that Mr. Lopez's crimes did not involve moral turpitude, that doesn't change the fact that he was arrested for breaking the law for driving a motor vehicle without a license. Twice. This, of course, after he broke our country's laws by entering illegally nine years ago."

Juan grabs my sleeve. "Wait, is he saying we can't stay?" he says. His voice is frantic.

I don't know how to answer, so I continue to listen to the judge's verdict.

"Finally, in regards to the medical condition of Alexandra Lopez, it is the opinion of the court that type-one diabetes is a sufficiently common condition that we couldn't possibly reverse every removal order for those who suffer from it. Therefore, Juan and Alexandra Lopez will be returned to Guatemala City, Guatemala, pending reception of the Bag and Baggage letter, which will be sent promptly."

"Oh, my god," Juan says, echoing exactly what I'm thinking. I just can't wrap my mind around what I'm hearing. They're going to be deported. It feels like a death sentence for Alexandra, and I'm afraid that might not be far from the truth.

"Mr. Cashman," Juan says desperately. I lean my ear toward him and listen to his tortured voice. At first, I can't believe what he's asking. Apparently it's true that desperate times require desperate measures. Because what he's asking me to do is pure desperation. But it's what he wants, so I clear my throat again.

"Your honor," I say, panicked. "I'd like to request that Alexandra Lopez be allowed to stay in the United States if, in exchange, Juan Lopez agrees to voluntary removal at his own expense."

I see Juan nodding vehemently out of my peripheral vision. The judge scowls at me. I read that offering voluntary removal is supposed to happen at the Master Calendar Hearing if it's going to happen, not after the order for removal has been judged on. But something about the little girl wearing red, white, and blue must get to the judge, because he hasn't shot down my request. So, feeling my heart thump in my chest, I stand up and continue to speak.

"Mr. Lopez could save the U.S. government the expense of deporting him. He'll buy his own plane ticket. Plan the entire departure. But we ask the court to consider . . . no, we beg you, please, to let Alexandra Lopez stay in the United States. For the sake of her health. She's never known any country other than this one."

The judge considers my offer for what feels like a very long time. "Does she have other family in the United States? Legal residents?"

"No, your honor."

"Then who would take care of her? Where would she live? I'm very hesitant to break up a family unit, especially if there's no extended family nearby."

"We have systems for this type of situation," I say. "Foster homes. Anything is better than being deported. Her chances of survival in Guatemala will be very low."

The judge doesn't even hesitate this time. "Not good enough. Without family, without a legal guardian, I can't allow her to stay."

"I know who she could stay with." It's Juan, standing right next to me now and speaking with desperation in his voice. "This man," he says, and I know without looking that he's gesturing toward me.

"Juan, please," I say. I just wish he would sit back down. He doesn't understand—I can't do what he's asking.

"He has come to know my daughter well," Juan continues. "He is a caring man. He made a list of wishes with Alexandra and together they have been making them come true. He is good and kind, and I trust him. He could be my daughter's guardian."

The judge stares at Juan openmouthed. He's understandably surprised that a father would suggest legal guardianship of someone that, to the judge anyway, must seem like a random person. A random person who can't even function without portable oxygen. After giving Juan a long, incredulous look, he turns to me.

"Well?" the judge says. When I don't answer immediately, he continues. "If the girl's own father trusts you enough, I'd be willing to allow her to stay in the country, since she was a toddler when she was brought here illegally. If you will become her legal guardian, that is. Are you willing?"

So many things bombard me at once. Whether I could actually act as a parent to a preteen girl is the first. How doing so would change my life in so many ways is another. But more than anything else, I consider my heart.

The doctors have made it clear that it won't last much longer. Not that I needed their expertise. I know Tiegan's heart well enough to know it is almost done with the extra time it has given me on this earth.

And I couldn't possibly take on this kind of responsibility, knowing that I'll die soon and leave Alexandra on her own, without parents or a guardian of any kind. But the only solution to that problem—getting a second transplant—is out of the question. Cutting Tiegan out of my life, out of my body, is unthinkable. I couldn't possibly do it. Not after what she did for me. That's no way to repay her for saving my life.

I continue to go back and forth in my mind, because leaving Alexandra to face deportation is just as unthinkable. If I did that, and she were to die as a result, I'd never be able to forgive myself.

It seems I've put myself in an impossible situation. And as the judge stares me down, awaiting my response, I have no idea what to do.

"Your honor," I say. "I'm going to need some time."

His scowl deepens, and I think he's going to tell me I don't have any time. But instead, he reaches for his gavel and says, "It is currently eleven o'clock. We'll reconvene at noon, at which time I need your answer. And not a minute later."

He slams the gavel, and I stare at it, unable to move. All I can do is try to ignore the probing looks I feel from the desperate people beside me.

■　　■　　■　　■　　■

I leave the courtroom in a trance. Not Juan's questioning voice, nor Alexandra's pleading eyes, nor even Rachel's touch of my forearm can force me out of it. I stumble through the threshold, blindly walk through the exit, and find my car without conscious thought.

I want nothing more than for time to stop. To not have to make this terrible decision. Or even better, if I could rewind time, if I could turn back the clock, then I could avoid this entire situation altogether. I would never come back to Lemon Grove, never meet Alexandra Lopez, and never have to deal with this impossible choice.

Who am I trying to fool? I wouldn't choose that even if I could. The little girl has grown to mean so much to me. But to be her legal guardian? Could I handle that, even if I am able to survive?

Yes, is the answer that comes, emphatically, to my mind. Yes, I could. I could become a father figure for her. I would never replace Juan as her actual father, but I could help her, guide her, teach her what I know. I could navigate the process of becoming a U.S. citizen so she could visit her father in Guatemala with the security of knowing she'll be allowed back into the U.S., the only home she's ever known.

I could do it. I could take on that role. I'd be honored to do it. The hole in my life would be gone, filled by a sweet eleven-and-a-quarter-year-old girl.

Except for what it would do to Tiegan.

How did I get myself into a situation where, no matter what I do, I'll hurt someone I care about? Could cutting Tiegan out of my chest be the right thing to do? More than anything else—more, even, than sadness—I feel utterly confused.

My phone alarm goes off, which is strange because I don't remember setting it and don't know why I would have set it for 11:16 a.m. But now I realize it's not my alarm. It's the same ringtone, but a different phone. I pull the hospital cell phone out of my jacket pocket and actually laugh when I realize what's happening. Of course, there's not the least bit of humor in it.

"Hello?" I say. "Is this a prank?"

"No, it's the real thing, Jason." The sound of her voice startles me more than I expected.

"Rachel," I say. I was with her in the courtroom only moments ago. How could she be calling me on the hospital phone now? Through my confusion, Rachel's voice comes through clearly, urgently.

"I know you're not a religious man, Jason, but hearts don't become available left and right like this. And for it to happen just minutes before you have to make your decision?"

"I've already made my decision. You know that. I can't cut Tiegan out."

After a long silence, Rachel's voice has a stern quality to it. "You could have told them to take you off the list, you know. When you turned down the first heart for Andy? But you didn't. You told them you weren't able to make it in time, so they kept you on the list."

"So?"

"So, I think you did that on purpose. Because somewhere, deep inside, you know you want to live."

"You don't understand—"

"I do understand," she says, her voice soft and empathetic. "At least as much as anyone without Tiegan's heart inside them can understand."

"There's also Gary to consider," I say.

After a long pause, Rachel's voice is even more curt. "Gary Johnson? You used the stolen list again?"

"He has a son," I say, ignoring the question. "He wants desperately to reunite with him, but he needs more time."

"Of course, he does. But do you know who else needs more time? You. Because you have a little girl depending on you. I'm going to the hospital right now, and you should, too. Maybe Juan can tell the judge you accept the deal, or at least postpone the hearing. I'm sure this qualifies as a legitimate reason."

"Look, Alexandra is no worse off now than she was before I met her," I say, reciting the line I've been using in my own mind to rationalize what I'm doing. "She's actually better off for having the wishes. She was able to live the American dream for a little while."

"You can tell yourself whatever you want," Rachel says. "But I'm going to tell you what I think, and I want you to listen closely. I think you're scared. You're scared of what your life will be like without Tiegan's heart guiding you. You're scared you won't be the same person. That you won't recognize yourself. So you're doing what cowards do, which is nothing at all. I don't think you're actively choosing Tiegan," Rachel says. "I think you're choosing to do nothing because you're scared. And I don't understand it, Jason. I don't. Don't you remember what you said last night? About what's happening to people like Alexandra and Juan?"

I squeeze my eyes closed, trying to shut out her words. I want to say something but can't decide if it should sound angry or injured or conciliatory. In the end, I say nothing. Maybe that proves Rachel's point.

For several moments, the only sound I hear is the hum of the tires through the phone as Rachel speeds toward the hospital. I adjust the nasal cannula and try unsuccessfully to fill my lungs. I guess Rachel finally realizes I'm not going to say anything, and when she speaks, it's in a voice so soft and fatalistic it makes the back of my throat ache.

"Okay. You win. I'm going to give you this hour, whether you want it or not, because we know where Gary is and we know he'll be able to get here in time. But when the hour is up, if you haven't come to your senses, I'll do what you ask. I'll call Gary and let him know there's a heart waiting for him. A heart that should be yours."

With that, the line goes dead.

■   ■   ■   ■   ■

I don't know where to go. I don't know what to do. I should have told the judge I couldn't do it and been done with it. Maybe the fact that I didn't is more proof that Rachel is right about me. I am a coward.

And once again, I'm lost. I know my mom said I could always go home, but that's not what I do. Maybe I'm too ashamed, but for whatever reason, with only forty minutes until I'm due back in court, I end up at the church. Predictably, Father James is waiting for me.

"Jason."

I join him in the front pew. We sit side by side for several long moments.

"The situation we feared," he says. "It has come to pass?"

"Yes," I say. "But I can save her if I'll become her legal guardian." I dread the only question that could possibly come next.

"What will you do?"

"I can't cut Tiegan out, Father. No one seems to understand, but I just can't."

He nods as if he does understand.

"She has been a very big part of you as far back as you can remember," he says, and I nod hard. "You feel her inside you. Not just as a beating heart, but as a presence. As a friend. Alive, almost."

"Yes. Exactly. How could I possibly remove her? Just cut her out? You do understand."

A small shrug. "Deciding life or death is God's job, not mine. And, of course, it's complicated. For example, whose life are we talking about? Yours? Tiegan's? Alexandra's?"

The church is so empty Father James's words echo off the walls and hit me again. When I don't answer, he continues.

"You've already given up one heart to someone in need, just as Tiegan did. And if this was just about you, I'd support letting another person on the list jump ahead of you. It's a selfless act, Jason, I believe that. But this isn't just about you. Since the day you met Alexandra, it never has been."

I shake my head. "But what about Tiegan?" I say. "It always comes back to Tiegan. She gave me her heart."

"What Tiegan did for you was amazing. But she wouldn't have wanted to make you a slave to her memory."

"I'm not a slave to her—"

"Jason," Father James says, cutting me off. His voice is firm now, almost angry. As if he's done letting me talk in circles. "Think about what you're considering doing," he says. "You've said yourself that Alexandra will likely die if she's sent back. And yet you won't help her."

"You don't understand."

"I do understand. More clearly than you do. Because your thoughts and emotions are clouded. I know what I'm talking about."

This gets my attention. In all my time knowing Father James, I've only known him to talk about how much he doesn't know, the things he can't understand or explain. So when he of all people says he understands more than I do, I can't help but listen.

"You feel such intense guilt for surviving when Tiegan died that you have dedicated your life this far to her wishes. It has been noble, but it has also been destructive. Now, finally, it is time."

"Time for what?"

"Time to let Tiegan go."

I stand abruptly, knocking the heavy pew back several inches. I'm out of breath and a stabbing pain makes me double over. But I force myself to continue.

"You're wrong," I say, heaving to catch my breath. "You don't have her heart in your body. You can't feel what I feel."

"True. But I know—"

"No you don't! You think you know, but you don't have any idea what I feel. So don't try to tell me you do. Because you don't. And you never will."

I don't allow myself to look at the sadness in his eyes. I won't allow him to poison my thoughts, and I won't let him change my mind. I stumble for the exit, cursing under my breath as the oxygen concentrator bounces on the stone floor behind me. I pick it up and toss it over my shoulder, but before I can escape, Father James cuts me with a few last words.

"You'll regret it, Jason. If you do this, for the rest of your life, you'll regret it."

■   ■   ■   ■   ■

Everyone is against me. No one understands. How could they? No one else has Tiegan's heart in their chest. No one else has lived with her for the past twenty years.

But if I'm honest, Rachel was also right about something: I'm scared. In fact, I'm terrified beyond anything I've ever felt before. Nearly dying as a ten-year-old kid didn't hold a candle to the terror I feel right now.

I'm terrified of what I'm about to do.

As I walk back into the courthouse, the sun shines from a pure blue sky, as if the universe is unaware of the turmoil in my heart. I pull out my phone and stare at the time—11:40 a.m. Twenty minutes until I have to give the judge my final answer. Three hours and thirty-five minutes until Gary needs to begin surgery to get the new heart.

Since I can't seem to pry my eyes from the ticking clock, I probably would have walked right past Gary if he hadn't reached out and grabbed my shoulder. I'm startled, which makes my heart pound with a small amount of adrenaline, which almost brings me to my knees.

"I'm sorry," Gary says, his eyes widening with surprise. "I should have known not to do that. Me of all people."

I try to figure out what's happening, but my mind is foggy. Or maybe the opposite. Maybe I'm so focused on the one thing I have to do that anything else feels foreign and confusing. "What are you doing here?" I ask. "Did Rachel already call you? You need to get to the hospital."

"I'm just happy to be out of jail," he says. He giggles his giggle. "Oh, I got me a little escort," he says, and points to an armed security guard down the hall. "They'll get me back there soon enough. Even with good behavior, I have a little more time left to serve."

"But Gary, you have to get to the hospital *now*."

"Oh, I know. I got me a phone call, same as you. That's why I'm not in jail right now." He lowers his chin to give me a serious look. "The way I hear it, the only reason I got the call is that your girlfriend thinks you might turn that heart down. Wanted to know my thoughts on the matter. Since she knows we've met, and all."

I nod hard, trying to feel sure of myself. "You need that heart. You need more time, for Aaron."

"Aaron's right here," Gary says, motioning down the hallway. Sure enough, Aaron is facing a painting, which he seems to be studying intently. But he must hear his name because he turns to look at us and smiles. It's a nice smile. I didn't realize until now that I haven't seen it before. Gary's voice is choked up when he continues. "He told his mother he wanted to visit me. Insisted on it, actually. My son says he's going to visit me every day now, thanks to you. And we're starting over, Mr. Jason. A real father and son this time. If I die today, I'll die a happy man." He reaches out a heavy hand and places it on my shoulder. "Now it's your turn to make a difference in that girl's life."

I try to take it all in. To understand what he's saying. He and Aaron have reconciled. He no longer needs that time to make up with his son.

"Don't do it," he says, watching my expression. "Don't you even think about it."

"Don't do what?"

"Look up who's next on the list. I know that's what you're scheming."

"What if it's someone who really needs another heart?"

Gary shakes his head. He sits on the nearest bench, out of breath, and I join him, equally out of breath. "I understand," he says. "You have a good heart, a good soul. You want to help people. But it's your turn now. And this isn't just about you," he says, echoing Father James.

He makes an exaggerated motion toward the entrance of the courtroom, where Alexandra stands with her father, wearing her red, white, and blue outfit.

"Only one of us is going to get that new heart," he says. "Which means one of us needs to get ourselves down to that hospital, and fast." He dips his chin and looks at me with a serious expression. "I can promise you this much, Mr. Jason: this time, it ain't gonna be me."

■   ■   ■   ■   ■

After my conversation with Gary, I'm feeling more and more like I'm alone on an island. I'm the only one who can understand why I can't cut Tiegan out of my life. But finally, I see someone else who knows.

My very last hope.

Della.

The only explanation I can think of for her being here is that she somehow found out about the noon deadline and wants to be sure I keep Tiegan alive. When she sees me, she looks straight at my chest. As if she's been needing time with her daughter. Without speaking, I lead her to the same alcove I hid in after the first hearing.

"You know," I say, "You know about what the judge said?"

Her brow furrows, as if she can't figure out what that would have to do with anything. In her eyes, I see her longing: her daughter's heart is in the same room. She needs to be close to it. To feel its life. What could a judge's words possibly have to do with that?

Tentatively, we sit on the only bench in the alcove. She barely makes a sound, she's moving so cautiously. "Rachel called," she says. "She just said I should come. That a decision had to be made, and I should be here for it. Does it involve me somehow?"

"Well, it's Tiegan," I say. "And it's Alexandra. And it's me. And yes, it's you." I toss my hands up in surrender. "It's hard to tell the difference sometimes."

"I don't understand." Her eyes flick to my chest, as if it contains the drug she so desperately craves.

I consider how much to say. In the end, I'm as concise as possible. "Alexandra can stay, but only if I become her legal guardian, and I can't do that knowing that I'll die soon. I would have to get another transplant. And a heart is available. Right now."

Della's sharp intake of breath startles me. "But . . . Tiegan's heart."
"I know."

This, finally, is what I need. I need someone to tell me I can't get the transplant. I need support for my decision, in the form of someone telling me I have to keep Tiegan's heart and accept whatever consequences may come. And for that, I need someone who loves Tiegan every bit as much as I do.

I need her mother.

In what looks like slow motion, Della stands from the bench. She faces a corner and stares for a long time. At what, I don't know. I wonder if she knows.

"It's okay," I say. "I know some things have changed. I've met Alexandra and we've had her wishes. But I'll figure something out with her. I don't know what, but something. One thing that will never change is my commitment to Tiegan. I won't ever cut her out of my life, I promise."

She remains facing the corner, but her slow nod gives me comfort. It gives me the strength I'll need to go through with this.

"I understand," she whispers. "I, more than anyone, understand. But, of course, that can't be."

The alcove is so quiet I can hear her soft, steady breathing. I try to wrap my mind around her words, but I can't seem to comprehend what she means. "What can't be?" I finally ask.

"You can't keep Tiegan's heart any longer."

My heart jumps in my chest. "What are you talking about? Of course I can keep Tiegan's heart. I have to."

"For what?" Della says. She turns to me with tears in her eyes. "So you can die with her? She's already gone. She's been gone for a very long time. And our holding onto her? It's been fine. It's been a comfort. But that was when there were no consequences. Now, things are different. Now, there's another little girl. One who is very much alive. And who very much needs you."

My vision spins. I fight with all my mind, trying to keep thoughts of Alexandra away. "How can you say that? Tiegan is inside me. She's a part of me. Alive—"

"She's *not* alive!"

I stare at Della, unable to believe what I'm hearing. When she continues, her voice is soft again. "All this time, I've taken comfort in the idea that while Tiegan was here, I taught her to be strong and brave and kind. But there's nothing strong or brave or kind about telling you to go to your grave with Tiegan's heart when there's a little girl who needs you. And there's nothing strong or brave or kind about you turning your back on Alexandra for the sake of someone who won't even benefit from it."

I realize my fists are clinched and I'm holding my breath. I loosen my hands and take a deliberate, slow inhale of oxygen. I know now that I'm the only one who truly understands. I'm the only one who could possibly understand.

"You're wrong," I say. As quickly as I can so I won't have to see her expression, I turn my back on her and leave the alcove.

■   ■   ■   ■   ■

I don't know where to go, but I need to get out of here. I wander circles for several minutes until I can't take it anymore. I peek my head into the courtroom, hoping the judge is ten minutes early and I can get this over with. But he's in the middle of a hearing. Juan is sitting near the back, and near him is Della, who apparently is staying, I'm sorry to see. I thought she was an ally, but it turns out she's just like everyone else.

Gary and Aaron are still here, too. I know I should tell Gary, again, that he needs to get to the hospital. Wasting a donated heart would be such a tragedy, on top of everything else. But I can't stay here, with them, for the last ten minutes until noon. So I look for an empty room where I can have some peace. My final ten minutes of peace, before I tell the judge what I, alone, know I must.

Near the end of the long hallway, I find a room that appears empty. It's a chapel, I realize. But when I step inside, it's not empty. Alexandra is sitting by herself on the back pew. She has the tail of her shirt in her mouth, and she's injecting her abdomen with insulin. It pains me to see her innocence and vulnerability. Instinctively, I stop in my tracks and hold my breath. If I back out slowly, she might not know I was here.

But I can't do that. If I honestly believe what I'm doing is right, I should be able to defend it. So I don't back away. Instead, I look to where Alexandra is sitting, in the corner where a few candles are burning. Just like she was in the church, when I first met her. It seems so long ago. How did we ever get from there to here? I approach and sit next to her, leaving more space between us than I normally would. She notices. And she's smart enough to understand what it means.

"You can't do it, can you?" she says. "You can't become my guardian. Because you can't get a new heart."

"No," I say, forcing the words out. "I can't."

She nods, as if it's just another piece of information and not the equivalent of a death sentence. "Because there isn't one available? Or because you don't want it."

"Alexandra, it's not that I don't want it. I want it more than anything. I want to get a new heart, get a new lease on life, become your legal guardian, help you finish your final wish. I want all of that. But it's not that simple."

"I understand," Alexandra says. "It's because of Tiegan."

"Yes," I say. "Her heart saved my life. I can't just cut it out of me."

Alexandra looks at me with her big, round eyes. I'm blown away by her selflessness. Of all the people in my life, it takes a child, an eleven-and-a-quarter-year-old girl, to say she understands. "She must have been a great friend," Alexandra says. "Tiegan, I mean. She must have been really special."

"She was," I say.

"I'd like to hear about her. I'd like to hear what she was like. Then maybe I can try to be like her, and then I'll be special too."

I cover my face with my hands and try not to weep. "You are so special," I say. "And if there was any way . . . any way I could have it both ways. I would have been honored to be your guardian."

Alexandra flinches, as if my attempts to make her feel better are only making things worse. "But you can't," she says. "You have to choose. Me or her." She shakes her head. "That's not fair to you. I'm sorry."

I search my mind over and over but can't come up with anything to say that will help. I want to get away. Run as far from this place as I can. As far as possible from Alexandra and what I'm doing to her. But before I can move, she scoots along the pew until she's right next to me. She leans her head on my shoulder, and for the first time, I don't feel awkward.

"You've done so much for me," she says. "I've only known you for a little while, and you've given me some of the best times of my life." The room is so quiet I can hear the candles flicker, nearly burned to the bottom of their holders. When Alexandra sniffles, I can no longer hold back my tears. "Thank you, Mr. Cashman," she says.

I'm unable to respond. So we sit there, leaning against each other, and watch the candles until they burn themselves into darkness.

■　　■　　■　　■　　■

The noon deadline has come.

I walk to the front of the courtroom without looking at anyone. I sit and lean my face into my hands, hiding.

When the judge enters the room and tells me to stand, I force myself to my feet. "I assume you have made a decision regarding the option discussed earlier today, of becoming legal guardian to Alexandra Lopez?" the judge says.

"I have, your honor."

For the first time, I allow myself to look around the courtroom. Juan has a resigned look on his face. Alexandra's looking at the wall, away from me. But I can tell even from the side of her face that she's terrified. And that's what gets me. Her terror. Even more than her selflessness, more than her sweetness. At the same time I see the look of terror on her face, I feel something in my heart that I've never felt before. It's a strong, resounding signal, so powerful it's as close to an actual voice as it's ever been.

It's Tiegan's voice.

"Well?" the judge says. "Please announce to the court what you have decided, Mr. Cashman."

I swallow hard. Time is up. I wish with all my might there was another way, but there's not. I know there's not because I've thought it through from every possible angle, a dozen times over. A hard choice has to be made, there's no way around it.

"Your honor," I say, and I close my eyes briefly again, checking and rechecking this new feeling in my heart. Trying to decipher what it means. Trying to figure out exactly what Tiegan is telling me.

When I finally hear it clearly, when I finally understand what Tiegan is telling me, I fight it. For the first time in my life, I rebel against her. It can't be true. I must be misunderstanding. I can't do what she asks.

But it's clear. In fact, it's easier to understand than anything she's ever told me before. Tiegan is guiding me, one last time. Whether I like it or not.

Before I feel completely ready, I open my eyes and take a deep breath. And with the strongest voice I can manage, I allow my best friend to speak through me. "Your honor," I say. "If it pleases the court, I've decided to become the legal guardian of Alexandra Lopez."

There's a collective intake of breath from everyone sitting near me. I turn around and the first person I see is Gary. I wonder what he thinks now that he knows he'll have to wait for another heart. I shouldn't be surprised when he gives me a thumbs-up along with a silent, bouncing giggle, then stands from his bench and walks to the exit of the courtroom with his arm around his son. A prison guard meets him there.

I wish Rachel was here. She's probably made it to the hospital by now, preparing for whatever role she'll have in the transplant, unaware that it's me they'll be cutting into. But even if Rachel was here, I wouldn't be able to gaze at her like I'd want to, because there's someone else I need to see.

And then I find her. Tiegan's mom.

I study Della's expression, wondering if she still feels the same now that she's heard the words telling her that her daughter's heart will be cut out. That for the first time since Tiegan was born, it will stop beating.

She's staring at me, and I'm unable to tell if she's sorry she encouraged me. But I do recognize the anguish. Abruptly, she turns and strides toward the exit. As the doors swing closed, her sobs echo throughout the courtroom.

The judge, undoubtedly experienced with the agony that his proceedings can cause, rushes through the rest of the hearing. He instructs me to begin the process of becoming Alexandra's legal guardian as soon as possible so it is done before Juan leaves the country. As soon as the gavel slams, Juan and Alexandra swarm to me. They wrap me in a hug, both crying tears of joy. But I can't stay.

I pull myself away and rush to the exit Della burst through. I look down the hallway, hoping I can catch her, but she's nowhere to be seen.

It doesn't matter. I already know where she's going. Because it's where I need to go, too.

■　　　■　　　■　　　■　　　■

The green canopy of tall oak trees is starting to turn orange and yellow. A bluebird flits through the branches as I drive up a small hill and begin to weave my way deeper into the cemetery. By the time I see the stone chapel hidden among the forest, I feel miles away from the city.

Lemon Grove is a half-hour drive from Chicago, where the hospital with my new heart is waiting. If I had four hours to begin the surgery from the time I received Rachel's call, I'm running out of time. Which is why Rachel's voice is frantic when she calls.

"Jason?" she says. "Is everything okay?"

"It's fine," I say, but I'm not sure if *fine* is the right word. I'm not sure there is a word for what I'm feeling.

"I just talked to Juan. He said you told the judge you'll be Alexandra's legal guardian. Is that true?"

"It is. I guess I finally listened to what everyone was trying to tell me." I don't add that by "everyone" I really mean Tiegan.

"Then, the heart. You have to hurry. It's already been almost two hours. Where are you?"

The panic in her voice is palpable. And I understand. If I were to miss the window and the donated heart went to waste, well, the tragedy of that would be beyond words.

"I'm at the Lemon Grove cemetery."

"The what? Jason!"

"I know," I say, and my voice is strangely calm. "I'm sorry. But I didn't have a choice. This can't wait."

"Okay," Rachel says. "Okay. This is okay. Everything will be okay."

"Who are you trying to convince?" I say, and I hope she hears the joking in my voice.

"This is serious, Jason."

So apparently she did.

"I know. I'm sorry to cut this so close. But I have to do this."

There's a moment of silence, in which I can only imagine the panic she's feeling. "Please hurry. I don't have to tell you how important it is that you get here absolutely as soon as you possibly can."

"No, you don't. And I'll hurry as much as I'm able. I promise."

"Jason?" she says, and I hear the hesitation in her voice. "Thank you for doing this."

"Anytime," I say.

I hang up and ease the car onto the side of the road. I put it in park, grab the oxygen concentrator, and walk around the gray stone structure. When I get to the back, sunlight filters through the trees, illuminating Della's graying hair as she sits next to Tiegan's grave.

I've only been here once. Shortly after the transplant, when I was ten years old. It's a beautiful place, full of color and life, but I could never come back after that first visit. I told myself it was unnecessary. I had Tiegan's heart, alive in my chest. Why would I need to visit the place where she was dead?

But the truth is, it simply hurt too much. I couldn't face the idea of reliving what had happened. I couldn't handle reliving the guilt I felt when I saw the engraving on her headstone.

Tiegan Rose Marie Atherton
3/19/1988 - 8/22/1998
SBK. Always.

I approach silently and sit on the opposite side of the headstone from Della. For a long time, the only sound is the singing of the birds. I try to ignore the seconds ticking in my mind. Della deserves this time.

"I'm sorry," I finally say.

After a long moment, she looks to the sky. "I know I told you to do this. I know it was the right thing. But still . . . "

"I know. But you should know something. It's true that you told me to do this. So did everyone else in my life, it seems. But that's not the reason I'm doing it. Until just seconds before I spoke in that courtroom, I still wasn't going to. Despite what you said. Despite what you or anyone else wanted."

A deep furrow creases Della's brow. "Then why did you do it?"

"Tiegan," I say simply. "I heard her. I became absolutely certain, without any doubt whatsoever, that it's what she wanted me to do. She's the one I listened to. She's the reason I'm doing this."

Della's shoulders sag in relief, as if a giant weight has just been removed. "Thank you," she says.

In the silence that follows, I consider what she must be going through. Now, and over the past twenty years. I've never allowed myself to imagine what happened the night I received Tiegan's heart. I've been terrified of the horror I would feel. But Della doesn't have that luxury. She had to live through it. The entire thing. The accident. What happened to Tiegan. And she had to make the terrible, terrible decision to overcome her horror, call the hospital, and save a life. My life.

"Do you believe in heaven?" Della says.

I'm startled by her voice. It's as if, after the silence settled in, speaking here is unnatural. "I don't know," I whisper. I want to say yes, because she needs the comfort. I should say that of course Tiegan is in heaven waiting for us and we'll see her again someday, exactly as she was in life. And it will be like no time has passed at all and we'll have eternity together.

But I have no idea if that's true. Maybe it is, maybe it's not, how am I to know? But that's not what Della needs to hear, so I just shake my head and say, again, "I don't know."

"I think there is," Della says. "Maybe not like in paintings or the movies. But something. There has to be something more, doesn't there? Otherwise, how do you explain what existed before time, or what will exist after time? Why can't we comprehend eternity? Why can't we explain how the very first speck of matter came to be? Not even the most accomplished scientists in the world claim to know that. So there has to be something more. Doesn't there?"

A squirrel jumps from one branch to another, carrying an acorn in its mouth. A mere blink in a giant, unfathomable universe. I watch it for a long moment as it scurries around. "I think so," I say. "I don't know what it is, but yes, it only makes sense that there's something more."

Della looks at me for the first time. "I'm happy for you, Jason. That you get a new heart. That you get to live. I want that for you, you know."

"I know," I say, and I reach over and take her hand. It's wrinkled and frail, and I think again of all she's been through. But we're in this together. We're the only ones who can really understand. "I miss her," I say.

Della flinches at some internal thought. "You know what the hardest part is?" she says. "It's that, as much as I miss her and as much as I feel bad for her, for the fact that she didn't get the full life she deserved—and I do have those feelings, very strongly. But even more, even more overwhelming and persistent, is the thought that it was my fault. It's the guilt."

"Della, it wasn't—"

"I was driving the car. I lost control. I crashed, and Tiegan died. You can say it wasn't my fault as many times as you'd like, but nothing can change the fact that it was."

I wish I could let her know that I understand. That I feel the same about receiving Tiegan's heart. But the words that could fix things simply don't exist. Sitting next to Della, looking at Tiegan's grave, I'm tempted, over and over, to change my mind. To keep Tiegan's heart until it fails, and then to be content to join her in heaven. But each time, as I'm about to verbalize my intention to Della, I'm revisited by the image of Alexandra at Nationals Park. Stuck halfway through *The Star-Spangled Banner* and needing my help. And I know that her life is precious. And that if I'm in a position to help her and her precious life, I have an obligation to do it.

After all, Tiegan told me so.

I look again at Tiegan's mother. No one I know has acted on that sense of obligation I'm feeling, that sense of selflessness, more than the woman beside me right now.

"You need to go," Della says. The sun is noticeably further west than when I arrived and I wonder for a moment how long we've been here. "You have my blessing. There's only one thing I ask of you before you go."

"Anything," I say. "Just name it."

Della wipes a tear from her cheek. "Let me be with her? One last time. Let me say goodbye to my baby girl."

Wordlessly, I lean back against Tiegan's headstone. Della scoots next to me and leans in. She lowers her head to my chest, directly atop her daughter's beating heart. As the shadows grow longer through the old oak trees, Della and I lay quietly. The soft, rhythmic beating of a heart is the only sound.

And with that, we say our final goodbye to Tiegan Rose Marie Atherton.

.   .   .   .   .

The drive to the hospital in Chicago is surreal. It's like I'm falling headlong to my death, instead of toward something that can prolong my life. But in a very real way, part of me will die today. An important part that has guided me through the last twenty years of my life. Not just keeping the blood flowing, but showing me right from wrong. I wonder, when I have a new heart in my chest, a heart from a complete stranger, will I feel different? Will I be a different person?

I park in the hospital lot and try to hold myself together as I walk through the automatic doors. I'm not surprised to see Alexandra and Juan in the waiting room. Rachel is with them, looking worried until she sees me. She and Alexandra bounce up from their chairs and rush toward me, while Juan exhales the tension that has been building as they waited for me.

"Jason," Rachel says. "We thought maybe you changed your mind."

"No," I say, and I lean over to give Alexandra a hug. "I just needed some time to say goodbye."

They understand what I mean. I see the empathy in Alexandra's eyes. It makes me wonder about her heart, and how it became so full.

"Things are prepped and ready," Rachel says. "The surgeon is scrubbed in. Let's get you back there."

It's not until now, when I hear those words, that the fear I've had turns to panic. I've tried to think about Alexandra and what this will mean to her. I've tried to think about Della and what it will mean to her. I've spent the most time thinking about Tiegan and what this will mean to her.

But now I think about me.

For the first ten years of my life, Tiegan was my best friend. For the last twenty, she's been in my heart, quite literally. In every breath I've taken since I can remember, Tiegan has been a part of my life. In a few moments, if I follow Rachel down the hallway, she'll be gone.

"Jason?" Rachel says. She puts her hand on my cheek. It's soft and gentle. And it's electric. It pulls me from my trance. But I'm still short of breath, and it has nothing to do with her touch.

"I don't know if I can go through with this," I say.

"Yes, you can."

"I'm terrified. What if something goes wrong and I don't survive?"

"You will."

I look her in the eyes, unafraid of showing her my vulnerability "And what happens if I do survive?"

There's so much in that question, but Rachel seems to understand. She squeezes my hand and looks at Alexandra, guiding my eyes there. "It will be okay," she says.

Timidly, Alexandra leans her head against my side. And I know Rachel is right. It will be okay.

I kiss Rachel on the cheek.

I bend down and hug Alexandra.

Then I turn and walk down the hallway.

■   ■   ■   ■   ■

The world changes. It continues to turn.

Time marches on. It waits for no man.

I blink my eyes open, feeling weak and groggy from the anesthesia. Immediately, I feel different. Immediately, I know.

My friend Tiegan is gone.

Chapter Twenty-Two

Over the last hundred years, I've learned a thing or two. Maybe not as much as I should have, but at least a thing or two. One of the things I've learned is this: We all get older, every single day. We lose people we love along the way. No matter how much we want to hold onto a moment, it always slips on by. Things change. Life goes on, for those of us still here. Moment by moment by moment.

But you know what the surprising thing is? That's exactly what makes life precious, that's what.

—From the Journal of Murray McBride

Airplanes have always amazed me. In my career as a magician, I flew around the world. Sometimes it felt like I spent more time in planes than on the ground. But it never got old. I never lost the wonder I felt the first time I ever flew. I've always been keenly aware of the engineering marvel that is manned flight. Rocketing through the sky at more than five hundred miles an hour? The fact that I could climb onto a plane, take a nap and watch a movie, and disembark on the other side of the world? It's amazing.

Life is amazing.

I've realized that fact all over again since waking up in the hospital with a new heart—again. Although I may never get used to the fact that I can't go backwards—meaning I'll never see Tiegan again, or feel her in my heart the way I used to—I do understand the beauty that is a human life on earth. The magic of it.

And I'm spending that life doing what I've learned is important. I'm using my life for the good of others. For the good of Alexandra. I'm doing my best to spread joy.

Alexandra is huddled in the back seat of my car—my own car now, not a rental. Juan is next to her, looking scared but also enjoying these final moments with his daughter before he flies off to Guatemala.

More than anything—more than the palm trees or howler monkeys or avocado trees—he says he's looking forward to seeing the school Alexandra is helping build. I wish I could see it, too. Someday, maybe.

As for me, breathing comes easy now, and the sharp chest pains that used to be so common are a thing of the past. I miss Tiegan's guidance. I miss the feel of her presence within me. But I don't regret my decision. Not for a minute.

Our goodbye is brief. There are tears shed by all and no shortage of guilt on my part. It was my responsibility, after all, to try to get Juan permission to stay in this country. I failed, and a family is being torn apart as a result.

But then again, another family is starting. Not taking the old one's place, surely, but adding to it. Our focus, Alexandra's and mine, will be to propel her along the path of citizenship as quickly as possible. Once she's officially American, she'll be able to visit her father at will.

After a final hug that lasts several minutes, we watch Juan walk through the airport entrance with only one checked suitcase and one carry-on. Then we head back to Juan and Alexandra's house, where I've taken over the lease so Alexandra can stay in her childhood home. Who knows? Maybe I'll even start performing again. My days of constant travel are over, but maybe in Chicago, anyway.

Rachel is at the door when we arrive, eagerly awaiting the news.

"He's off," I say. "You really could have come, you know?"

"I know. But I didn't want to be a distraction."

"A distraction might be nice for the next twelve hours or so," I say, watching Alexandra open a book and stare at the same spot on the page.

So the three of us go out to dinner, but the conversation is stilted. Every few minutes, one of us says something like, "I hope he's okay," or, "He's probably taking off right now."

We go back to the house and the comments turn to, "I hope the men from El Remate are waiting for him when he arrives" and "If everything is going well, he should be into Guatemala by now."

Finally, we all fall asleep on the couch. Or at least I think we do. When the alarm goes off, telling us it's time for the FaceTime call, Alexandra's eyes don't look sleepy at all. She already has the laptop computer pulled up and is staring at the screen, waiting for the call from Zuri.

When it finally comes, fifteen minutes later than the agreed upon time, a small, Guatemalan girl stares at us through the computer screen.

"Lo siento," she says, then shakes her head. "Espere aqui." She darts away from the camera, and a moment later, a boy's face appears. He's a few years older than the girl but also has a wide smile.

"I'm sorry," he says. His English is heavily accented, but he has a sparkle in his eye. "Our internet did not work, and Zuri can write English, but she does not speak good English."

"No problem," Alexandra says. "Is my dad there? Did everything go okay?"

"No," the boy says. When he doesn't elaborate, all of us on our side of the call stiffen. But then the boy shakes his head. "I mean, he is not here. But he is on the way. My mother talked to them as they were leaving the city, before the signal goes away."

Until they arrive safely, I'll have nerves that cause a tightening in my chest. It's a feeling that is still unfamiliar. Over the last twenty years, I became so perfectly attuned to the feelings of Tiegan's heart. It was like a trusted partner. A friend I could rely on. This new heart—it pumps my blood, it keeps me alive. But it has none of the extra feelings I used to get from Tiegan's. None of the intuition or the guidance.

It's going to take some getting used to. I can't help but feel alone.

A chorus of whooping and shouting pulls me back into the moment. I look to the computer screen, but it's nothing but chaos. Either an earthquake has just begun or somebody is carrying the computer, bouncing through the house and out the door.

Finally, the computer settles on what looks like a different world. Palm trees are mixed with other trees with fruit hanging from the branches. Even though the screen is small, I can see mangos and starfruit, as well as several I don't recognize.

"There," the boy's voice says. "Under the ramon tree."

I don't know which tree is the ramon tree, but a moment later, I make out the form of several people walking toward the computer. Next to me, Alexandra jumps up like she was just electrocuted. We all stare silently at the computer as the figures get closer. Alexandra is the first to recognize him.

"Daddy!" she yells, and I'm surprised that the form of a man seems to hear Alexandra's voice. He drops his bags and runs to the computer. Soon, I realize it is, indeed, Juan, looking tired but perfectly happy.

"You're okay," Alexandra says when Juan's face enters the screen. "They helped you to El Remate?"

Juan laughs. "They talked about you the whole way. And when we got to El Remate, the people welcomed me like a hero. I've spent the last two hours talking with all the people you've helped here. They insisted on showing me the school right away. It looks amazing. I can't wait for you to see it. I can't wait for you to visit."

They talk for a full hour. It's like they haven't seen each other in years, even though we were all in the car together this morning. And when they finally end the call, Alexandra remains still, staring at the computer screen as if her father is still there.

"He's okay," she finally says. She looks at me and Rachel with shimmering eyes. "Everything's going to be okay."

Chapter Twenty-Three

I'm an old man, and I know I haven't got much time left on this earth. It has been a good place and I've been given a good life, most of it with my beloved Jenny. The fact that I met the kid changed the last part of it, that's for sure. And the girl? Tiegan Rose Marie Atherton? How's that for a mouthful? She's quite a kid, that's what.

I worry about Jason, and that's the truth. But if he doesn't make it, I look forward to seeing him at the pearly gates. And I'll tell him, I'll say, "Jason, I'm glad I met you. You saved my life." And then we'll come up with more wishes. And together, we'll see if heaven is as much of a hoot as earth has been.

—From the Journal of Murray McBride

"What are you reading?" Alexandra says.

I wipe a tear from my eye and put the old journal down. Murray's cursive has become difficult to read, and I use that as an excuse for rubbing my eyes.

It's been two days since Alexandra's first call with Juan. They just finished chatting again and Alexandra's smile is still going strong. The weight that has been removed from her shoulders is evident in every movement, every expression. It's a beautiful thing to see.

"It's a journal," I say. "Written a long time ago by a very dear friend of mine."

"Murray McBride?" she says.

I don't know why I'm surprised to hear her speak his name. It's not like I've kept Murray a secret. In fact, I remember telling Alexandra about him the first time we met. But they feel like two separate lives—my life with Murray and my life with Alexandra—separated by twenty years of working to make Tiegan's wish come true.

"Yes," I say. "It's Murray's journal."

Alexandra sits across from me in a way so familiar it warms my heart. Whether it's mine, Tiegan's, or this new one, that feeling is the same.

Alexandra peers over my shoulder, squinting to read Murray's handwriting. "Can you actually tell what that says?"

I chuckle. "Most of it. Some of it takes a while to decipher."

"What happened here?" she asks, pointing to a spot where the perforation is jagged. "Is it missing a page?"

"I think so," I say. "I don't know when it fell out, though. It's very old."

"He wrote about your friend, Tiegan, too," Alexandra says, leaning her head in close to the journal. After a few long moments, she says, "Do you think you'll ever tell me about her?"

The request takes me by surprise, although I'm not sure why. Maybe because of that feeling of separation. The sense that Tiegan and Alexandra are from two different lifetimes. But it only makes sense for Alexandra to wonder. After all, I've made no secret about how important Tiegan is to me.

"Tell you what," I say, and I close Murray's journal gently. "Come with me and I'll tell you all about her now."

"Can we call Rachel? I like when she's around."

"Of course," I say. "I like it when she's around, too."

■   ■   ■   ■   ■

"SBK, Jason. It's good to see you."

Della greets all three of us with hugs. I can tell it takes everything she has not to break down. She welcomes Rachel, tells Alexandra how happy she is for her, and forces a smile at me each time she looks at me. But her eyes continue to flick to my chest. Each time they do, a palpable sadness enters her eyes.

But she's strong; always has been. She's had to be, with the hand she's been dealt.

"Do you think we could see Tiegan's bedroom?" I ask. "Alexandra was hoping I'd tell some stories about her."

"Of course," Della says, and her eyes brighten at the prospect. It's a poor consolation—the reality that when someone is gone, all that's left is memory. Unsatisfying memory. We can try to make it seem like it's enough, but deep inside, no one is able to fool themselves that thoroughly. Memory can never, ever be enough.

But it's all we have. And right now, it's all I can offer. Or maybe it's Alexandra's offering to me.

"I'll give you some privacy," Della says, leaving us at the entrance of the bedroom.

When we step inside, I have to catch my breath. Nothing has changed since the last time I was here, more than twenty years ago. The same Third Eye Blind poster. The same quilted bedspread her grandmother made. Even the smell has somehow been preserved, unless it's just the memories that bring it back. Rachel, sensing the power of what I'm feeling, intertwines her fingers with mine.

I lead her around the room, touching everything I can. With every moment that passes, I thank Tiegan again and again for the life she gave me. Before and after. After several minutes of exploring the bedroom, Rachel and I sit on the bed next to Alexandra.

"So," Alexandra says. "What was Tiegan like?"

"My babysitter," I say, and Della's laughter bursts from the hallway, where she's apparently listening. "Come join us," I say toward the door. A moment later, Della walks in like a contrite schoolgirl, except for the smile on her face.

"She was your babysitter?" Alexandra says, confused.

"She might as well have been," Della says, her grin widening.

"Remember that time she stopped me from jumping off the roof onto the pile of leaves?" I say.

Della throws her head back in laughter. "Which time?" she says. "You tried three different times, according to Tiegan."

"She told on me?"

"Of course she did. We told each other everything."

Alexandra's eyes sparkle as she watches us reminisce.

"Not everything, I hope," I say.

"Third grade? Behind the garage? Oh yeah, she told me everything."

"Sounds interesting," Rachel says, nudging me with her elbow.

It's strange that I'm still embarrassed by the memory, but I would accept all the embarrassment in the world for the small distance we close with our memories of Tiegan.

So we spend the next hour and a half telling stories. It's not enough—not nearly enough. But it's all we have.

Finally, I get to the point where I can't think of anything else to talk about other than the events that saved my life; saved mine and ended hers. I swallow hard and Della seems to know what's coming. Tears glisten in her eyes, and I wonder if she'll ask me not to tell Alexandra the story. But then she gives me a small nod, stands from the bed, and walks out of the room.

I understand. Unlike the memories we've shared until now, this one isn't a story she wants to relive. Once Della is gone, Alexandra sits very still, as if she knows that what I'm going to tell her next will be life changing.

I take her hand, this girl who is now my responsibility. I squeeze, then let go, still unsure of the best way to properly express affection for her. I clear my throat and look to a random spot on the ceiling.

"It was midnight," I say. "Murray picked me up to take me to Chicago for one of my wishes."

I finally chance a look at Alexandra. She leans forward, eyes wide. Completely taken in by the idea. It relaxes me and for the first time in my life, I look forward to telling the story. A story I hope will live on long past the end of my life. A story of friendship, love, and sacrifice.

"Murray and I were arguing about how much I had packed," I say. "Little did we know, we had a stowaway in the back seat of his Chevy . . . "

"Was it Tiegan?" Alexandra asks.

"It was Tiegan."

Her giggle is pure and innocent. "I like her already," she says.

I don't know whether to laugh or cry, so I do both as I say, "She would have liked you, too."

One Year Later

It has been a year since my second heart transplant. I feel better than I have in years. Maybe better than I have ever felt. Alexandra is a big part of that.

She amazes me every day. With her zest for life, with her eternally optimistic attitude, and with her uncanny ability to brighten my world. I can't imagine life without her.

And I won't have to, although soon I might have to deal with some separation. Juan, who Skypes with Alexandra every single day, is always telling us how safe the journey is, how beautiful the land is, and how friendly and generous the people are. And soon the opportunity to visit will be available to Alexandra. Tomorrow, in a ceremony at the same courthouse where her father was sentenced to deportation, Alexandra Lopez will officially become an American citizen.

I've never seen a twelve-and-a-quarter-year-old so excited.

But she's studying now, making sure she keeps her straight-A report card. And I'm sitting on the edge of my bed in the same house Alexandra grew up in. I still sleep in the basement, in the hope that one day Juan will be able to return. If that happens, his bedroom will be waiting for him.

Rachel and I have talked many times about her moving in, but it hasn't seemed right. Maybe it's the timing, or the fact that it's still Juan's house, or maybe we just want to take it slow. There's something about the moment I first see her, which happens nearly every day, that still feels new every single time. I like that, and I don't want to give it up.

In my hand is a folded sheet of paper. I found it earlier, while vacuuming in the computer room. At some point, a page from Murray's journal must have fallen out and been lost behind the desk where the computer sat. Leave it to me to let a year go by before I actually move anything to vacuum behind it.

I hold the paper in my hand, but I hesitate to open it. Recently, there have been far too many endings to various chapters of my life. As soon as I read whatever is on this page, it will be the last time I'll discover anything written by my old friend Mr. Murray McBride. Besides, I don't know when he wrote it. Was it a good day? A bad day? One of the days when he wasn't sure he wanted to continue living? Or a day when we did something fun together? I just don't know.

So I rub the paper, feeling its texture. I stare at it, appreciating the discoloration of age. And finally, I open it.

I take a deep breath and allow the anticipation—and if I'm honest, the apprehension—to surround me. Then I turn my eyes to Murray's slanted handwriting, and I read.

Whoever said being a hundred years old came with horsefeathers must not have been a hundred years old. Today, I feel like I could fly.

Well, okay, that's what's called a good old-fashioned exaggeration. But I could walk around the block and still have energy to spare, after a good, long nap. That's how good I feel. Because today I was young again. I got out an old ball bag, a beat-up bat, and took the kids to the sandlot. Well, Old Lady Willamet's garden, but you get the point.

Being out there, I haven't felt so young in decades. And it's all because of the kid. Actually, make that the kids. Being around those two, so much younger than me, you'd think I'd feel old. But that's not what happened. Today, I felt indestructible.

I guess that's the difference. People. Living by myself since Jenny died, I became old and crabby. I stopped seeing the brightness in people's eyes, and stopped feeling any kind of connection at all. With anyone. And without connection, without people, we don't have a darn thing—no matter what else we might have.

I know I don't have many days left, but however many the Good Lord might grant me, I'm going to spend them in the presence of the people I care about. And then, when I'm at my hour of death, I'll know I lived myself one heck of a life.

God, I love those kids.

I fold the piece of paper and sit perfectly still on the side of the bed. In my hand, I hold the secret to a happy life, written by my good friend, Murray. A blueprint of sorts. And I decide right here and now, as much as I'm able, I'm going to try to follow it.

"Jason!"

Alexandra's voice drifts down the stairs. Finally, after a few months of resistance, she's calling me by my first name.

For some reason, I stay where I am, perched on the side of the bed, with the lost page of Murray's journal in my hand. It feels like Murray is here with me, and I don't want to leave that. "Yeah?" I yell.

"What do you think about picking up Rachel and getting some ice cream?"

I smile so wide my cheeks hurt. "I think that's a great idea."

Her footsteps rumble across the floor until she's at the top of the staircase. I stand from the corner of the bed and walk to the base of the steps so I can see her, but not so far that I lose Murray's presence. Alexandra is in her red, white, and blue, of course, along with her fanny pack. And that perpetual smile that lights up her eyes. Her happiness buoys everyone she meets.

"Vanilla or chocolate?" I ask.

Her eyes widen in anticipation, and she gives the same answer she's given for quite a long time now.

"Chocolate," she says. "Definitely chocolate."

It's a good answer. The answer I was hoping for. "I'll meet you in the car, okay?"

She darts away, her footsteps thundering across the floor again.

I look back to the corner of the bed. It's strange, but I swear Murray is right there, somehow. I stare for a long moment, remembering the very first time I saw him, in the hospital, where he joined me at my video game.

And I find myself on the brink of tears. We've been through so much, Murray and me. But here, finally, our journey ends.

"Goodbye, Mr. McBride," I whisper. "Thanks for being my friend."

I turn off the lights, climb the stairs, and go to join Alexandra for some chocolate ice cream.

Because with her, every day is the most amazing day ever.

The End

El Remate, Guatemala

In the summer of 2018, I took my wife and two daughters on a "volunteer vacation" to El Remate, a beautiful, peaceful village near the Mayan ruins of Tikal in Northeastern Guatemala. We saw the kindness and generosity of the people firsthand, as well as the poverty and need. We helped build a cement floor for a home with no floor at all—only dirt—and volunteered at the Women's Center, the Child Development Center, and the new medical clinic. All of these projects are organized, funded, and staffed by volunteers in collaboration with an organization called Project Ixcanaan.

The co-founder of Project Ixcanaan is a Canadian woman named Anne Lossing, who has lived in Guatemala for more than twenty years. Anne is a selfless person who has devoted her life to helping the people of the village in everything from finding volunteers for the medical clinic to organizing a project to bring running water to those on the edges of the village. Having spent some time with Anne, I'm confident in saying that a donation to Project Ixcanaan will be well spent. So if you'd like to make life a little better for people like Zuri—a real girl who joined us on a hike and braided my daughter's hair—please consider helping Project Ixcanaan however you can.

Maybe, if you're lucky, that will include a visit to the village. The current dangers of Guatemala City compel me to recommend flying into Belize City and taking ground transportation to El Remate; my family's experience doing so was perfectly peaceful and one that I highly recommend. It truly is a wonderful place.

To learn more about Project Ixcanaan, please visit https://ixcanaan.com/.

All the best, and enjoy your adventure.

- Joe

Note from the Author

Word-of-mouth is crucial for any author to succeed. If you enjoyed *The Final Wish of Mr. Murray McBride*, please leave a review online—anywhere you are able. Even if it's just a sentence or two. It would make all the difference and would be very much appreciated.

Thanks!
Joe

About the Author

Joe Siple is the award-winning author of *The Five Wishes of Mr. Murray McBride*, which was named "Book of the Year" by the Maxy Awards, 1st Place in the National Indie Excellence Awards, and Finalist in several others. He lives in Colorado with his wife and two daughters.

Thank you so much for reading one of **Joe Siple's** novels.
If you enjoyed the experience, please check out Book One
of the *Mr. Murray McBride* series for your next great read!

The Five Wishes of Mr. Murray McBride by Joe Siple

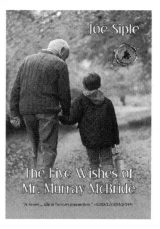

2018 Maxy Award "Book Of The Year"
"A sweet...tale of human connection...
will feel familiar to fans of Hallmark movies."
–Kirkus Reviews

"An emotional story that will leave readers meditating on the
life-saving magic of kindness."
–Indie Reader

BLACK ROSE
writing™